PRAISE FOR

Rag and Bone BY Michael Nava

A *Library Journal* Best Book of the Year

"In a perfect world, Michael Nava's conscientious lawyer-sleuth, Henry Rios, would have been made a judge long ago, because he deserves it. In *Rag and Bone*, the seventh and final book in an out-standing series, it looks as if this California criminal lawyer is going to get his just reward. . . . Or maybe he won't. Before he wins his last case—which has him defending a niece charged with killing her abusive husband—Rios has to survive it. Not since the death of his lover from AIDS has he been in such bad shape to take on an emo-tionally demanding investigation like this one. Estranged from his sister, lost without his lover, and weakened by a near-fatal heart attack, Rios can find no reason to go on living—until he meets the ten-year-old grandnephew who shows up on his doorstep with his bruised and battered mother . . ." —*The New York Times Book Review*

"This seventh Henry Rios mystery should bring both pleasure and sadness to admirers of the gay Mexican-American defense lawyer. Pleasure because Nava is in top form; sadness because of his announcement that this is the last Rios novel. . . . The challenges L.A.-based Rios confronts are as complex and involved as the man himself: a heart attack, a possible appointment to a judgeship, the discovery of an unknown niece and grandnephew, a new love, and the most personally daunting case of his career."

—*Publishers Weekly*

"Explores new emotional levels. . . . Sensitively portraying the con-flicts of a man intent on helping his family, Mr. Nava has filled *Rag and Bone* with carefully drawn characters with complex motiva-tions."
—*The Dallas Morning News*

continued...

Michael Nava

Rag and
Bone

BERKLEY PRIME CRIME, NEW YORK

RAG AND BONE

A Berkley Prime Crime Book / published by arrangement with
G. P. Putnam's Sons, a division of Penguin Putnam Inc.

PRINTING HISTORY
G. P. Putnam's Sons hardcover edition / March 2001
Berkley Prime Crime trade paperback edition / June 2002

Berkley Prime Crime trade paperback ISBN: 0-425-18470-6

Visit our website at
www.penguinputnam.com

The Library of Congress has catalogued
the G. P. Putnam's Sons hardcover edition as follows:

Nava, Michael.
Rag and bone / Michael Nava.
p.   cm.
ISBN 0-399-14708-X
1. Rios, Henry (Fictitious character)—Fiction.   2. Los Angeles (Calif.)—Fiction.
3. Mexican Americans—Fiction.   4. Gay men—Fiction.   I. Title.
PS3564.A8746 R34   2001   00-051729
813'.54—dc21

Berkley Prime Crime Books are published by The Berkley Publishing Group,
a division of Penguin Putnam Inc., 375 Hudson Street,
New York, New York 10014.
BERKLEY PRIME CRIME and the "B" design are trademarks
belonging to Penguin Putnam Inc.

PRINTED IN THE UNITED STATES OF AMERICA

10   9   8   7   6   5   4   3   2   1

· · ·

. . . Now that my ladder's gone,
I must lie down where all the ladders start,
In the foul rag-and-bone shop of the heart.

W. B. YEATS
"The Circus Animals' Desertion"

I.

THE WALLS OF THE COURTROOM OF THE COURT OF APPEAL
on the third floor in the Ronald Reagan State Office Building were
paneled in gray-green marble the color of money while the justices'
dais and the benches in the gallery were gleaming wood that had
been stained the deep, coagulated red called oxblood; the same red
as the tasseled loafers of the big-firm lawyers who regularly prac-
ticed in this venue. The $350-an-hour crowd were set apart not
only by their shoes but also by their haircuts, which appeared to be
the result of a microscopic process by which every hair was, in fact,
individually cut. Needless to say, these lawyers were in civil practice. We in the criminal bar were incapable of the insouciance that
seems to be issued with platinum credit cards and corner offices.
We tended to be solitary creatures, easily identifiable by our
bulging files, tattered briefcases, hair in need of cutting, suits in
need of pressing and attitudes of weary cynicism. The deputy attor-
neys general who filed down from their offices on the fifth floor to
represent the state in criminal matters were mostly kids a few years
out of law school who produced earnest, moot-court–style briefs
but with the law largely on their side; in the defense bar, we joked
that they could have submitted photocopied pages from the phone

book and still won. They slouched into the courtroom in off-the-rack suits, carrying cheap leather briefcases stamped with the Great Seal of the State of California: a woman warrior clad in a Princess Xena breastplate pointing at San Francisco Bay and presumably exclaiming the state's motto, Eureka! I have found it. She represented the mythical Queen Calafia, whom Spanish explorers believed had ruled over the race of Amazons in the land that now bore her name. Perhaps, I thought, studying the Great Seal on the wall above the dais, she was actually pointing to Oakland, home to a large lesbian population, including my sister, Elena, and her partner.

I wasn't usually so dyspeptic this early in the day, but I had the world's worst heartburn, undoubtedly the result of a breakfast that had consisted of four cups of coffee, a bagel that was half-burned and half-frozen—I really needed a new toaster—and a handful of vitamins. The bitter aftertaste of the pills lingered at the back of my throat. Also, now that I noticed it, my right arm was throbbing. Great. When I was a teenager, I'd suffered through growing pains; at forty-nine, I was suffering through growing-old pains.

The young deputy A.G. beside me pored over his notes and muttered to himself, as if he were about to argue before the United States Supreme Court rather than a three-judge panel—two white-haired white men, one graying black lady—of the intermediate state appellate court. His knee knocked nervously against mine and I glanced at him. He was a handsome boy with that luminous skin of the young, as if a lantern were burning just beneath the flesh.

"'Scuse me," he murmured without looking up.

"Your first appearance?" I asked.

Now he looked. His eyes were like cornflowers. "Is it that obvious?"

"Don't be too anxious," I said. "They've already written the opinion in your case."

"Really?"

"Really," I said. "Oral argument's mostly for show. It's hardly worth bothering to show up."

"Then why are you here?"

"I'm a criminal defense lawyer," I said. "Tilting at windmills is my specialty."

He smiled civilly, then returned to his notes.

"We will hear *People* versus *Guerra*," the presiding justice said.

I pulled myself out of the chair and made my way to counsel table. The young A.G. beside me also stood up.

"You're Mr. Rios?" he said as we headed to counsel table.

"None other," I replied.

He held open the gate that separated the gallery from the well of the court where counsel tables were located, and said, "Great brief. I had to pull an all-nighter to finish my reply."

I remembered his brief had had the whiff of midnight oil. "Thanks. You did a good job, too."

I set my file on my side of the table and was gripped by a wave of nausea so intense I was sure I was going to vomit, but the moment passed.

"Counsel?"

I looked up at the presiding justice, Dahlgren, who was not much older than me and quite possibly a year or two younger.

"I'm sorry, Your Honor."

"Your appearance, please."

"Yes, Your Honor," I grunted. "Henry Rios for defendant and appellant Anthony Guerra."

"Mr. Rios," the lady judge, Justice Harkness, spoke. "Are you all right? You went white as a ghost a second ago."

"Heartburn, Justice Harkness. I'll be fine with a little water." I poured a glass from the carafe on the table. My hand was shaking.

"Tom Donovan for the respondent, the People," the A.G. was saying.

"Mr. Rios, if you're ready," Dahlgren said.

"Yes," I replied, and went to the podium. The justices regarded me dubiously. "Not to be impertinent, but I can see from Your Honors' faces that you're less than thrilled with another Three Strikes case on your docket."

Harkness permitted herself a smile, but Dahlgren said, "It's fair to say, counsel, that you're not the first lawyer to argue that Three Strikes is cruel and unusual punishment, so maybe we can cut this short. Every appellate court that's considered the issue has held that sending repeat felons to prison for life upon conviction of their third felony does not violate either state or federal constitutional proscriptions against cruel and unusual punishment. What's your pitch?"

"My pitch, Your Honor," I said "is that this law is an abomination. In this case, it's sending my client to prison for the rest of his life because he got into a tussle with a security guard in the parking lot of a supermarket from which he had stolen a case of infant formula for his eight-month-old daughter."

Justice Harkness leaned forward. "He was convicted of robbery," she said. "The law doesn't distinguish between stealing diamonds and stealing baby food, Mr. Rios, where the theft is accomplished by force or fear."

"He committed robbery only in the narrowest sense of the statute because he bumped the security guard with a shopping cart. Technically, that's force, but come on, this is L.A., where people shoot each other for parking spaces."

Justice Harkness shook her head. "The security guard was a woman who was five inches shorter and forty pounds lighter than your client."

"Your Honor, with all due respect, she was asked on cross-examination if she was afraid, and she said no. There was no fear and the force was minimal. The Three Strikes law doesn't distinguish between stealing diamonds and stealing baby food, which is why this court must."

The third justice, Rogan, said, "I agree."

"You do?" The surprise was so evident in my voice that the lawyers in the gallery burst into laughter. But it wasn't surprise they had heard; it was the shooting pains in my arm and the waves of nausea that continued to sweep through me.

"I do," Rogan said when the laughter subsided. "But Mr. Rios, Three Strikes doesn't just punish the current felony, it also punishes defendants for past serious felony convictions. Your client has a record as long as Pinocchio's nose."

"But only two convictions are qualifying strikes," I said, "and those were insignificant burglaries . . ."

"Insignificant by what standard?" Harkness asked.

"They were nonviolent, the losses were small, my client pled." I saw a flash of lights and then groaned as someone with very cold hands squeezed my heart.

I heard the alarm in Justice Harkness's voice when she said, "Mr. Rios, are you sure you're all right?"

I gasped, "If I could just have another minute."

Dahlgren said, "Actually, counsel, your time has expired."

I keeled over.

I didn't completely lose consciousness until I reached the emergency room. I had this vision of myself as a very small boy—maybe three or four—holding a seashell to my ear to hear the ocean, but instead of a gentle reverberation, I heard a thunderous swell of water rising from a black depth. Terrified, I dropped the shell, but the roaring did not stop and I began to wail. Slowly I turned around and found myself standing at the edge of an ocean shimmering with light. Like shifting plates of glass reflecting the sun, the movement of light mesmerized me. I stopped crying and my terror evaporated. I felt a dim but widening awareness that if I stepped into the tide, everything would be all right, and it seemed to me at some point the water ceased to be water and revealed itself instead to be a brilliant sentience that called to me with such benevolence I rushed toward it. When my foot touched the light, I felt a kind of ecstasy, but then someone hooked her arms beneath my armpits and dragged me away. I looked up and saw my sister, Elena, as she had been at eight or nine. Her grave dark eyes communicated love and terror. I tried to struggle out of her grip to run back into the light. "No, *m'ijito*," she said, holding me against her body. *"No es tu tiempo."* Then a male voice shouted, "He's back," and an excruciating sensation roiled though my body that left me gasping with pain. I groaned my sister's name.

I woke up in the middle of the night in a narrow bed, groggy, disoriented and scared. Across the foot of the bed, a window looked out on the nurse's station, from which light filtered into the room. I was pinned to the bed by tubes, lines and catheters and felt more specimen than human. In the darkness, a chair squeaked and I realized with a start there was someone else in the room. Laboriously, I turned my head toward the noise. When I saw who it was, I was sure I was either dead or crazy.

"Mom?"

The woman inclined her face toward the light. "No, Henry, it's Elena."

Only her voice persuaded me my mother had not risen from the grave. My mother, though born in California, was the daughter of Mexican immigrants. Spanish was her natal language and she spoke English with a slight but unmistakable Mexican accent. My sister, Elena, spoke in the educated tones of her profession—she was a professor of English at a small private college near Oakland. Her hair was the same dense black shot through with white as our mother's had been. At fifty-five, her face was worn to the same grave lines, with the same smooth olive darkness of skin, and her eyes were the same unrevealing black. She leaned forward and the resemblance ended. Elena was thin, whereas our mother's body was a mound of flesh that only seemed soft until you touched it and discovered its laborer's strength.

Elena touched her palm to my forehead as if she was taking my temperature. "How are you feeling?"

"Where am I?"

"The hospital. The intensive care unit. Do you remember that you had a heart attack?"

"I remember the judge wouldn't let me finish my argument." Her presence confused me—who had told her I was in the hospital? When I tried to express my bewilderment, it came out with unintended harshness. "What are you doing here?"

Hurt, she replied, "You asked for me. Just after your heart stopped."

"My heart stopped."

"For a few seconds, and then they resuscitated you. You don't remember?"

The boy with the seashell. That incandescent light. My sister dragging me away. "Why didn't you let me go?"

"What do you mean, Henry? Let you go where?"

I wanted to explain, but my head was a jumble of thoughts and images. A red-headed male nurse had materialized at the nurse's station, and I thought I was hallucinating again because I recognized him. "Which hospital is this?"

"I think it's called Westside," she said.

"The AIDS ward is one floor down. This is where I brought Josh the last time he was hospitalized." I roused myself as best I could and stared at her. "He's dead. So many people, friends, also dead. Why not me, too? I'm not afraid and there's nothing . . . nothing left to do. More of the same. I don't want it. Why didn't you let me go?"

She grasped my hand. "It's not your time yet."

. . .

And then it was morning, that day or the next. A doctor—a cardiologist named Hayward—came to examine me. Elena excused herself. Hayward perched at the edge of my bed. He was a small man who wore round tortoiseshell glasses beneath which were quick, bright eyes that beamed rays of ironic intelligence. Despite his thinning hair and slight potbelly, he retained the air of a precocious child but he had the beleaguered smile of a man with too many demands on his attention.

"How do you feel today, Henry?"

"Forget the soothing bedside manner," I replied. "Just tell me what happened to me."

"You had a heart attack—actually we call them myocardial infarctions, now, or M.I.'s—and you lost about twenty percent of your heart."

"Lost?"

"It died," he said. "That's what M.I.'s do. They kill a portion of the heart muscle. The quality of life depends on what the remaining capacity can handle."

"How can I even be alive if twenty percent of my heart died?"

"Well, fortunately," Hayward said, grinning, "the body is rather overengineered with excess capacity."

"What, like an SUV?"

He laughed. "Something like that."

"Am I going to require some kind of surgery?"

"Not necessarily," he replied. "If there's arterial blockage, we can often open it up with angioplasty, and there are also preventive treatments. Surgery is a last resort."

"My sister said my heart stopped."

He nodded. "Yes, you died for almost a minute. When you came back, you were asking for her. In Spanish. I speak enough to understand what you wanted, so we tracked her down. That took some doing. She wasn't in your medical power of attorney. I had to call your lawyer to find her."

"I know. My sister and I aren't close."

He looked at me quizzically. "It seemed urgent to you that she come."

"Thank you," I said, declining his implicit invitation to explain.

"Sure," he said. He hopped off the bed and patted my head. "I'll see you tomorrow."

For most of our lives, we had been brother and sister in name only. My father's drinking and violence had made for an unpredictable and terrifying childhood. My mother retreated into religion, leaving Elena and me to fend for ourselves. We each survived in our own way; I, simply, began to disappear, spending more and more time away from home, at school, at the houses of friends, at the city library, at the track field, anywhere I could find a refuge from my father's rage and my mother's sadness.

While I found ways to escape my family, Elena stayed behind but learned how to occupy space without calling any more attention to herself than a chair did. She was obedient, dutiful and quiet; I could only look bad by comparison. But children reveal themselves to each other in ways that are not apparent to grown-ups, and there were moments when I understood she was not quite the girl she pretended to be at home.

My most striking memory of this was when I saw her with her friends one afternoon while I was taking the long way home from school to eat up time. I passed a hamburger joint where a group of teenage girls—I was nine or ten—were sitting at a picnic table drinking Cokes and smoking cigarettes. I noticed them because they were wearing the blue-and-white uniforms of the parochial high school Elena attended. One of the girls was sitting with her back to me, having her hair brushed by a girlfriend. When the first girl turned slightly to address the second, I saw it was Elena. Her hair, which at home she wore in a long braid, spilled down her back and across her blue-sweatered shoulders. I was as startled as if one of the nuns who taught at my elementary school had suddenly removed her wimple. Even more shocking, she lifted a cigarette to her lips and inhaled with perfect aplomb. After a moment, I continued on my way without her having seen me and wondered what to do with this information. In the end, I could see no way of using it to my advantage, so I kept it to myself, but I looked at her differently after that. When she sat quietly at dinner as my father raged at my mother or me, delicately cutting her food into small bits that she pushed around her plate without eating, I knew she was also silently plotting her exit. A week after she graduated from high school, she entered the convent of the Sisters of the Holy Cross. I would not see her again for five years, and by then we were strangers to each other. We had remained strangers for many years, until she asked my help in a legal matter that forced us to reveal parts of ourselves to each other that we had kept hidden. Elena, who had by then left her religious order, came out to me as a lesbian; I told her about my own struggles with my homosexuality and alcohol. She met my lover, Josh, who eventually died from AIDS, but while he was alive, he badgered me to keep in touch with her and we had formed the fragile bond of two people who had survived a catastrophe—the cataclysm of our childhood. After Josh's death four years ago, Elena had tried to keep the connection alive, but I had only sporadically responded to her calls and e-mail. I had been startled by her appearance in the hallucination I had had in the emergency room, and I was still puzzled by why I had called for her and why she had come.

Elena had gone to call her partner, Joanne Stole, a painter who taught in the art department at the same school where Elena taught in the English department. I knew almost nothing about Joanne except that she seemed to disapprove of me.

When she returned to the room, I said, "How is Joanne?"

"She's fine, Henry," Elena said. "She sends her best wishes." She picked up her book.

"I'm sorry I caused all this trouble for you."

"You're my brother."

"Joanne's your real family."

She put the book down and studied me for a moment. "The first time the hospital phoned, they told me you were dead," she said. "Two minutes later, they phoned again and explained they'd made a mistake, but the sadness I felt after that first call was indescribable."

"It's not like you to be sentimental."

"I'm not sentimental," she said. "But I trust my feelings. I felt that terrible grief because we have never resolved the things that have estranged us all these years."

"What things?"

"To begin with, you could forgive me."

"For what?"

"For not protecting you from Dad when we were children."

"That wasn't your job."

"I know that now but at the time I thought it was, and so did you. You looked to me for protection."

"I don't remember anything like that."

She reached into her purse and handed me an old snapshot. A little girl in pigtails happily held a laughing toddler in her lap. With astonishment, I recognized them as the children in my emergency-room hallucination. Elena and me. In the picture, her skinny arm encircled my waist possessively, as if to keep me from squirming away. I remembered how, in the hallucination, she had dragged me back from the light. The sensations came back with such clarity and force that it seemed like a real memory, not a dream.

"When you were first born, I wouldn't let you out of my sight," she said. "I cried when they made me go to school because I didn't want to be separated from you, and Mom said you fussed until I came home. She called me your little mother." She took the picture from me and studied it. "We may not consciously remember the first loves we form, but they stay inside of us. I have always loved you, Henry. You called for me when you thought you were dying.

What was that except your way of remembering how much we loved each other? I couldn't be there for you then. I can now, if you'll let me."

I replied with the sobs of a little boy and buried myself against her.

2.

Dr. Hayward returned the next day to perch leprechaunlike at the edge of my bed, his feet not quite reaching the ground. After the standard Q-and-A about the state of my physical well-being, he cleared his throat sententiously and said, "You know, it's not uncommon for survivors of heart attacks to have pretty wild emotional swings."

I was too tired to be anything other than irritable. "Duh."

Undaunted, he went on. "Your body failed you. In fact, you died for almost a minute. That's one of the most traumatic experiences anyone can have. Your recovery may be slow and difficult and you'll be having a lot of feelings. If you were already depressed before the heart attack—"

I had been slowly sliding beneath the blankets, struggling to stay awake. Now I sat up and demanded, "Who said I was depressed?"

He glanced at my sister, who had been quietly reading, or pretending to read, a biography of the poet Elizabeth Bishop. She lowered the book to reveal a guilty expression.

"I never told you I was depressed," I said to her.

"The first night I was here, you talked about dying, Henry," she said. "About wanting to die."

"I had just had a heart attack, Elena. I felt like roadkill, plus I was pumped up with pharmaceuticals. I was out of my head."

Her nostrils quivered, which I remembered from childhood was a sign of anger, but she restrained herself and replied mildly, "This wasn't pain or the drugs. You mentioned Josh and other friends who had died from AIDS. You said, 'Why not me, too.' You said you had nothing left to do."

"I don't remember saying anything like that, and if I did, it was babble."

Hayward, who had been watching our back-and-forth like a spectator at a tennis match, said, "I could prescribe Zoloft."

"I'm not depressed by anything but this conversation," I said. "And I won't take happy pills."

He eased himself off the bed. "Have you been up yet?"

I tugged at my IV line. "What do you think?"

"I think you should try walking down the hall."

"I can't even walk to the bathroom to take a leak."

Hayward answered with a smile of great kindness. "I know it's frightening to feel so weak, but that's why you've got to get out of bed. Rejoin the land of the living. It's that or the Zoloft. Your choice."

After he left, Elena helped me out of bed and into my bathrobe and we went for a walk to the window at the end of the corridor, a distance of maybe fifty feet. After four days in bed, viewing the world vertically was shockingly disorienting. I tottered against my sister, pulling my IV behind me, taking tiny steps.

Elena said, "This reminds me of when you were first learning how to walk."

"You can't possibly remember that," I huffed.

"I was five years old when you were born, Henry. I remember most of your childhood."

Further conversation was impossible as I concentrated on reaching the smear of light at the end of the hall. I tried to keep my gaze straight ahead but sometimes my glance fell into one of the rooms, where figures lay huddled beneath thin hospital blankets as TVs flickered soundlessly overhead.

"We made it," Elena said, a little breathless from shouldering my weight.

The window was double-paned to minimize the shriek of traffic from the street below, but I could still feel the heat of the sun when I pressed my hand against the glass.

"Why did you have to rat me out to the doc?" I asked my sister. "Now he thinks I'm mental."

"The way you were talking worried me. I know you don't remember what you said, but—"

"I remember," I said, resting my forehead against the window. The April wind rattled the palm trees that lined the boulevard. I had never seen anything so beautiful. I turned my face to Elena, resting my cheek on the glass. "If I explain, will you promise not to tell him?"

She struggled with that for a moment. "I promise, Henry."

"I didn't feel depressed before the heart attack, not in the usual way people feel depressed. What I felt was—I don't know. AIDS, Elena. How I can explain it to someone who hasn't crossed off half the names in their address book as one friend after another died?"

"There are treatments now," she said quietly. "Effective treatments."

"I know and no one talks about AIDS anymore. For most people, it's as if it never happened. But it did happen, it's still happening. While it was going on for me, so many friends were dying before their time, I think I subconsciously assumed that I would also die before I got old."

"You're not HIV positive," she said.

"So? For fifteen years, being gay has been like sitting in a trench on a battlefield, watching people get picked off right and left. Who got the virus and who didn't, who died and who lived, all began to seem completely arbitrary, and as you staggered from hospital room to memorial service, it started to look like it would never end and there wouldn't be anyone left." I rolled my back against the window and stared down the hall of the hospital where I had sat the death watch for half a dozen friends. "And then one day I woke up and people I knew weren't dying anymore and I was looking at the rest of my life, a life I had not expected to have. A life I was completely unprepared to have. Does any of this make sense?"

"When I left the convent, I think I felt something similar," she said. "My experience as a religious wasn't tragic, though. It didn't leave me half-dead."

"Yes, that's how I felt. Half-dead. Readier to go the rest of the way than step back into the world." I looked at her and smiled. "I didn't try to commit suicide by inducing a heart attack. Honest. I wasn't suicidal at all, but I was finding it hard to come up with reasons to be alive. I didn't feel needed."

"Your friends need you. So do your clients."

"My friends love me, they don't need me. As for my clients, well, lawyers are fungible. There is no one to whom I am irreplaceable. They've all died."

"You don't know that there won't be others," she said.

I looked away from the ghost-filled corridor to my sister's kind, worn face and said, "I wish I could believe that."

After two days of walking the hall, we graduated to the hospital's small interior garden. I was liberated from my IV lines and rode down in the elevator in a wheelchair but discarded it once we got outside. Our course was a circular flagstone path that ringed a dozen rose bushes now in florid bloom, their scent mingling with banks of rosemary and lavender. But after only two laps, I began to tire and said, "Look, there's a bench. Can we sit for a minute?"

The bench was of snowy marble carved with clawed lion's feet.

Embedded in the stone was a small brass plaque that read, IN MEMO-RIAM, CHRISTOPHER GRAYE, 1963–1992."

"God," I said. "I knew Chris Graye."

"AIDS?"

I nodded and then didn't want to talk about it anymore. For a moment we listened to the buzzing of bees and the distant thrum of traffic. I closed my eyes. The sun on my face and neck was like the warm breath of a lover. I was ruefully surprised that I could remember that sensation, given how long it had been since I had actually experienced it. Even before the heart attack, I concluded there was not much chance I would meet someone; and while my reflex was to regret it, when I actually thought it through, I felt relief. Love is very strenuous; only the young really enjoy it and I was not young. Now, my damaged heart seemed the perfect metaphor, and I was ready to let go of that part of life.

"This reminds me of the garden in the convent," Elena said.

I waited for her to continue, because she rarely spoke of her years as a religious. Elena had been an honor student in high school, but because she was a girl, our father decreed it was unnecessary for her to attend college. One day, I came home from track practice and found three nuns in full habit sipping tea with my parents in the living room. They belonged to a teaching order called Sisters of the Holy Cross that was affiliated with a number of small Jesuit colleges. The sisters had come to ask my father's permission for Elena to join their order. Though they were white women, they addressed him in fluent Spanish in firm, almost lecturing tones, while he sullenly shrugged and nodded. Elena knew that no one else could have persuaded our father to let her leave home and attend college except the representatives of a religion that, though he did not observe it, still exercised a primeval influence over the Mexican *campesino* who lived beneath his thin Americanized veneer.

Yet, she had once told me, after she joined the order she discovered a vocation, or at least enough of one for her to have spent six years as Sister Mary Joseph. The few times I had seen her during this period, she had radiated a calm, purposeful energy and seemed very happy. I assumed she would remain a nun for the rest of her life and was surprised to receive a brief letter from her announcing that she had left the order and could be reached through the English department at Berkeley, where she had been accepted to graduate school. I lost track of her altogether during most of the Berkeley years. Her remark a couple of days earlier about her disorientation at returning to the secular world came back to me now.

"What happened after you left the nuns?" I asked lazily.

"I went to Cal, you knew that."

"All I know is that's where you got your Ph.D. I don't know anything about your life there. Isn't that where you came out?"

She didn't respond for such a long time that I thought she hadn't heard me. I opened my eyes and found her staring into the middle distance, at a hummingbird zipping in and out of the roses in a blue-and-yellow blur.

"Elena? Are you all right?"

Slowly she turned her face to me and managed a pained smile. She said, "I always wondered how I would tell you about this. Or even if I would."

"Tell me about what?"

"I had a child, Henry. A daughter. I gave her up for adoption the day she was born, almost thirty years ago now."

A dry breeze rustled through the garden. I said, "What?"

"I started at Berkeley in nineteen-seventy. Do you remember what nineteen-seventy was like on college campuses?"

"I remember what it was like to be a junior at Stanford," I said. "I had hair to my shoulders and the halls of my dorm smelled of patchouli oil and pot."

"I was twenty-five. My hair was still growing out—we really did shave our heads in my order—and if you had asked me about pot, I would've thought you were talking about cookware. Needless to say, I knew almost nothing about sex. Mom had told me the bare minimum. The novice mother supplied some other clinical details but strictly in the interests of hygiene. We had taken a vow of celibacy, after all."

"You had no feelings toward any of your sisters?"

"I had plenty of feelings toward them," she said. "But I didn't recognize them as being sexual. I really was very, very naive. When I walked around Berkeley, I felt like I was branded with a scarlet V."

"I don't understand."

She shot me a look. "Virgin, Henry. All the other students seemed so sophisticated and experienced. I felt like a dress that had never been worn and I very much wanted to be worn. To be part of the excitement around me. To be young. I met a boy. A law student, actually. We went to a party and got drunk and I told him I was a virgin and he said he could take care of that."

"Did he rape you?"

"God, no," she said. "Though I can't imagine it was much fun for him. I was very awkward the first few times."

"The first few times?"

"I went out with Charlie for a couple of months."

"Charlie?"

"Charlie Tejada," she said. "He was the first Chicano I ever met. He couldn't speak ten words of Spanish and his dad was an accountant in L.A., but he lectured me about *la causa* and told me that studying American literature was assimilationist." Her tone was rueful but affectionate. "He dropped me for a girl from Chile whose father was in Allende's cabinet. I was hurt and relieved. Grateful to him for teaching me about sex. He was kind and patient in bed. But not," she added, "very careful. I knew about birth control pills but I didn't start taking them until after we'd had sex several times. I remember complaining to one of my housemates that the pressure of studying was making me sick in the morning. She said, very casually, that I was probably pregnant. I went to the student health center. She was right."

"What did you do?"

"Panicked. I was frightened and ashamed and I didn't know who to turn to."

"What about Charlie?"

She shook her head. "As inexperienced as I was, I still knew there was nothing to our affair. I mean, he wasn't going to marry me and I wouldn't have wanted that anyway."

"Why not?"

"I had begun to think I might be lesbian."

"Just like that, out of nowhere?"

"Those feelings I'd had for other women in the convent that I didn't recognize as sexual? I did after I started sleeping with Charlie. Sex was the missing piece that finally made sense of things. Do you know what I mean?"

I had a flash of myself at nineteen in bed with the first boy I ever made love to, and how, when he kissed me, it eliminated any doubt in my mind about who I was or what I wanted. "I think so," I said.

"I liked being with Charlie, but something was missing. I was on the verge of admitting what it was when I discovered I was pregnant."

"What did you do?"

"There was a professor in the department who was openly gay. I showed up at her office one day, told her I thought I was a lesbian, and begged her to help me deal with the pregnancy."

"Did she?"

"She arranged an abortion," Elena replied. "That was very brave of her, because abortion was still against the law and she could not only have lost her job but been prosecuted. I was grateful because my fall-back plan was to induce an abortion myself."

"Oh, Elena."

"That's what women did in those days, Henry. Thank God for Nora."

"The professor?"

She nodded. "The doctor's office was on Grant Street in China-town above a restaurant. I remember sitting in the waiting room with Nora, trying not to be sick from the food smells coming up the vent from downstairs. To this day I don't much care for Chinese food."

"But you didn't go through with it. Why?"

"The doctor scheduled the abortions late at night, after her regular hours. There was no one else in the waiting room except Nora and me. I went over to the window and looked outside at the neon signs and the people crowding the sidewalks and the shops, and slowly my own reflection emerged in the glass and I saw myself and realized I could not go through with an abortion."

Her face had a vulnerability I had never seen before. I reached for her hand. "I wish you hadn't had to go through that alone."

"I wasn't alone," she said, and for a moment I thought she was alluding to her professor, but then I understood.

"You think God told you not to go through with the abortion? But you're not antiabortion. Are you?"

"My God is not an unpleasant old man who lives in the sky and forces people to make desperate choices and then condemns them if they get it wrong. For me, God is the clear inner voice that guides us to the choices that are right for us, if we're willing to listen. The choices are different for everyone. For some women, an abortion makes sense. I just wasn't one of them."

"What happened after you decided not to go through with it?"

"I told Nora. We left the office and went to a coffee shop, where we talked for hours. She was the first person to whom I ever told my life story, and when I finished she said I was an exceptional woman. No one had ever said anything like that to me before. Her saying it gave me the courage of my convictions. Nora got me a leave of absence from school and convinced me to move in with her so she could help me through the pregnancy."

"And the baby?"

"I held her for a few minutes before I turned her over to a nurse from the county adoption agency," she said.

"Do you know what happened to her?"

"In those days you relinquished control completely," she said.

"And you never saw her again?"

She released my hand and sighed. "Around the time I turned forty, I developed some medical problems that eventually required a hysterectomy. I had never wanted another child, but losing the ability to bear them was surprisingly hard on me emotionally. I had a kind of breakdown, or at least I wasn't acting very rationally, and I was obsessed with two things—you and my daughter."

"Me? Why?"

"Because of what we talked about the other day. The guilt I felt at not protecting you when you were a child. That was nothing to the guilt I felt about putting my daughter up for adoption. I went looking for her."

"Did you find her?"

Elena nodded her head. "Yes. The agency was very helpful. They encouraged me because, well, you see, Henry, she was not one of their successes."

"What do you mean?"

"Thirty years ago, brown-skinned girl babies were not very placeable. She was never adopted. She grew up in foster care and group homes. She was at a group home when I found her. A Catholic charity group home that was run by my former order. I arranged to visit the home without disclosing who I was."

"Why?"

"I thought it would be less shocking to her if she got to know me first as a person before I told her I was her mother. I went ostensibly to talk to the girls about going to college, and I saw her. She was fourteen or fifteen. A chubby little girl squeezed into pants two sizes too small for her, with teased hair and too much makeup."

"Did you talk to her?"

"Not directly. I went around the circle and asked each girl what she wanted to be when she grew up. When it came her turn, she said beautician."

"So?"

"The two girls before her gave the same answer. She was simply imitating them. Seeing her, hearing her, exposed the foolishness of my fantasy."

"What fantasy?"

"I thought she would be like me at that age, but she was like the *cholas* we grew up with, Henry. The bad girls, the gang girls. I tried to imagine bringing her home, but I couldn't." She closed her eyes as if in pain. "My maternal instincts weren't even as strong as my snobbery." She fell silent. "A few years later, when I had grown up a bit, I tried to find her again. I was ready at that point to establish whatever relationship I could with her, but by then she had turned eighteen and was long gone. I learned she was married and had had a child. At the hospital where her son was born, I found a social worker who knew where she was, but she refused to give me my daughter's address. I persuaded her at least to give her my name and how to reach me. But I never heard from Vicky, so I don't even know if she got the information."

"Vicky?"

"That's what they named her. Victoria Maria."

"That's a lovely name."

"Isn't it?" Elena said. "I'll never see her again."

I reached for some consolation and found the same one she had given me when I worried about being needed. "You don't know that, Elena."

After a moment, she said, not very hopefully, "I'd like to believe that."

3.

AFTER TEN DAYS, I WAS RELEASED FROM THE HOSPITAL. Dr. Hayward came in as I was laboriously dressing. He stood at the doorway and watched me clumsily attempt to button my shirt. After a moment, he entered the room, gently moved my hands aside and delicately looped the buttons into the buttonholes, applying the same single-minded attention with which I imagined he performed heart surgery.

"Top button, too?" he asked. His warm breath glanced my cheek, smelling of coffee and peppermint.

"No," I said. "I'm not a geek."

He stepped back as if to admire his handiwork. "How do you feel?"

"Like nothing happened," I replied. "And like nothing will ever be the same."

He dug out a tube of breath mints from his white jacket and peeled two. "Mint?"

I accepted. He sat down lightly at the edge of the bed. I now realized he perched on beds not to create rapport with his bedridden patients, but because he was always tired and took every opportunity he could to rest. Like most good people I had known, he was seriously overworked, a condition that did not lend itself to treacly saintliness. He was unsentimental, direct and caustic, but acted out of such palpable kindness that I could not take offense.

"Everyone dies of something, Henry. What you now know is that the probabilities are you'll die of heart disease. Even if you follow the treatment plan I gave you and do it all perfectly, given the severity of your heart attack, your lifespan has still been shortened by probably ten years. If you don't follow my treatment plan, you could be in serious trouble a lot sooner."

"You're telling me this to scare me into taking my niacin?"

He crunched his mint. "To a point. I'm also telling you this because now is the time for you to start thinking about doing whatever it is in life that you've been putting off till your old age."

"I don't have any secret fantasies, Doc," I said.

"I can give you a regimen to keep you alive," he replied. "I can't give you a reason for living."

"Has Elena been talking to you again?"

"No," he said. He slid off the bed and put his hand on my shoulder. "I've been doing this a long time. Most of the time when people survive a heart attack as serious as yours, along with everything else they feel exhilarated, euphoric. You seem disappointed."

"You pushing antidepressants again?"

"If I thought they would help." He gave my shoulder a friendly squeeze. "You're still a relatively young man. You'll be around for a while. Make the best of it, Henry. Live every moment as fully as you can, even if all you're doing is eating a bowl of soup." He moved toward the door. "I'll see you next week. You have my number if there's an emergency."

"On automatic dial," I said. "Doc, I appreciate everything you've done for me. Even the bromides."

"Remember that when you start getting the bills," he said, and was gone. A few minutes later, Elena arrived with the wheelchair that she had gone off to fetch just before Hayward had turned up. I settled into it and we left.

. . .

My house was built atop a canyon on a dead-end street in the hills above Franklin Boulevard, east of Hollywood. Gray-green undergrowth filled the canyon; the views from my deck were of the Santa Monica Mountains to the west and, on clear days, the San Gabriels to the east. These brown, craggy mountains were a reminder that, although its boosters like to claim Los Angeles was the gateway to the Pacific Rim, it was essentially a western city. However crowded the city got, it was still pervaded by that western sense of unlimited space, vast emptiness and hidden wilds. The isolation that was so much a part of the city's psyche, the feeling that its ten million people were all living parallel lives that never intersected was, in part, a function of this landscape in which we were all like pioneers engaged in solitary struggle over the mountains to some distant valley of repose. I had lived in the city now for more than ten years, and of the hundreds of people I'd met, only a few had stuck. Many of them were at my house when I arrived home. They had cleaned my house, filled it with flowers and, as I later discovered, stocked my freezer with casseroles. They were waiting for me in the living room, which they had decorated with streamers and balloons and a WELCOME HOME, HENRY! sign strung across the doorway. On the dining room table, amid bowls and platters of food, was a chocolate cake in the shape of a heart.

"I can't believe this," I said.

Elena said, "It was Edith's idea."

Edith Rosen bustled toward me, a small, plump, gray-haired woman of sixty, a psychologist whom I had met while working on a case involving the drug and alcohol rehab where she had worked. She currently worked for the county's Department of Mental Health Services, providing therapy to all those crack babies of the late 1980s and early '90s who were now on the verge of adolescence with problems that started at attention deficit disorder and got worse from there.

"Sweetie," she said, hugging me. The top of her head came to my neck, her frizzy hair tickling me. She stepped back, assessing my appearance. From the sudden dampening of her eyes, it was clear she did not like what she saw, but she made a joke. "There was a lot of discussion about whether to shout surprise when you came through the door. I'm glad we didn't." She led me into the room. "Come and sit. We won't stay long, you probably need to rest."

"I've done nothing but rest," I said.

I eased into an armchair and looked around the room at all my friends. One of them murmured, "Speech," but I shook my head, too moved to speak.

The party broke up early, and one by one as they were leaving, my friends came up to say a few words of affection and encouragement. Edith, who had been cleaning up, came last.

"Thank you for doing this," I told her.

She tried to smile, but her eyes glistened. "You're much too young to have come so close to dying."

"The doc says if I follow his orders I'll have pretty much the usual life span."

"Well, just in case," she said. "Take this." She handed me a leather loop. A pendant hung on it, a dark red stone, smoothed and polished and cut into the shape of a heart.

"What is it?"

"The stone's called red jasper."

I slipped the loop over my neck, tucked it into my shirt. The stone was warm against my flesh. "Thank you."

"It's a spare, Henry. Don't lose it." She grinned. "Well, maybe to the right man."

Elena had volunteered to stay with me for a little while until she was sure I was all right. I was awakened early the next morning by the urgent murmur of her voice talking on the phone. I pulled myself out of bed and fumbled around in the closet for my bathrobe. There was a quick knock at the door and then she came in. Her expression stopped me in my tracks, the robe hanging limply over one arm.

"What happened?" I asked.

"I've got to fly home," she said. "I've talked to Edith. She'll come by this afternoon to look in on you."

"Is it Joanne?"

She shook her head. "It's my daughter. Vicky. She turned up black and blue at our doorstep last night, with her son, begging for help."

"Help for what?" I said after a long moment, still befuddled by sleep.

"Her husband beat her," she said. "She told Joanne she had been in a shelter for battered women, but they'd asked her to leave and she didn't have anywhere else to go where he wouldn't find her."

"How did she find you?"

"I don't know," she said. "The social worker from the hospital must have given Vicky my address after all."

"That was years ago. How can you be sure it's her, Elena?"

She answered impatiently, "I can't until I get home." Then, relenting, "I'm sorry, Henry. This has taken me completely by surprise." She half-smiled. "The other day in the garden, you told me I might see her again. It must have been a premonition. I've got to pack. I feel terrible leaving you on your second day home from the hospital."

"Don't worry about that," I said.

I slipped my bathrobe on and followed her into her bedroom, where she began packing in a distracted manner, as if her mind was coursing along a half-dozen tracks.

"It's odd," she said, carefully folding a slip. "My two regrets in life were that we weren't close and that I had lost my daughter. Now suddenly you're both back in my life." She tossed the slip into her suitcase, undoing the folds. "In each case a crisis brought us together." She threw some blouses on the bed. "I've always believed good can come out of suffering. This proves it, doesn't it?"

"I know I'm grateful for you," I said. "I'm sure she will be, too."

I hoped she would not detect the skepticism beneath my minimal response, but the notion of a stranger showing up in the middle of the night with a hard-luck story, claiming to be family, awoke my professional instincts, which naturally suspected the worst. Had Vicky turned up on my doorstep, I'd have a lot of questions before I embraced her into the warm bosom of the family. I hoped that once her excitement wore off, the same questions would occur to Elena.

"Her last name is Trujillo," Elena said, cramming the last of her clothes into her suitcase. "Her little boy's name is Angel. Angelito." She gave his name the Spanish pronunciation: *Ahn-hel-ito*. "Joanne said he looks like he's nine or ten. I'm a grandmother, Henry. Can you imagine?"

"How did she get Trujillo as a last name?"

"It must be her husband's name." She took a step back from the bed and her suitcase popped open. "Damn!"

She sat on the bed and began to weep. I sat down beside her and put my arm around her. "What is it, Elena?"

"I've prayed for the day when I would see my daughter and now I—I'm afraid."

Gently, I asked, "Afraid of what?"

"The girl I saw fifteen years ago in that group home didn't have much of a future ahead of her," she replied. "I might have made a difference then, but I was a coward. She must be almost thirty now. God knows how she turned out. It's not a good sign that she's running away from an abusive husband. Maybe her coming isn't a blessing, Henry. Maybe it's a reproach."

Although she had articulated some of my own doubts, my fueling them would only make the reunion harder. "Whatever trouble she's in, we'll deal with it together."

"You? You shouldn't even be out of bed," she said, wiping her eyes, but I could tell she was reassured.

"Let's start with the packing," I said, and together we repacked her suitcase so that everything fit.

I woke in the middle of the night and realized that, for the first time since I'd had the heart attack, I was completely alone. My stomach began to churn anxiety while my head went spinning on *what ifs. What if I had another attack and couldn't reach the phone? What if the paramedics couldn't find the house? What if I died this time and didn't come back?* I lay there with my finger pressed to my pulse. After a minute, I wondered whether I was really prepared to spend the rest of my life obsessively monitoring my pulse and worrying if the next heart beat would be the last. Hayward was right: Everyone died of something and I would probably die of heart disease. Fretting about when would not delay the moment. I relaxed, took a deep breath, and closed my eyes. I did not fall asleep immediately, but when I finally did, I didn't wake again until it was light.

That afternoon I was sitting on a chaise-longue on the deck with my shirt off, taking in the sun and nodding off over a volume of Supreme Court advance sheets, when I heard a woman exclaim, "Henry!"

I opened my eyes and turned my head. Inez Montoya was poised above the back of the chaise, about to grab my shoulders.

I barked out a grumpy, "Don't do that."

"*Dios mío,*" she said. "They told me you almost died and I find the door unlocked and you out here not moving." She dug into her purse and pulled out a cigarette, clicked her lighter on, then stopped. "Shit, I guess I shouldn't smoke around you."

"Just be careful not to ignite the canyon. What brings you down from Sacramento?"

She pulled up a chair and sucked on the cigarette impatiently; the same way she went through life. Her clothes hung on her—she was in a thin phase—and her strong bones showed in her long, dark face, which had always reminded me of the face of a female Aztec deity. Inez was not, however, the presiding goddess of a local volcano, she was something called the secretary of state, a position to which she had been elected the previous spring in the Democratic landslide that gave California its first Democratic governor in sixteen years. We had known each other for more than two decades, first meeting as young public defenders. She had gone into politics, as tough-minded and hard-nosed as the men with whom she competed, until slowly but steadily she climbed the political ladder to become the first Latina to hold statewide office, albeit an office that no one, including Inez, seemed to know the function of exactly. That wasn't the point: It gave her national visibility, which she planned to put to good use when the senior senator from California retired in six years. Why she maintained our friendship was a mystery to me, since I imagined I was a great disappointment to her.

"I have a fund-raiser in Santa Monica tomorrow. Movie ladies. Plus I wanted to see you. Who's taking care of you?"

"Different friends drop by," I said. "Today it's the Kwans from next door. Everyone brings a casserole. Where's yours?"

She crushed her cigarette beneath an elegant sandal and said, "Listen, *m'ijo*, my cooking would send you back to the hospital. Anyway, I brought you something better than a casserole."

She dropped a diskette into my lap.

"What's this?"

"Judicial application," she said. "I had one of my staff download it for you."

"You want me to apply for a judgeship?"

"The governor got eighty percent of the Latino vote," she said.

"I figure I'm responsible for twenty percent. That's worth a couple of judges."

"Oh, I see. For a minute there, I thought it might have something to do with my qualifications."

She lit another cigarette. "Spoken like a true male," she said, clicking her lighter shut. "Don't tell me it never crossed your mind when you were arguing to some *payaso* in a black robe, that you couldn't do a better job."

I temporized. "They're not all clowns. All right, yes, I've thought about it."

"*Pues*, I can do this for you. Just fill out the form."

I picked up the diskette. "All right. It can be my occupational therapy."

"Always a smart-ass remark," she said. She put out her cigarette and studied me with an expression that seemed to mingle concern for me and fear for her own mortality. "You're skin and bones. How bad was it?"

"They tell me I actually died for about a minute," I said. "If you stand close enough, you can still smell the sulfur from the fire and brimstone. Have you figured out what the secretary of state does yet?"

"She runs for senator," she said, then added in her bossiest voice. "And don't die again."

Elena called that evening, and from the weariness in her voice when she greeted me, I knew the reunion had not been one of unmitigated joy.

"Is she your daughter, Elena?"

"Yes," she said. "She is definitely my daughter." Her words were emphatic, but her tone was neutral, cautious. "She showed me the paper with my address on it that I gave the social worker. She's also the spitting image of Mom."

That startled me. In our generation, my mother's genetic heritage had been overwhelmed by my father's, whom both my sister and I resembled. "Then she doesn't look like us," I said.

"No," she said, "but Angel looks exactly like you when you were ten. It's eerie. I keep calling him Henry."

That was more startling still. "Does he know about me?"

"I showed him a picture of you when you were a boy. He kept asking to see it, so I finally gave it to him."

"What are they like?"

In the silence that followed, I discerned that she was choosing her words carefully. "A step or two up from street people," she said. "Vicky's had a hard life but it hasn't made her hard. She is pretty closed-mouth, though. But then I was the mother who abandoned her, so I can't expect her to trust me right away."

"Has she told you anything more about why she came to you?"

"She said her husband was in prison for beating her until last month, when they released him. The first thing he did was find her and beat her for having gone to the police the last time. She went to a women's shelter in San Francisco, but they asked her to leave. Everyone she knows also knows him, so she came here."

"Why was she asked to leave the shelter?"

Another careful silence. "She said it was because she's a Christian and the women who ran the shelter weren't."

"That doesn't make sense."

"She belongs to one of those storefront Pentecostal churches that have sprung up in the barrios the last twenty years. You know, what we used to call Holy Rollers. Vicky's very serious about her religion. Most women's shelters are secular, to say the least. I can imagine her giving her born-again spiel to a lesbian social worker."

"Has she given it to you and Joanne yet?"

"She's let drop a couple of disapproving references to lifestyles, but so far we haven't had that conversation." She added quickly, as if in mitigation. "Don't misunderstand, Henry. I respect her faith. I think it's all that has kept her from the kind of street life I was afraid that she had had."

"No evidence of drugs?"

"No," she said. "She really doesn't seem the type."

"What's the boy like?"

Without hesitation, she replied, "He radiates intelligence and he's so self-possessed you forget he's a child."

"Children who don't seem like children have generally had a pretty rough time of it," I observed. "Has he been abused, too?"

"If he has, it wasn't by her," she said. "They're so close they're almost telepathic. Vicky's intelligent, too, Henry, though she didn't get much education. I think she sees Angel's potential and she's tried to give him stability, but this man she married, he sounds like her worst mistake."

"Has she told you what she wants?"

"She says she needs a little time to get herself together."

"Does she work?"

"She told me she was a maid at a hotel in the city. She gave up her job because she was afraid her husband would turn up while she was at work."

"What's her husband's name?"

"Peter. Peter Trujillo."

"Do you know what prison he was in?"

"San Quentin. Why?"

"I can probably pull his rap sheet."

"His what?"

"His criminal record. It would tell us what he was convicted of, when he was paroled and under what conditions. If he was convicted of some kind of spousal abuse crime and he's stalking her, he could be tossed back into the prison on a parole violation."

I could tell she was tempted, but she said, "I need to establish trust with her. What you're suggesting sounds too much like going behind her back or trying to run her life."

"These domestic violence situations can be terribly volatile, Elena, and they tend to escalate. I don't like the idea of this guy showing up at your house with a gun and a grudge."

"According to Vicky, he doesn't know anything about me. That's why she came here."

"That's hard to believe if they were married any length of time," I said. "Finding out who your natural mother is, that's big news. Don't you think she would have told him?"

"I think she always meant for me to be her last resort," Elena said.

"I'd still be worried."

"Don't be," she said. "As hard as this is, Henry, I can't tell you how happy I am that she and Angel are here. All I want now is to spend as much time as I can with them. I'll tell her what you told me about her husband being in violation of his parole, and maybe we can find a lawyer who specializes in domestic violence cases."

"I'll get you a referral," I said.

"Good," she said. "Let's talk tomorrow, and, Henry, don't worry. You should be happy, too. Overnight, our family's been doubled."

Yeah, I thought, *not counting the psycho husband*. "I can't wait to meet them," I said.

The next morning, I called around and got the names of a couple of lawyers in the San Francisco area who handled domestic violence cases. Then I called a contact in the sheriff's office and persuaded him to get me Peter Trujillo's rap sheet. A few minutes later, I called him back and asked him to pull the criminal history, if any, of my niece as well.

4.

THE FAX MACHINE IN MY OFFICE WENT OFF WHILE I WAS watching Fred MacMurray in *Double Indemnity* having one of the longest death scenes in cinematic history. I went to retrieve the fax, and when I returned, he was still dying. I switched the TV off and examined the fax. The cover sheet bore the letterhead of the Los Angeles County sheriff's office. In the space for remarks, my sheriff pal had written: "Who are these losers?" I flipped to the next page, my niece's rap sheet.

Victoria Mary Trujillo, a.k.a. Victoria Maria Rios, born twenty-nine years earlier; five foot five; one hundred and twenty pounds; brown hair; black eyes; a small butterfly tattoo on her right ankle; a San Francisco address that I recognized as the Tenderloin. Probably a welfare hotel. Three arrests and three convictions, the first when she was twenty-two, the last when she was twenty-six: the first conviction was for Health and Safety Code section 11350, the second for Penal Code 647(b) and then another for 11350. In English, she'd been busted once for prostitution and twice for possession of a controlled substance, all misdemeanors. The prostitution charge had been knocked down to a 415, disturbing the peace, the standard plea bargain for a first-time offender. On the first possession charge, she was allowed to enter a drug diversion program; the second time, she did 90 days in the county jail. That was three years ago and she'd gone without convictions since. I tried to give her the benefit of the doubt, but if her son was now ten, she'd incurred all of her arrests after he was born. Each time she had been convicted, she had risked losing him to the same system of foster care in which she had grown up. Hardly mom-of-the-year material. Still, something had happened within the past three years. The type and sequence of her offenses pointed to the beginning of an all-too-familiar story: female drug addict who turns tricks to support her habit. I could even guess her drug of choice. Crack. A quick, cheap high that didn't screw around like heroin or yuppie cocaine, but took its users down fast and hard. My niece, however, seemed either to have learned her lesson or learned discretion. Elena said she'd found Jesus. That might well be, but when I'd seen it happen over the years to the occasional client, he was eager to testify to his prior wanton ways, the more dramatically to contrast his present state of salvation. I gathered that my niece had not mentioned to my sister her stint as Mary Magdalene, pre-Jesus.

Peter Trujillo, a.k.a. Solo, born thirty-four years earlier; five foot ten; one hundred and sixty-five pounds; brown hair; brown eyes; numerous gang tattoos; a healed bullet wound in his right thigh and, for further identifying marks, a sixth toe on his left foot. The same San Francisco address as my niece. I glanced down the lengthy list of his arrests and convictions, and thought, *Whoa. This looks familiar.* Generically familiar, that is—Solo's three-page rap sheet told the story of an entire generation of poor Latino boys: gangs, guns, drugs, jail and early graves. He had gotten off to a seriously bad start: juvenile convictions for robbery and attempted murder that garnered him a seven-year sentence at the California Youth Authority—"prison with training wheels" an old supervisor of mine at the public defender's office used to call the CYA. Still, Solo had been lucky. Sixteen-year-olds who committed the same offenses today were automatically tried as adults and skipped CYA for prison. There followed the classic rap sheet of a drug addict. Theft offenses alternated with drug arrests, and while he never again committed as heavy a crime as he had when he was sixteen, he racked up the usual low-grade felonies of someone supporting a ravenous habit: second-degree burglary, receiving stolen property, grand theft, petty theft with a prior. He was fortunate only in that Three Strikes hadn't been in effect while he had piled up most of these convictions, but it was in effect the last time he'd been convicted of felony possession of heroin with intent to sell. His juvenile convictions counted as strikes and he should have been sentenced to life upon his plea to the possession count. Instead, and incredibly, he got off with a 36-month sentence. He must have had a hell of a lawyer to persuade a judge to dismiss the prior strikes and sentence him to the lowest term for possession. His record ended with the notation that he had been paroled from San Quentin four weeks earlier, with the usual drug conditions.

Wait, I thought. Didn't Elena tell me that Vicky said her husband had gone to prison for beating her up? I rechecked the last entry. Straight drug possession. Of course there could have been misdemeanor spousal abuse charges that were dismissed as part of a deal. Dismissed charges weren't always picked up by the Department of Justice when they prepared criminal histories. Drug-addict/wife-beater was a pretty common combination, but it was odd that none of his prior arrests or convictions were for any of the usual domestic violence offenses. Which in my experience could mean only one thing—she never called the cops on him when he hit her. And what that meant to me was that she would eventually return to him.

Edith Rosen showed up that evening with a bag of groceries and cooked me a meal of baked chicken, baked potatoes, and stringbeans, with strawberries for dessert. Afterward, we sat on the deck and watched the sunset while drinking a special green tea that she insisted had helpful medicinal qualities. It tasted very much like it smelled, and it smelled like the moldering woods in a poem by Edgar Allan Poe.

"Edith, what do you know about wife-beating?" I asked, tossing the contents of my cup over the railing. "Professionally, I mean."

She poured me another cup, saying mildly, "Honey helps, now drink it. What about domestic violence?"

"The women so often go back to the men who beat them. Why is that?"

"Often because they have no economic choice, especially if there are children. They need the man's income even if they pay for it with bruises and broken bones. Drink your tea, I mean it. My rabbi swears that it's a blood cleanser."

I put in another two tablespoons of honey and essayed a sip. It still tasted of the tomb. "I feel my blood getting cleaner by the moment. I meant what's the psychological reason they go back to their abusers?"

She leaned back and pulled her sweater around her as a cool breeze trickled up from the canyon. "This is a little out of my field, but battered women's syndrome is a fairly widely accepted explanation of that particular dance of death. You begin with a woman with low self-esteem and a man who alternates between being attentive and being violent. The attention bolsters her self-esteem, the violence tears it down. She's a little like Sisyphus, you know. She rolls the rock up the hill and then it rolls down and flattens her. Why are you asking me this?"

"I'm trying to understand my niece," I said.

She set her cup down. "Yes, Elena said something to me about an abusive husband the other morning."

"I looked at his criminal history. No convictions or even arrests for domestic violence. She's never called the cops on him."

"You don't know that," Edith said. "The police are often called and leave without making an arrest or bothering to take a report."

"They've been together ten years, give or take his jail and prison time. If he hit her habitually and she reported him, someone would have noticed."

Edith smiled grimly. "Really, Henry, you know the criminal system as well as I do. The cracks are big enough for whole populations to fall through, and poor women are the first to go."

I swallowed some tea and made a face. "She finally went to a shelter. If she knew enough to do that, she must have had some sense that the system could protect her. She didn't report him, Edith. She'll go back to him."

"Have you talked to Elena about this?"

"No," I said. "When I offered to run his rap sheet, she told me not to. I ran Vicky's too. Arrests for drugs and prostitution."

Edith counseled kids who were facing murder charges. Vicky's record did not impress her. All she said was, "Current user?"

"I don't know. Elena doesn't think so, but she does live in that ivory tower. Vicky's last drug arrest is three years old."

"And the prostitution arrest?"

"Seven years." I conceded. "That may not mean anything except that she got smarter."

"You seem determined to think the worst of her," she observed.

"I don't want my sister to be hurt."

She poured herself more tea, raised the teapot in my direction. I crossed myself as if to ward it off. "Very funny," she said. "Elena's a very able woman, Henry. She can handle this situation without you having to run background checks."

"She feels so guilty about having put her daughter up for adoption that she's an easy mark."

"Realistically, Henry, what do you imagine your niece can do to her?" she asked, in the modulated tones that therapists use when they want to let you know you're being an idiot.

"She can get herself emotionally invested with a masochist," I said. "A woman involved in what you called the 'dance of death' with an abusive husband. I don't want my sister dragged into that kind of ugliness."

"I don't know whether to be touched by your sibling loyalty or annoyed by your male chauvinism," she said. "So I repeat—Elena can handle the situation. You might think about your hostility to your niece."

"This isn't my issue."

"Pulling the girl's rap sheet is not exactly avuncular behavior, sweetie," she observed over the rim of her cup.

I knew better than to argue with her when she was in full therapist efflorescence, so I drank the wretched tea.

The following morning, I decided to return *Double Indemnity* myself instead of calling the video store and asking them to pick it up, a service they performed for shut-ins like me. This meant taking my most ambitious walk yet, all the way down the hill from my house to Franklin where the store was located, a distance of about five blocks. In the warm May morning, the big white Mediterranean-style houses drifted like galleons on lush lawns. Hummingbirds burst through the smoky air, bullets of green and yellow. Cars and trucks streamed continuously up and down the broad boulevard, creating a constant low rumble broken by the occasional shriek of brakes at an intersection where the stop sign was almost hidden by a stray branch of flame-colored bougainvillea. I felt almost maniacally alive on the way down, but halfway up the hill on the way home, my legs turned into sandbags and I was nearly gasping for breath.

I felt like I had drifted into the deep end and the water was closing over my head. I told myself not to panic. Hayward had cautioned me that I would experience these moments of exhaustion— "You've been dragged down a bad stretch of road by a Mack truck," he said. "The body has great recuperative powers, but you're not in control of them. Sometimes you're going to wear out." Still, it was terrifying to feel my fragile heart pounding in my chest as if looking for the nearest exit. Knees creaking, I lowered myself to the curb to catch my breath. Fatigue seeped through my entire body, a kind of weariness I had never felt in my life before the heart attack. At that moment, I would happily have died rather than get up. I pulled out my cell phone and dialed information for the number to a cab company. Then I heard heavy footsteps coming down the driveway behind me, turned my head and saw a pair of battered construction boots, the laces broken and retied, the leather cracked. I snapped the phone shut as I raised my eyes to bejeaned legs, a plaid shirt and the dark, inquisitive face of a man wearing a red baseball cap with the words DeLeon & Son stitched across a stenciled lion's head.

"Hey," he said. "You all right, man?"

"Is this your yard? Sorry. I didn't mean to trespass."

"Don't worry about that. You don't look so good."

"I just have to sit for a minute."

His face came into focus; skin the color of walnuts, short curly reddish-brown hair, a darker goatee flecked with gray. His eyes were narrowed in what appeared to be the permanent squint of someone who spent a lot of time in the sun. When he stooped down, I saw they were green. I guessed he was a few years younger than me but slightly more battered; deep lines bracketed his mouth, the flesh sagged beneath his eyes. He was long-legged, with a workingman's heavily muscled arms and chest. A potbelly pressed against his shirt. He grinned as if we were old friends and not two strangers meeting under peculiar circumstances.

"What happened, man? You tie one on down at the corner cantina?"

"I'm recovering from a heart attack," I said. "I went for a walk and ran out of gas. I'll be fine in a couple of minutes."

His eyes were thoughtful "Heart attack, huh? You seem way too young."

"They run in the family."

"I'm Johnny," he said, then quickly amended. "John."

"Henry Rios," I said. "Are you DeLeon or son?"

"Huh?"

"Your hat."

"I'm the son. Where do you live, Henry?"

I pointed to the top of the hill. "Up there."

He straightened himself up. "Come on, I'll drive you."

"If it's no trouble."

He shrugged, pulled me up from the curb with a powerful arm and pointed to a red Ford pickup truck in the driveway. "That's my truck. Can you make it?"

"Sure," I said. "You live here?"

"No, I'm a contractor. The owner wants to add a master bedroom and bath. I dropped by to give him an estimate. Let me get that door for you."

"I got it," I said, but not fast enough. He opened the door, helped me up into the cab, and closed the door behind me. I wanted to reassure him that I wasn't about to drop dead, but I couldn't really vouch for it. "Thanks, John."

He looked at me for a moment and said, "I'm thinking maybe I should get you to an emergency room instead of taking you home."

"It's not that bad, really."

"If you say so," he said, then went around the truck and climbed in. As he reversed down the driveway, he asked, "How long you been out of the hospital?"

"Four days."

He looked at me incredulously. "You should be in bed, man, not trying to hike up hills."

"My doctor wants me to be up and around," I said. "Take the next left. It's three houses from the corner on the right. There's my driveway."

He pulled in, and before I could thank him, got out of the truck, came around and opened the door for me.

"Thanks for the ride."

"Someone inside to take care of you?"

"I'll be fine."

"I'm coming in," he said simply.

Part of me wanted to shrug him off, but then I took stock of my-self and figured it might not be a bad idea if he hung around for a couple of minutes until I was sure I was all right. "All right," I said. "I appreciate it. Thank you."

Once inside, I asked, "You want something to drink? I don't have any liquor in the house, but there's lemonade and cranberry juice and some other stuff."

"Lemonade would be great. I'll get it, you sit down."

"It's quicker if I do it," I said, heading into the kitchen.

"I'm not in any hurry," he said.

When I came out, he was in the living room, standing at the fire-place holding a framed picture of Josh and me. He put it back on the mantel with a slightly guilty grin and accepted the glass I held out to him.

"That's a sturdy-looking deck," he said, glancing through the glass doors. "You do the work?"

"No," I said. "I can change a light bulb and hang a picture. After that I have to call one of you guys. You want to go out?"

We went outside and stood at the railing, looking across the canyon. John said, "You got a real nice setup here."

"Where do you live?"

"Up on Mount Washington," he said. "It's like this, but wilder and even quieter. I spend all day around saws and hammers and whatnot. When I go home I don't want to hear nothing but birds and the wind in the trees."

"You must not have kids."

"They're grown," he said. "My boy's a junior up at Cal. My daughter's married. I'm a granddad."

"So it's just your wife and you."

He gulped some lemonade. "Divorced."

"I'm sorry to hear it."

He turned his back to the canyon and said, "It's okay." He seemed to be thinking something over carefully. I knew what it was.

The picture of Josh, me alone up here with no apparent family. He had figured out I was gay. My stomach clenched. I'd been out of the closet for a long time, but this moment always set me on edge because I could never predict how the news would be received by some new person who entered my life, even as briefly as this nice man with his sad eyes. He showed no visible disgust, but sometimes they didn't at first, but would then say something stupid or foolish or evil. And what had been a pleasant conversation would become an argument.

"How come your boyfriend's not here to take care of you?" he asked. I heard nothing in his voice except concern that I'd been left alone in such bad shape.

"Josh died awhile ago," I said.

"AIDS?"

"Yeah."

"Man, that's rough. I'm real sorry."

He's a genuinely nice guy, I thought, but I didn't want to be having this conversation. Although I no longer felt in imminent danger of keeling over, I was still exhausted. "I need to lie down for a while."

He must have seen from the fatigue in my face that I wasn't blowing him off. He nodded and said, "I'll wash up these glasses and get out of here."

I stretched out on the couch, listening to him shuffle around in the kitchen. He turned the tap off and then came back into the living room, sat at the edge of the couch and said, "You gonna be all right?"

"Yeah, I get tired, then it passes."

"You need anything?"

"Thanks, John, but I'll be fine. My friends drop by and check up on me."

"That's good," he said. He stood up. "It was real nice meeting you, Henry."

"Same here. Thanks for getting me home. I'd still be sitting on the curb if you hadn't come by."

"That's cool," he said. "Listen, I think I'm going to get that job, so I'll be in the neighborhood. Maybe I could drop by too, huh? See how you're doing."

"Sure," I said, fading. "That would be great."

He smiled. "All right, then, I'll be seeing you." I fell asleep as soon as he left, and when I woke up a couple of hours later it was as if I had dreamed the whole thing.

When Elena called that night, she heard the fatigue in my voice and forced the story of my expedition to the video store out of me.

"Oh, Henry," she said. "I'm flying down tomorrow."

"No," I said. "I talked to Hayward and he said my panic was psychological, not physical. He told me he wouldn't have released me from the hospital if I couldn't handle it." To forestall further conversation about my health, I asked, "How are things going with Vicky?"

She accepted the change of subject. "I mentioned to her your idea about reporting Pete being in violation of his parole, but she said no."

"Why?"

"She gave a kind of garbled explanation," Elena said. "She's very evasive."

Alarms went off. "About what?"

"Pete," she said. "The bruises on her face are still visible from the last time he hit her, but I think—"

"She wants to go back to him?" I suggested.

"I've walked in on a couple of furtive phone calls," she replied.

"To whom?"

"I can't be sure, but who else would it be but him?"

I summarized my conversation with Edith about domestic violence, omitting, of course, any reference to anyone's rap sheet. "You have to be prepared for the possibility she'll want to hook up with him again."

"Really, Henry," she replied impatiently. "You talk as if I don't know anything about women who put up with violent husbands."

"I didn't know you did," I said, slightly piqued.

"Have you forgotten?" she asked incredulously. "We were raised by one."

Our mother. And then I understood how deeply my sister was already invested in her daughter and her daughter's fate.

"You think it's a case of history repeating itself?"

"Not if I can help it," she replied.

Afterward, it occurred to me that what Edith had described as my hostility to my as-yet-unmet niece might have something to do with my memories of my mother. Another weak woman in thrall to a violent man, with a child whom no one was protecting. Yes, I'd seen that movie before.

5.

My mother had been dead for more than twenty years. She had been so self-effacing it was difficult for me to remember what she looked like, though I could still see her hands, covered with flour from making tortillas or clasped tightly together in prayer as she knelt beside her bed. When I was very small, I prayed beside her, but as her God seemed unable or unwilling to control my father's rages, I soon drifted away from her and her faith. In the prison of my childhood, she was halfway between an inmate and a guard. Sometimes she was the object of my father's fury, but more often she seemed to be his collaborator, making excuses for him, admonishing me to stay out of his way, denying the reality of his brutality by pretending he was no more than an average disciplinarian even when he left me black and blue. The time he broke my arm, it was my mother who took me to the emergency room and told the doctor I had fallen from a tree. My hatred of my father kept him vivid in my memory for decades after I had left home, but my mother had faded away, leaving only the faint residue of contempt. Adult life had taught me that she was as much his victim as I was, and he himself was a victim of a culture in which Mexicans were viewed as a simple race of gardeners and maids. With his thick ac-

cent, dark skin, and Indian features, every encounter with the outside world was an assault on my father's dignity. Unable to strike
back at the Americans on whom he depended for his living, he took
it out on his American son. I had come to terms, if not peace, with
my father, but I had simply dismissed my mother without trying to
make sense of my feelings about her. Perhaps this niece had tapped
into them and maybe that was why, sight unseen, I was ready to
think the worst of her.

I didn't have long to ponder the connection between Vicky and
my mother before my sister called with a development that seemed
to render the issue moot. She and Joanne had gone away for the
weekend on a long-planned vacation. When they'd returned, Vicky
and Angel were gone.

Before I could stop myself, I asked, "Anything missing?"

In a flat voice, she replied, "Some cash. A credit card." Before I
could respond, she added, "Don't tell me to call the police, Henry."

"I wasn't going to."

"I would have given her money."

"Do you think she went back to her husband?"

"I don't know." Something in her tone told me she was equivo-
cating.

"That seems the likeliest explanation," I prodded. "You said you
thought she had called him—"

She cut me off. "The Thursday before we left, I had a long talk
with Vicky. I tried to explain why I put her up for adoption. It was
painful for both of us, but I thought we were getting close to some
kind of understanding. Then I reminded her about the time I had
gone to the group home when she was fifteen. She didn't remember
it at first, but once she did, she was furious that I had found her and
then left her again."

"What did you say?"

"What could I say? When I put her up for adoption, I was struggling to start my own life. Giving her up was the best choice I could
make for both of us, but I couldn't justify giving her up a second

time. That was just fear. I couldn't explain it, I could only ask her to forgive me."

"How did she respond?"

"She told me she was sexually molested in that group home, that it was probably going on around the time I came to visit. When Joanne and I returned from the weekend, Vicky and Angel were gone."

"You think that's why she left?"

"I think she decided her chances were better with a husband who beats her than a mother who deserts her," she said.

"If she went back to him, Elena, it's because that's her pattern."

"You didn't see her face when I told her," she replied.

"When she's had time to think about it, she'll realize that whatever happened in the past, you were willing now to take her in and help her."

"Joanne says the same thing," she replied. "I just want to know that she's all right."

"Have you canceled the credit card?"

"No," she said. "Why?"

"Don't cancel it for a while and find out what charges she makes on it. That may lead to her."

"Yes, that's a good idea," she said. "Thank you, Henry. I haven't even asked you how you're feeling."

"Better every day," I replied.

In fact, however, three weeks after the heart attack there were many days when my body simply stalled and it was all I could do to stagger out of bed and into the living room, where I would fall asleep on the couch only to be roused in the afternoon by whichever friend was dropping by that day to check up on me. After eating something, I went back to bed, and when I opened my eyes, it was the next morning. I was having that kind of day when, one afternoon, I was awakened from the couch by the doorbell.

I thought it might be the pair of Mormon missionary boys I'd spotted Mrs. Byrne running off her property earlier. She was a born-again harridan, and in her book, Mormons were no better than devil-worshipers. They were not going to get a much friendlier reception from me. I composed my face into a scowl and opened the door. John DeLeon smiled and said, "Hey, how are you doing?"

He was wearing pretty much the same clothes as he had when he'd given me a lift home a week earlier—maybe the flannel shirt was a different plaid—and looked like he had just come off work.

"John," I said. I canceled the scowl and put up a hasty—and I'm sure unconvincing—smile of my own. "I'm fine. How are you?"

He wore a small gold hoop earring in his right ear, almost hidden by a graying lock of hair. I felt the glow of his physical vitality. Rarely had I met a person of such palpable warmth. It made me all the more aware of the chill of my ill-health.

He took in my pajamas and bathrobe. "Am I catching you at a bad time?"

"I was asleep."

He stood irresolutely at the door. "I thought maybe you might want to get a bite to eat."

"That sounds great, but can I take a rain check? I'm really not up to it."

He nodded. "Yeah. Hey, I'm really sorry if I woke you up."

"Don't worry about it," I said.

"Okay, then. Later."

"Good-bye, John."

I stood in the doorway and watched him head down the driveway to his truck. There was something in the movement of his shoulders—the momentary droop of a small humiliation—that made me think this visit had not been as casual or as easy for him as he had made it sound. I thought about him driving off feeling bad because his kind impulse had been rejected, while I wandered back into my house for another long evening of dozing and waking and feeling sorry for myself.

"Hey, John," I said. "Wait a minute."

He turned around and walked back. "Yeah?"

"Actually, I think it would do me good to get out of the house for a while."

"I won't keep you out late." He grinned. "I know this great place not too far from here."

"Come in for a second while I get dressed," I said, and stood aside to let him pass.

I angled my feet around the toolbox on the floor of the cab. A medallion of the Virgin of Guadalupe dangled from the rearview mirror, and stuck in the sun visor was a prayer card that depicted Michael the Archangel with a fiery sword and Satan prostrate at his feet. We rolled down the hill, past the red-faced Mormon kids, in the warm May twilight. A baseball game was playing on the radio in the background. He was telling me that he'd been hired at the house where he'd picked me up the other morning.

"Should take about three months," he said. "Damn!"

"What's wrong?"

"Braves scored."

"What?"

He glanced at me. "The game. Dodgers playing the Braves. You don't follow baseball."

"Not since I was a boy," I said. "I used to root for the Giants. You're a big fan?"

"I played," he said, in a voice resonant with quiet pride. "Played in the minors for the Dodgers organization. I made it up to the bigs for two games. Four innings."

"That's impressive."

With a self-deprecating grin, he said, "It was a long time ago, man. Twenty-five years."

"What position did you play?"

"Pitcher," he said. He took a sharp left turn off Santa Monica and pulled up to the curb in front of a brown stucco building with a tattered blue canopy over the door and a small red neon sign on the wall blinking the words MARIA'S RAMADA. "This is it."

Across the street was a long, three-story brick building with an institutional look. Over the door, however, was a bas relief depicting an angel.

"What is that?" I asked, pointing to the building as we got out of the truck.

"Nursing home," John said.

"That looks like a chapel, with the angel over the door."

"Could be," he said. "I'll have to ask my dad. He lived around here when he was a kid."

We headed toward the restaurant. "Did you grow up in this neighborhood?"

"Me? No. I grew up in Pasadena. That's where my parents moved after my dad started making money from his business."

"DeLeon and Son. Does he still work with you?"

He shook his head. "He's seventy-seven now. He takes care of his garden, spoils his grandkids." He smiled. "Gives me lots of unsolicited advice about the business, but damn if he isn't usually right." He pushed open the door to the restaurant and put his hand on my shoulder. "It's nothing fancy."

Piñatas dangled from the ceiling over booths separated from one another by bamboo screens. On one wall were garish movie posters advertising Mexican movies of the 1940s and '50s with Cantinflas or Dolores Del Rio; on another, a velvet painting of a pneumatically muscled Aztec warrior lifting a maiden with breasts like projectiles. The floor was covered with sawdust. Dusty paper flowers and strings of small earthen jars stretching across the ceiling completed the décor.

A smiling teenage girl greeted John as if she recognized him and led us to a booth. On the table between us was a candle, a jar of pickled vegetables, a Dos Equis beer bottle holding a paper rose, and a metate in the shape of a pig carved from volcanic rock filled with chile so hot I could smell it.

"My grandmother had a metate exactly like this one."

"Every *'buelita* had that metate," John said.

The girl left for a moment, then returned with water, a basket of tortilla chips, a bowl of fresh salsa, flatware and menus. She laid them before us with shy efficiency and eye-averted modesty.

"That girl seemed to recognize you," I said.

"I know the family that owns the place. The Huertas," he said. "I did some work for them. The girl is a niece or something. They brought her up from Mexico." He unfolded the menu. "Everything's good here, but especially the fish. You like fish?"

I nodded, looked around the garish room and asked, "So what part of the décor are you responsible for?"

He grinned. "The kitchen."

The restaurant was almost empty when we arrived, but the booths soon began to fill. The clientele seemed about equally divided between *mexicanos* in straw hats playing Javier Solis on the jukebox and would-be Anglo bohemians from nearby Silverlake, complaining to the waiters about the loudness of the music and anxious over whether the refried beans were vegetarian or not.

The young waitress brought our drinks and took our orders. After she left, I asked him, "What happened with baseball?"

"I tore a ligament in my pitching arm," he said. "Nowadays, they just take a tendon from somewhere else in your body and transplant it, but not back then, not for a minor leaguer."

"You must have had some talent to get called up, even if only for a couple of games."

"I was a lefty, and there's never enough of those to go around, so I got more attention than maybe I deserved." He dunked a chip into the hot salsa and munched it. "*Hijole*, that's hot. Don't get me wrong, Henry, I had decent stuff when I could control it." He tried another chip. "They may have been able to make something out of me, but when I ripped up my arm, that was it was *adiós*, Johnny."

"Just like that?"

He gulped some water. "I was pretty immature. I don't think they were that sorry to see me go."

"You must have been barely out of your teens," I said. "Immaturity goes with the territory."

"I was a big blowhard, Henry. I was sure I was going to be the next big Latin star. Roberto Clemente, Juan Marichal, and me. The only problem was I didn't have their talent and I didn't like to work all that hard, either. That's a bad combination. I'm suprised I lasted as long as I did."

"How long was that?"

"Five years," he replied. "I was recruited right out of high school. Man, my dad wasn't happy about that."

"Why?"

"He wanted me to go to college like my brothers and sisters," he said. "I got three of each, and they're all white-collar but me and my sister Josefa. She dropped out of college to get married. After baseball got done with me, I never made it back to school."

"You went to work for your dad?"

Our food arrived on enormous, thick white platters. John had a whole fish while I had ordered the snapper Vera Cruz. There were piles of rice and beans on the side and a big bowl of salad to split, with a fragrant stack of corn tortillas. The food made me think of my mother, who was a wonderful cook. She frequently cooked dishes that she knew I particularly liked. The platters of *chile rellenos* and bowls of *picadillo* were messages from her to me seeking forgiveness. I would pass them, untouched, to my father.

As he separated the flesh from the bone of his fish, John said, "I didn't go to work for my dad right away."

"What did you do?"

"Partied," he said, sprinking the fish with lemon. "*Buen provecho*," he said, and for a few minutes we ate. "Yeah, I partied for five solid years. Even getting married and having my kids didn't stop me. When I wasn't high, I was drunk."

"And then?"

"I woke up in jail," he said, piling beans on a piece of tortilla. He stuffed it into his mouth, chewed, swallowed, sipped his Coke.

"DUI?"

He nodded. "With injuries, mostly to me, but the girl who was with me in the car, she got hurt some, too. Oh, yeah, and she wasn't my wife. Wasn't my first arrest, either. My folks had bailed me out before. This time my pop told me I could either come back home and learn a man's trade, or rot in jail." He smiled. "It was a harder decision than you'd think. My father, he's a great man, Henry, but a little on the severe side."

"I know something about severe Mexican fathers," I said.

"He told me loved me," John said. "But that he didn't respect me. You know things like that sound a lot worse when you say them in Spanish. He thought I was, you know, *un* playboy. When it came to construction, I couldn't tell a hammer from a hole in the ground, so he put me on his crew and I learned." He grinned. "I didn't get special treatment for being the boss's son. Some days, the nicest thing he called me was *pendejo*. If my mom knew how he talked on the job, she'd make him go to church twice on Sunday. After a while, I started to get the hang of things. I even found out I had some talent for designing stuff. My dad saw it. He offered to send me back to school to study architecture or something, but I told him I was happy where I was."

"That still true?"

"There were years when I couldn't watch baseball because it hurt too much to think about what I'd thrown away, but I'm forty-three now and whatever career I coulda had in the bigs would be over by now, so I guess I don't have regrets I can't live with."

"That's philosophical."

"Yeah," he said, smiling. "That's me, Johnny DeLeon, philosopher. What about you? What do you do?"

"I'm a lawyer. Didn't I tell you that the other day?"

"You were kind of out of it the other day, Henry. Wow, an *abogado*. I'm impressed, man. What kind of law?"

"Criminal defense."

"Helping the people," he said, nodding.

"Since the heart attack, my new career seems to be sleeping."

He finished his Coke and signaled the girl for another one. "You don't have family to take care of you?"

"My parents are dead," I said. "I have a sister who lives in Oakland." I decided not to tell about Vicky and her son, as it seemed a moot point.

"Man, I can't imagine what I'd do without my family."

"For me, it was good, not really having a family. I was able to live my life my own way without worrying about how the fallout might affect them."

"You mean being gay."

"Not just that," I said. "I've tried to be true to who I think I am in other ways, too."

He looked at me and said, "I think you're brave, man."

"Being brave is doing the things you're afraid of doing, not the ones you were born to do."

"There ain't too many people can do either one," he said. "I bet you've done both."

"But I never pitched in the majors."

He laughed. "Okay, I guess I'm embarrassing you. How are you feeling?"

I ran a quick check. "I feel pretty good."

"You wanna go home, or would you like to get coffee somewhere?"

"Coffee."

We fought over the check, but as it turned out our meals were on Mr. Huerta, who came over and thanked John effusively for the work he'd done in the restaurant's kitchen, for which, I pieced together, he'd only charged for supplies. When I mentioned it in the truck, he shrugged and changed the subject.

We ended up at a coffeehouse on Beverly at the edge of West Hollywood as austere as Maria's had been over the top: concrete floors, metal tables, actor-waiters clad in black and Edith Piaf singing softly beneath the din of cell phone conversations.

"This is different," I said at the doorway.

"I was the contractor on this place," he said. "There's a table by the window. Grab it, I'll get coffee."

I comandeered the table and watched him approach the counter, completely out of place and totally comfortable. After a moment, I realized I was admiring his body: the long legs and wide shoulders and even the lap of love handles over his belt. The young athlete was still present in the easy way with which he carried himself. His body had never failed him. He returned to the table with two cups of coffee and a large piece of chocolate cake with two forks. He said, "You're gonna love this cake."

We dug in. "Why did you get divorced?" I asked John, picking up the conversation we'd started in his truck.

"After I stopped drinking, things changed. I changed." He cut off a chunk of cake and wolfed it down. "You know what that's like. A year later, you're an entirely different person. Five years later, and it's like another lifetime. I hung in there until the kids were in high school, but at the end, it was either a divorce or hit the bottle again."

"Things were that bad with you and your wife?"

"There wasn't anything wrong with Suzie." He mashed cake crumbs beneath his fork. "It was all me. The divorce was hard on her, hard on the kids, too. My daughter still holds it against me."

"I'm sorry," I said.

He looked at me for a moment. "What about you? After your friend died, why didn't you hook up with someone else?"

I had the feeling this was not what he had intended to say, but something to divert the conversation away from him. I had been in what Josh used to call my cross-examination mode, and in that mode I sometimes overstepped. Maybe he was just showing me he could also ask painfully personal questions.

"It's not that easy, John," I said. "I never believed in just hooking up. A friend of mine once told me that my problem is that my dick's connected to my heart."

The words were out of my mouth before I considered that a gay man referring to his dick might push the limits of John's tolerance, but all he said was, "Me, too."

"You think you'll get married again?"

"If I met the right person. I been dating this girl off and on for a while now, but it's real casual. How are you holding up, man?"

"The caffeine and sugar rush is wearing off. I think it's time for me to turn in."

We drove back to my house in companionable silence, listening to a Mexican radio station.

John pulled into the driveway. I said, "I had a great time, John. Thanks for coming over."

"I was wondering if you'd like to go to a ball game sometime."

"You know, I've lived here ten years and I've never been to Dodger Stadium."

"Then it's time," he said. "I'll give you a call tomorrow. We'll figure out a day."

"Great. Good night, John."

I held out my hand but he reached over it and hugged me. For a second, his cheek brushed against mine with that familiar sensation of stubble and heat. He released me, patted my back and said, "Sleep tight, man."

I was asleep as soon as my head hit the pillow. I dreamed I was in a pawn shop on Spring Street, a neighborhood that seemed like it belonged in Mexico City rather than L.A. A greasy old woman stood behind the counter, arms crossed, an unlit cigarette clamped between her lips. I was frantically searching my pockets for my pawn ticket while she barked in Spanish, *"Apurete, señor, quiero cerrar."* Finally, she came out from behind the counter, went to the door and was about to turn the sign from OPEN to CLOSED, when I found the ticket and waved it in her face. Grudgingly, she grabbed it out of my hand, went back around the counter and through a door that led into the dark recesses of the store. When she returned, she opened her palm. I saw the glint of gold and then I woke up.

6.

I GOT OUT OF BED FILLED WITH ENERGY, AND AFTER breakfast went into my office for the first time since the heart attack. I turned on the computer and spent a couple of hours organizing my calendar, which showed about twenty appeals in various stages of progress. On most I was either waiting for oral argument to be scheduled or for an opinion to be filed. Fortunately, as it turned out, just before the heart attack I had been trying to clear the decks for a death penalty appeal with a ten-thousand-page transcript. The handful of trial court matters left on my docket I could either continue or hand off to other lawyers. When I finished working out my calendar, I saw the disk with the judicial application that Inez had brought me and copied it onto my hard drive. The application ran to ten pages, with almost a hundred questions, many of which, in typical legal fashion, had subpart piled upon subpart. The bar exam had been less complicated. The first question was easy enough, though: applicant's name.

I had worked on the application for nearly an hour when the phone rang in the kitchen. I let the machine take the call, but when my office line rang, I picked it up.

"Law offices."

"Henry? Is that you?"

"Hi, Elena. Did you just call on the other line?"

"Yes, when you didn't answer, I called this number. Are you working?" she asked with a note of concern in her voice.

"A little."

"Is that wise?"

"I'm not doing any heavy lifting. How are you?"

"I heard from Vicky."

"She called?"

"She wrote me a letter," Elena replied. "She said her husband found out she was staying with me and that's why she left. She apologized for taking the money and she returned the credit card."

"Did she use it?"

"I haven't called to check."

"Where's the letter postmarked from?"

There was a pause, a rattle of papers. "San Francisco."

"Well, at least you know she's still up there."

"Do you have any ideas about how I can find her?"

"She's not missing, she's hiding. She doesn't want to be found." An alarm went off in my head. "She said her husband learned she was staying with you. Did she tell you how?"

"No," Elena replied. She was silent for a moment. "I wouldn't be surprised if she told him."

That tallied with my assumption. "Maybe she's gone back to him and she's ashamed to tell you."

"I doubt that my disapproval means much to her," she said. "If she was with Pete, she would have said so in her letter. I think she was struggling with what to do, and in a moment of weakness, called him and told him to come get her and Angel, but then changed her mind and ran. Well, at least I know she didn't leave because she was mad at me. I've got to talk to her."

"What can you do for her that she can't do for herself?"

"Persuade her to do what you suggested and call his parole officer or, if that doesn't work, get a restraining order."

"What's going to restrain her if she changes her mind again?"

Exasperated, she said, "Henry, she needs help. She may not accept it from me, but she's certainly not going to get any out there on the streets and neither is Angelito." She paused. "Do you think I should call the police?"

"She's not missing and she's not the victim of a crime," I said. "They won't be interested."

"He beat her," she reminded me.

"And she didn't report it," I said. "They're not going to pick him up on a stale complaint. Did she mention a friend or someone she might have gone to or who would know where she is?"

"She seems to be close to her mother-in-law," Elena ventured.

"Pete's mom? Wouldn't she be on his side?"

"The way Vicky talked about her, she could have been her mother, too," Elena said. I could hear that the admission pained her.

"What's her name?"

"Jesusita. She lives down there in a town called Garden Grove. You know where that is?"

"Just south of L.A.," I said. "Jesusita. I assume her last name is Trujillo."

"As far as I know."

"I'll have my investigator try to track her down. If she's in touch with Vicky, maybe she'll get a message to her from you."

"Thank you, Henry."

"Elena, I know this is hard for you."

"I'll be all right," she replied. "You really sound like you're having a good day today."

"I feel good."

"Well, whatever you're doing, keep it up."

I called my investigator, Freeman Vidor, and gave him the assignment of finding Jesusita Trujillo. Freeman was suffering from a form of arthritis that was slowly crippling his spine and might have forced him to retire had his career not been saved by the internet. The dingy office he occupied on Broadway now looked like the headquarters of some dot-com startup.

"Of course," I told him, "Trujillo is a guess. She might have divorced and remarried."

"You don't have anything else? DOB? Social Security?"

"Just a name and a town," I said. "I thought you could get anything on the internet these days."

Freeman snorted. "You think the web's like a Ouija board. I'll get back to you."

The sky was clear and bright above the tiers of half-filled seats in Dodger Stadium. The typical Dodger fan, John had explained to me, arrived around the middle of the third inning and skipped out at the seventh inning stretch to avoid traffic. Out on the field, the visiting Giants were taking batting practice. The sight of the Giants' black and orange took me back to childhood and going with my father to Candlestick, when the Giants had more Latin players than other teams in the majors: Orlando Cepeda, the Alou brothers, José Pagan and Juan Marichal, the first living Latino player inducted into the Hall of Fame. Almost more than the game itself, I think what my father loved was the sight of those dark-skinned, Spanish-speaking men outplaying the *americanos* at their own game. Their heroics on the field, and a couple of beers, must have made him feel bigger in his own life—for a few hours, anyway. On the long drive home, we regaled each other by reliving the big plays of the game, a sweet catch by Pagan or a strike-out by Marichal or another Cepeda homer. Those were the happiest moments I ever had with my dad. By the time I was ten, our expeditions to *el béisbol* were over, and after that there were no happy memories.

"Hey, Henry," John said, nudging me. He'd gone off to buy a

couple of Dodger dogs and had returned to his seat while I was lost in the past. "You with me?"

"I was thinking about my dad."

"Must have been a good memory," he said. "You were smiling. Here's your dog. *Con todo*, like you said. Mustard, relish, onion— you sure it's okay for you to eat this with your heart and all?"

"If it's not," I said, biting into the hot dog, "I'll die a happy man."

He looked momentarily alarmed, then relaxed and grinned. He was wearing jeans and sneakers and a short-sleeved yellow silk shirt, half-unbuttoned to take in the sun. His Dodgers cap covered his graying hair and I could almost see the teenage prospect he had been when he played for the Dodgers farm teams. *He must have been a beautiful boy*, I thought, and then wondered who I was protecting by putting it in the past tense.

"You don't wish sometimes you were down there on the field?"

"Ancient history," he said, then relented. "Yeah, sometimes. I can remember going out to the mound at the beginning of the season and being totally focused on throwing the ball, like my whole life was behind that pitch." He slurped some lemonade. "Getting the ball over the plate was the easiest thing in the world and the hardest at the same time. I haven't felt that intense about anything since. Man, I was so alive I could feel the hair on the back of my neck. *Pues*, if I'd known at the time I was playing that this was as good as life was gonna get, I woulda paid more attention."

"That was the peak for you?"

"Sure," he said, cramming the last of his dog into his mouth. "There've been other things that were beautiful, like when my kids were born, but playing baseball, that belonged to me. That was my moment. You ever experience something like that?"

"Nothing that intense. Well, maybe my first couple of trials. You have mustard on your chin."

"I eat like a pig, don't I? Sorry. You ever play baseball?"

"Only as a kid. I was a decent batter and I could run, but I couldn't catch a watermelon."

The Giants finished up, and a local chanteuse came on the field and sang a breathy version of the national anthem that made it sound like a Cole Porter ballad. The line-ups were announced, Kevin Brown threw the first pitch—a ball—to Benard, the Giants' centerfielder, and the game began. Within seconds, I was eight years old again, mesmerized by nonchalant heroics on the field: balls that whizzed by at 90-plus miles an hour, a hop-up catch at the fence, a runner thrown out from across the diamond, a long slide almost beneath the baseman's cleats into second.

Somewhere around the bottom of the third, John said, "You having fun, Henry?"

"You can't imagine."

"I think I can," he said quietly.

I glanced at him. "Yeah, I guess you can." I put my arm around him and gave his shoulder a squeeze. He grinned without taking his eyes off the game.

We were out on the deck finishing a dinner of Chinese takeout and watching the sun set. I was still buzzing from the game. The sky was filled with dusty reds and pinks, and the moon had begun to emerge.

John, standing at the railing, pointed at the sky. "Pretty colors, huh? What would you call that one?"

"Pollution pink."

He grinned and said, "Gonna be a full moon. Want to do something wild?"

"Sitting out here without a sweater is as wild as I get at the moment. I had a great time today."

"Me, too," he said. "You tired? You want me to go?"

"No, not unless you have to . . ."

"Nah, I'm good."

"I thought maybe you had a date with your girlfriend."

He shook his head. "We're going out tomorrow to Catalina on her brother's boat."

"Sounds nice," I said, experiencing a fleeting jab of envy.

He sat at the edge of my chaise and looked at me with his sad eyes. "I don't know if you can even call Deanna my girlfriend. She doesn't want it to be that serious."

"Do you?"

"You know that thing you said the other night, Henry, about your dick being connected to your heart? And I said so is mine? Deanna's wired different." He sipped the Coke he had in his hand. "I asked her to marry me, she told me to lighten up. Things haven't really been the same since then. It's kind of winding down between us."

"I'm sorry to hear it," I said.

He looked at me for a moment, and I could see him working something out in his eyes, the same way he had the first afternoon right before he asked me whether I was gay. "Are you really sorry, Henry? Don't you like me?"

I was acutely aware of his hand on my leg. I looked down at it. "I like you fine, John."

"I like you, too," he said. He scooched up on the chaise and took my hand in his and threaded our fingers together. His hand was warm and callused, a workingman's hand. My father's hand. "I like you a lot, Henry."

It was as if my vision had been blurred, but now, abruptly, my focus returned and I saw him clearly and with such immediacy that my head seemed to snap back an inch. "Are you gay, John?"

He squeezed my hand playfully, then let it fall. "Life ain't baseball, Henry. There's more than two teams."

"Which one do you play on?"

"I never finished telling you about my divorce," he replied quietly.

"You said you were unfaithful. Was that with a guy?"

He bristled. "I fell in love with a guy. I figured that made me gay. Suzie and I got a divorce and I moved in with Tom. A couple of years later, when that broke up, I was back at singles bars hitting on women."

"Because you decided you weren't gay after all?"

He frowned. "I was real confused, but eventually I accepted the fact that I'm attracted to men and women. It's the person that matters."

"This guy—Tom—he was your first guy?"

"I had the feelings for a long time, but I liked girls fine so it wasn't something I needed to explore. More like I was curious, and if the opportunity had come up I might have done something about it. Playing baseball, that didn't happen. Baseball players are not real open-minded, plus there were always baseball Annies around for sex."

"No baseball Andys?"

He grinned. "Not that ever came on to me. After I got out of the game, there were a couple of times when I'd let some queen give me a blowjob, but I had to be real drunk and it never felt right. Plus I got married, had my kids, got into trouble. I had enough to think about. After I got sober, I went to some AA meetings where there were gay guys. First ones I ever really talked to. That's where I met Tom. I didn't even know he was gay at first. He was just a regular guy."

"That was important to you?"

"Look, Henry, you're *mexicano*, too, so you know the drill. Men are men. The only homosexual Mexican I ever met when I was a kid was one of my grown-up cousins who lived with his mom and wore more makeup than her. That's what I thought all homosexuals were like. I was attracted to men. Until I met Tom, I didn't know someone could be both." He grinned. "Tom helped me get over that machismo complex. He taught me there are all kinds of men, and some of them like to wear dresses sometimes."

"What happened between you and him?"

"When I was married to Suzie, I felt like part of me was buried under all the weight of being a husband. A couple of years with Tom, I had the same feelings about being his lover. It's like you have to choose a side and stick with it. Be all straight or all gay. Man, I like brunch, but I like baseball, too, you know? Whoever I'm with, I just want to be able to be myself." He looked at me. "You know what I mean?"

"I'm not bisexual, John."

"No, but you're real," he said.

"When did you decide that?"

He laughed. "When I walked into your house that first day. I saw the picture of your lover and then I looked around at your living room, and I thought, He's gay but he doesn't have gay furniture. Then we got to talking and I saw that you were just a decent guy. You reminded me of the boys I played softball with in the street when I was a kid. Most gay Latinos I meet are still pretty much into role-playing. One guy's the man, one guy's the woman. That's bull-shit. Gay Anglos, man, they treat each other like shit, like they're taking out on each other all the hate they have to deal with for being gay in the first place. You're different, Henry. You're just a person, like me. I think we could get something going. Something sweet. What do you think?"

"Not if being bisexual means you screw guys on the side but if anyone asks, you have a girlfriend."

His face darkened and he took a deep breath. "When I left my wife for another guy, I didn't lie to anyone. My whole family knew. Suzie went crazy. I had to get a court order to see my kids. Suzie and I are okay now, but my daughter still barely talks to me. I do things in the open, okay?"

He was so handsome at that moment—his chin tipped forward defiantly but his eyes unguarded and his hair mashed down from his baseball cap. I felt a surge of tenderness and affection for him. He was right—we were like the boys that we had grown up with, we spoke the same language, but we were familiar to each other in ways that didn't require language at all. I didn't know what else we'd end up being to each other, but I knew I wanted his friendship.

"I'm sorry if I was a jerk," I said. "You caught me by surprise. I thought you were just being nice to a sick guy who didn't seem to have anyone to look after him."

"Yeah, that too," he said. "You do need someone to take care of you, but *sabes que* that's not all I want to do with you."

I think I may have blushed. "You know, John, there hasn't been anyone since Josh. I'm way out of practice with this stuff."

"What stuff?"

I shrugged. "Don't embarrass me."

He hopped up and extended his hand. "Come on."

I let him pull me to my feet. "Should I get my mitt? You sound like we're going to play catch."

He grinned, then pulled my body against his and kissed me. He smelled like cotton left out to dry in the sun. When his tongue touched the inside of my mouth, it was as if I had awakened into my body after a long, gray sleep.

"See?" he said, releasing me. "You remember."

"Wait," I said, pulling him back. "I'm not sure. How does it go?"

"*Chistoso,*" he said, and then we didn't talk.

The doorbell rang.

"You expecting someone?" he whispered into my ear.

"No," I said. It rang again. I let go of him. "Someone really wants to talk to me."

I headed toward the door, but he grabbed my arm. "Wait up."

At the door, I peered through the peephole and saw a boy standing on the porch. He was maybe ten years old, shivering in a T-shirt and jeans.

"It's just a kid," I said. "Selling candy or paper subscriptions or something."

"At eight o'clock on a Saturday night?"

I opened the door. The boy looked at me with eyes that were both suspicious and hopeful.

"Can I help you?" I asked, recognition slowly dawning.

Then, from behind him, out of the darkness, a woman stepped forward. I had not yet made out her face when I heard her say, "Uncle Henry?"

7.

His hand on my shoulder, John repeated softly behind me, "Uncle Henry?" And then her face emerged, a smooth,
dark-skinned moon. She had a smaller, softer version of my own
beak of a nose, and the corners of her small mouth were turned up-
ward in a worried smile. Her large eyes were black as figs. She
stepped further into the light. Her dark, straight hair was pulled
back into a ponytail. She was wearing jeans and a rumpled blouse
and, unlike Elena and me, she was short and plump. A large crucifix lay between her breasts. The Vicky I had imagined was a street-
wise *chola* who applied makeup with a trowel and beamed attitude.
This woman quivered like a small, gentle animal that had barely
eluded a predator. And in this, as Elena had observed, she seemed
very much like our mother. I glanced down at the boy. There was
nothing childlike in the dark eyes that met mine and took my measure. He wore a mucky pair of jeans and a stained Giants T-shirt.
His greasy hair framed a small face that startled me with how familiar it seemed. Big saucer eyes, bird's beak nose, full Indian mouth,
skin the red-brown of cinnamon. Elena was right about him, too; he
looked so much like me at that age it was like peering at a mirror

into the past. From the way he continued to stare at me, it seemed he must be having the same experience in reverse.

I looked at his mother. "Vicky?"

She nodded. "This is my son, Angelito." She glanced at John. "I'm sorry to bother you . . ."

"You're not," I said. "Come inside. This is my friend, John DeLeon."

They murmured introductions as I led them into the living room. We all sat down.

"What a beautiful home you have," my niece exclaimed.

"Who's that man in the picture?" Angelito asked, pointing to the photograph of Josh on the mantel above the fireplace.

She slapped at the air between them and said, "Angel, *silencio.*"

"He was my friend," I said. "We just finished dinner, but there's lots of food. Are you hungry? Thirsty?"

The boy's eyes brightened at the mention of food, even as my niece politely refused.

"It really won't be any trouble at all to warm something up."

"Well," she said. "If it's no trouble . . ."

Angelito said, "I'm hungry."

"Come on, Vicky, let's take a look in the fridge. John can keep Angelito company. Okay, John?"

John winked. "Sure. Hey, Angelito, you're a Giants fan? Your uncle and me went to see them play the Dodgers today—"

I pulled open the refrigerator door and we surveyed the leftovers: macaroni and cheese; chili and a pan of cornbread; a stew; white cartons of Chinese takeout; half a pizza.

"Oh," she said. "There's so much."

"I've been recovering from a heart attack and my friends have been bringing me food so I wouldn't have to cook." I pulled out the macaroni and cheese, a bag of salad. "Will this be okay?"

"Yes," she said. "I'm sorry you were sick, Uncle Henry."

I distrusted the note of solicitude in her voice. "Call me Henry. The microwave will be faster than the oven."

"I'll do that," she said, taking the pasta.

I opened the bag of salad, poured it into a bowl and went back into the refrigerator for salad dressing. "What would you like to drink? There's mineral water, some fruit juice. After dinner, you and I have got to talk."

Her back was to me, her shoulder tensed. "I'll just drink water."

"Milk for Angelito?"

She turned around, her eyes tearing. "Thank you."

"Don't cry," I said. "Whatever's going on, we'll work something out. Elena will be relieved to know you're here. How did you find me?"

"I took your address from my mom's address book when I left her house," she said. "I'm sorry."

A host of questions came to mind, but they could wait until after she and the boy had eaten. "I'm glad you did," I said. "I wanted to meet you and Angel. You take care of things in here while I set the table."

I went back out to the living room and found John and Angelito on the couch watching clips from the day's baseball games on ESPN and chatting authoritatively about pitchers and pennants. John said something and the boy responded with a high, soft peal of laughter, the little-solider stolidity momentarily set aside.

"Angelito, come and have some dinner," I said.

He looked at me over his shoulder, his eyes neither friendly nor unfriendly, and said, "They're going to tell us the American League scores."

"You can leave the TV on. John, you want anything?"

John got up and said, "I'm going to cut out."

Angelito asked anxiously, "Are you coming back?"

"Not tonight," John said. "But I'm working down the street so I'll be around. Come and see me. H'okay?"

"H'okay," Angelito replied.

I thought, *John knows the kid ten minutes and they've already got a private language going.* But then John was a father. I began to panic.

What was I supposed to do with my wayward niece and her sullen son?

At that moment, Vicky came in with the food. "Aren't you staying?" she asked John.

"I gotta go," he said. "Nice meeting you. See you, Angelito."

"'Bye, John," the boy said, distracted by the smell of food.

I told Vicky, "You and Angelito eat. I'll be back in a minute."

Outside, the marine drizzle that moved into the city from the ocean at the beginning of the summer blurred the moon in the misty sky. The air was cool and damp. Leaned up against his truck, John shivered in his thin yellow shirt.

"I thought your sister was your only family," he said.

I gave him an abbreviated version of Elena and Vicky.

"Angelito could be your son," he said when I finished. "He looks so much like you."

"I noticed," I said. "You're the one he liked. You must have been a good dad to your own son."

He shrugged. "I learned from my own dad. Mostly, you have to listen and try to hear what they're really telling you and remember that, half the time, they don't know themselves. You must be real happy to find out you got other family."

"That remains to be seen," I said.

He looked at me quizzically. "You're not happy?"

I couldn't explain to him that my niece's unfortunate resemblance to my own mother, combined with what I knew about her criminal history and the worry she had caused my sister, had seriously predisposed me against her. Instead, I offered a lame, "I don't know what I feel at the moment, except sorry that Vicky chose tonight to show up."

He grinned. "We'll have other nights, Henry. Don't worry about that. Can I kiss you out here, or will your neighbors call the cops?"

"Let them," I said.

I stood in the driveway watching the taillights of his truck disappear around the corner, and then reluctantly went back into my house. As I approached the dining room through the kitchen, I heard my niece tell her son, "Don't talk back to me, Angel. You stay out of his way. And don't let him get you alone."

I pushed through the swinging doors and said, "Hey."

From the look the boy threw me, I knew she had been warning him about me.

After they finished their meal, Angelito cleaned up while Vicky and I went into my office to talk. She paused at the threshold of my office, looked in and stepped across warily. Unlike the rest of my house, furnished, as John said, with mismatched pieces bought on sale, this room was formal and deliberate. The walls were forest green; the bookshelves, the file cabinets and the long table I used as my desk were mahogany. On the wall above the black leather sofa was the usual collection of degrees and admissions to various courts, including the United States Supreme Court. My tall desk chair was of the same black leather. Since I never met clients at my house, the businesslike furnishings of the room were strictly for my own benefit; their conventional severity put me into work mode even if I stumbled in wearing a bathrobe and slippers. Josh had hated this room and told me he never entered it without expecting to be cross-examined. I could see it was having a similar effect on my niece. After overhearing her warning to her son, I felt a spiteful satisfaction at her discomfort, then felt ashamed of myself for it.

"Sit down," I said, as invitingly as I could. She perched at one end of the sofa like a small brown bird about to take flight. I sat down behind my desk. "I want to help you, Vicky, but I need to understand your situation."

"What do you mean?" she asked nervously.

"You told your mother you were running from your husband, but then you told him where you were, didn't you?"

"I didn't, Uncle Henry."

I leaned forward. "Vicky, I'm not like my sister. I've been a criminal defense lawyer for twenty-five years and there isn't much I haven't heard about people and their problems. Why did you tell Pete where you were?"

She stroked the cross that hung from her neck nervously, then said, "Brother Ramiro said I had to do what Jesus would do."

"Who's Brother Ramiro?"

"He was my pastor," she said. "I went to his church on Mission Street. That's where I was saved."

"I don't see what this has to do with your husband."

She folded her hands together in her lap as if in prayer. "Brother Ramiro told me that a woman should be submissive to her husband. He said the man is like God in his family, the woman is his helpmate. He told me to talk to Pete and tell him the good news about Jesus, and the spirit of the Lord would make us a family again."

"From the bruise on your neck, I assume the message didn't get through to Pete."

A tear coursed down her face. "It's my fault. I'm weak. The Lord says love those who abuse you, if they strike one cheek, turn the other, but I remembered how much Pete hurt me and I was afraid, so I took Angel and ran away from my mother's house back to Brother Ramiro. He told me to come here."

"Here? To me?"

"No," she said. "To the church down here where he studied to minister. He said they would take us in and protect us until I was strong and could face Pete, but it wasn't where he said it was. We got lost and I was scared. We didn't have any money, no place to go, so I came here. If you take us to the church, we won't bother you anymore."

"You want me to help you find people who are going talk you into going back to a man who beat you and got you to use drugs and prostitute yourself?"

"How did you know about—"

"Your arrests? I pulled your rap sheet. Pete's too. I saw the path you were on, Vicky, drugs, prostitution. Somehow you pulled yourself together the last time he went to prison. Are you going to throw all that away because some storefront preacher tells you your husband has a right to beat you up? Wasn't the last time enough?"

"You don't understand," she said. "Jesus got me off drugs. Now He wants Pete and me and Angel to be a family, a Christian family. I know you're not a Christian. I know what you are."

I heard the disgust in her voice, and it was as if I was thirteen again and my mother was chiding me for the stains my wet dreams had left on my sheets. It was all I could do not to throw her out of my house.

"A homosexual? Unlike Elena, I don't think I owe you anything and I don't care whether you approve of me. And doesn't your Bible tell you to remove the beam from your own eye before criticizing the mote in your neighbor's? You've made a wreck of your life, Vicky. Let's keep the conversation there."

"It was a mistake to come here," she said, her eyes furious.

"You didn't come here for yourself," I said. "You came here for Angel. Whatever you think of your mother and me, you know we can help him. Unless you want him to end up like Pete."

The anger went out of her and she deflated into the couch. I felt as if I'd kicked a kitten.

"I'm sorry I raised my voice," I said. "Elena said Angel is a special boy."

She nodded. "He is, Uncle, and I don't want him to end up in a gang, selling drugs and getting himself killed before he's a man."

In my gentlest voice, I said, "Then you have to dump Pete, because we both know drug addicts don't change."

Again she nodded. "I know. What should I do?"

"You and Angel are welcome to stay here and catch your breath. I'll call Elena and she can come down and we'll have a family meeting and figure out what's best. Do you have any luggage?"

"We hid our suitcase in the bushes outside."

"You better bring it in before it disappears."

"This is a rich neighborhood," she said.

"This is Los Angeles. Go get it, and when you come back, we'll call your mother."

As she opened the door, I caught a glimpse of Angelito, who had, it seemed, been standing outside while we talked. His mother ushered him away, but he looked back. Our eyes met and I saw in his gaze a tiny ray of hopefulness.

Elena was out, so we left a message. I showed my niece and nephew the guest room and bathroom, made sure they had clean sheets and towels, told them to make themselves at home, and went back into my office where I made another call, to Edith Rosen, my psychologist friend. We talked for a long time about Vicky and Angelito, and she agreed to come to dinner the next evening to meet them. I was on my way to bed when the phone rang. I grabbed it, thinking it was Elena, but it was John. We finished the conversation we had started on the deck and I slept a lot better than I thought I would.

Elena called at six-thirty the next morning. I got out of bed and remembered, just as I reached the door, to pull on a pair of pants and a T-shirt so as to spare my niece the shock of seeing me in my boxers. The door to the guest room was tightly shut, but I had the disquieting sense that they were awake in there. I picked up the phone in the kitchen.

My sister exclaimed, "Henry, I'm sorry to be calling so early."

"That's all right. I'm surprised you didn't call last night."

"We were at a play and didn't get home until after midnight. I can't tell you how relieved I was to get your call. How are they?"

"They seem fine," I said. "Vicky and I didn't exactly hit it off."

"What happened?"

"We discussed religion," I said, and gave her a synopsis of my conversation with my niece.

Elena replied, choosing her words carefully, "I don't have any sympathy for that kind of Christianity, but that church may have saved her life."

"The charlatan who runs the church is the one who encouraged her to call Pete," I said. "You're not suggesting we should turn her and Angel over to these fundies, are you?"

"That's her decision," she said, "but the fact that she keeps coming back to us tells me she's looking for an alternative. We have to offer her a substitute for what she'll lose if she gives up her church."

"What alternative?"

"A family, Henry."

After a moment, I said, "You were right about Angel. He's extraordinary. I want to help him."

She said, "Well, that's a start. I can't get away until tomorrow evening, but I've already made a plane reservation."

We talked logistics for a couple of minutes and then I let her go.

I went into the kitchen, put on a pot of coffee, and then came back out into the living room and stretched out on the sofa while it dripped. I closed my eyes and my head spun with fatigue. I struggled to stay awake, but the weight of my weariness dragged me into unconsciousness, sleep closing over me like water. When I opened my eyes, Angelito was standing in front of me, watching me as intently and as inscrutably as a cat. The room, which had been dim with the first light of morning, now blazed brightly around me. I heard the drone of the vacuum cleaner in the background.

Angelito watched me rouse myself into a sitting position, then asked, "Are you dying?"

"What?"

"You look sick."

"I was sick but I'm getting better. What time is it, Angelito?"

"I don't know."

"There's a clock in the kitchen, could you check?"

He withdrew a shade further into himself. "I don't know how."

I was still emerging from sleep and it took me a moment to understand. "You can't tell time?"

"I know the names of all the presidents in order."

"You do? That's impressive."

"Should I say them?"

"Could you bring me my watch first? It's sitting on the table beside my bed."

He looked at me as if I were making fun of him, but then he padded off, returning a moment later reverently carrying in the palm of his hand the heavy, gold-plated railroad pocketwatch that had belonged to my father and was the only thing of his that I owned. My mother had sent me the watch after he died, with a note reminding me that he had taught me to tell time on it. I had forgotten that, but I did remember watching covetously his nightly ritual of removing the watch from his pants pocket just before he went to bed and winding it for the next day.

"Thanks," I said when he reluctantly handed it over. It was past ten-thirty. I'd been asleep for four hours. "I learned how to tell time on this watch," I told Angelito. "I could teach you, if you want me to."

"Okay," he said neutrally, but his eyes were eager.

I lay the watch on the coffee table between us. "You see the numbers that go around in a circle?" He nodded. "Those are the hours. There are twenty-four hours in a day—"

"It only goes up to twelve," he said suspiciously.

"Every hour comes around twice, Angelito, once during the day and once at night. Right now it's ten-thirty in the morning. In twelve hours, it will be ten-thirty at night."

He nodded and said, "Twelve times two is twenty-four," but, after staring at the watch, "What's the thirty?"

Angel listened to my explanation of the workings of my father's watch with the absorption that marks a deep intelligence, and when I finished, he repeated to me my explanation in a way that demonstrated he had understood it completely. Then he began asking questions about the mechanics of clocks that quickly exhausted my paltry knowledge, and I had to give him an intellectual IOU.

"I want a watch like this," he said when we finished the lesson.

"It belonged to your great-grandfather, Angel. My dad. I inherited it from him after he died. I don't have a son, so you're next in line, kiddo."

He smiled. "I can have this when you die?"

I laughed. "Yeah, but I'm not dying anytime soon."

"My mom said—" he exclaimed, then caught himself.

"What did your mom say? You can tell me, I won't be upset."

He weighed my credibility as carefully as a judge. "My mom says you're a *joto* and probably have AIDS."

Jota was Spanish for the letter "J," but in the vernacular, *joto* meant, essentially, faggot. To hear the word from him was like being stabbed, but I knew better than to be angry with him, so I calmly explained, "*Joto* is not a nice word, Angel. Please don't use it again. I don't have AIDS and I'm not dying."

"My mom's friend Laura died. She got AIDS from a dirty needle."

"Does your mother use needles?"

"No," he said. His expression told me I had crossed a line.

"You were going to tell me the names of the presidents. Remember?"

The eager light slowly returned to his eyes. "Yeah."

"Go ahead. I'm listening."

"Angel, *que 'stas haciendo?*" My niece sounded one breath short of panic. I looked up. She was standing at the doorway with the vacuum cleaner.

"Nothing," he said, sullenly.

"I was teaching him to tell time. What are you doing with the vacuum?" I asked sharply.

"I was cleaning your house," she replied docilely.

"Angel, let's do the presidents later. I need to talk to your mom for a minute."

Without a word, he slipped out of the room.

"You don't have to clean my house," I said, still angry at what she had told Angel about me.

"I should do something to pay you back."

I got up and approached her, saying, "You can. Stop scaring Angel about me. I'm not going to hurt him."

"I know, Uncle," she said meekly, but her eyes were defiant.

"And I won't hear the word *joto* in my house again. Or *maricón* or any other gutter words you've taught him to use about people like me and your mother. Remember something, Vicky, our blood flows through your veins. Whatever we are, you and Angel carry inside of you."

"Not that thing," she spat.

"I know you think homosexuality is a sin, but that's because you've been taught by ignorant people. I've got to get dressed and do some work. Please put that vacuum away. You're a guest here, not the maid."

"Yes, Uncle," she said, but as soon as I turned my back, she started it up and vacuumed furiously for the next hour.

8.

EDITH ARRIVED THAT EVENING WITH A BAG OF GRO-
ceries, said to Vicky, "Will you help me with dinner, dear?" and disappeared with her into the kitchen.

"You need a hand in there?" I shouted after her.

"We're fine, Henry," Edith replied. "You *men* relax."

I smiled at my nephew. "Maybe we can catch some baseball
on TV."

We burrowed into the couch. I turned on the tube and flipped
through the channels until I found a Yankees–Indians game on cable. I listened with one ear to the murmur of conversation coming
from the kitchen but was unable to make out more than a random
word or two, so eventually I gave up and watched the game. Angel,
meanwhile, had scooted across the couch until he was almost
touching me. I put my arm around his shoulders. Without looking
up, he wriggled up against me. The Yankee shortstop made a jump
catch that ended the inning.

"Wow, that was a beautiful catch. Who's the short?"

Angel, who'd been watching raptly, said incredulously, "Derek
Jeter."

"I haven't followed baseball since I was about your age, so I don't know who any of the players are. Jeter's good?"

Turning his attention back to the game, Angel said, "He's the best shortstop, except maybe Nomar Garciaparra. He plays for the Red Sox. I play short, too."

"When did you play baseball?"

"When my dad was living with us, I played Little League."

"When was this?"

He shrugged. "I don't know. Before he went back to jail."

He must have felt guilty about telling me as much as he had, because he pulled away from me. I asked him about some of the other Yankees and soon he was back at my side giving me a running commentary on the game. As he reeled off stats, I remembered how knowing a pitcher's ERA or a batter's RBI or what phrases like "no hitter" and "fielder's choice" and "squeeze play" had made me feel when I was ten years old, like I belonged to the world of men. Listening to him reminded me that after baseball, another myth of men had captured my attention and introduced me to a world that had obsessed me as much as the major leagues, with a more lasting effect.

At a commercial, I said, "I bet you like to read, don't you?"

He looked at me and ventured a cautious, "Yeah."

"I'll be right back," I said, and went into my office, where, tucked on a shelf amid my twenty-five-year-old law school texts, was an even older book. The battered brown cover bore the imprint of water stains and grease spots. The binding was loose and the gilt lettering on the spine nearly indecipherable but I could still make out the title, *The Tales of Homer*, and still felt some of the thrill I had experienced when I opened it for the first time almost forty years ago. I turned yellowing pages that bore finger smudges from a smaller hand, but the illustrations still jumped off the page: the great wooden horse being wheeled into the city; a fragile ship hurtling toward a strait where on one side was a whirlpool and on the other jagged rocks; a beautiful woman with a wand standing among a herd of swine. I had been given this book—a prose retelling of the *Illiad* and the *Odyssey*—when I was eleven by a teacher who observed my interest in Greek mythology, but it had opened up more than that world for me. Reading about Achilles and Patroclus had, even in this bowdlerized version, intimated something about the love of men for one another that I scarcely understood but never forgot. Ulysses's long journey, filled with suffering and adventure, had in some obscure but palpable way consoled and encouraged me as I struggled through my own difficult adolescence.

"Here," I said, handing Angel the *Tales* when I'd returned to the living room. "You can look at it after the game."

He immediately opened the book at random and found the illustration of the Greeks pouring out of the great wooden horse.

Wonder in his voice, he asked, "What is this book about, Uncle Henry?"

"It's really two stories," I said. "The first one is about a war that happened thousands of years ago between people called the Greeks and the Trojans and how the Greeks won it with a trick, using this horse." I pointed at the illustration. "The second story is about how one of the Greek soldiers named Ulysses tried for ten years to get home to his family and about the monsters he met and the adventures he had on the way."

His eyes widened at the word "monsters." He began to turn the pages, glancing up at the game every couple of minutes, and when we were called for dinner he took the book with him. Just as I had done when I was a boy, he propped the book up against his water glass and read while he ate. His mother observed him with equanimity as if this was familiar behavior.

"Angel," I said, "we have a guest. Put the book away until dinner is over."

Only then did Vicky chime in. "Do what your uncle says, Angelito."

Grudgingly, he complied. He sat through the rest of dinner

without saying a word but attentively listened to the three-way conversation among his mother, Edith and me.

After dinner, I saw Edith to her car.

"Did you have any luck with my niece?" I asked her.

"I don't know what you mean, Henry," she said.

"I was hoping you might have some insight into her."

Edith smiled. "I'm a psychologist, not a psychic. Obviously, she figured out that I was here at your invitation to talk to her." She unlocked her car. "I don't think I'm the first mental health professional Vicky has dealt with. She knew the drill."

"What drill?"

"Try to figure out what you're supposed to say, and say it to make them go away and leave you alone."

"What did she say?"

"Henry, you know I'm not going to tell you that," she said. "In fact, you shouldn't have come out here with me, because now she'll assume we're talking about her and it will make it harder for me when I see her tomorrow."

"You're seeing her tomorrow?"

She nodded. "I'm taking her and Angel shopping and then to lunch. I want to see them together without you around."

"You can't leave me out to hang."

She got into her car and rolled the window down. "You want me to try to help her or spy on her?"

"Point taken," I said. "Sorry."

"Good night, Henry," she said and drove away.

When I returned to the house, Vicky and Angel were already in their room. Angel had taken the book in with him.

John called the next morning. I took the call in my office to avoid being overheard by my niece.

"How's the reunion going?" he asked.

"She seems to think I'm going to rape Angel if she leaves him alone with me."

"What are you talking about?"

"She told him I'm a fag who has AIDS. She called me *joto*. You're right—some things do sound worse in Spanish."

After a moment, John said, "She'll feel different after she's spent more time around you."

"Plus she's a born-again."

"You don't like Christians?" he asked in a tone that gave me pause. "Aren't you Catholic?"

"My mother was Catholic enough for my entire family," I said. "Are you religious?"

"I go to Mass every Sunday with my mom and dad. Is that going to be a problem?"

"My problem is with Vicky's religion, not yours," I said.

This got a dubious "Okay." After a further awkward silence, he said, "Hey, the reason I called is I can get tickets to the game on Saturday for you and me and Angel."

"I don't know if Vicky will let Angel out of her sight that long."

"Man, you're really angry," he said. "Let me talk to her."

"Now?"

"Put her on the phone, Henry."

I put the phone down and found my niece doing laundry. I explained that John, whom she had met the night she had arrived, wanted to ask her something. Reluctantly, she took the call in the kitchen. I went out into the living room where Angelito was curled up on an armchair reading the *Tales*.

"How's it going?"

He looked up. "They have funny names. I get confused."

"I know," I said. "In the first book, the important characters are Achilles and Patroclus, who are Greeks, and Hector, who's a Trojan. The second book is pretty much all about Ulysses. How far along are you?"

"The Trojans want a truce but not the Greeks." He put the book in his lap. "This part is boring. Do they start fighting again?"

"In a couple of pages."

His mother came into the room. "John wants to talk to you," she said to me. To Angel, she said, "John wants to take you to see baseball on Saturday. With your uncle."

Angel smiled. "Really, Uncle Henry?"

"Yeah, if it's okay with your mom. I'm going to get the phone. We'll talk later." I went back into my office and picked up the phone. "How did you do that?"

"I told her how much it meant when I took my son to his first big league game. As soon as she knew I had my own kids, she was okay with it."

"She thinks you're straight, so she'll trust you with her son?"

With an edge in his voice, he said, "Henry, don't get pissed off at me. I'm not the problem here."

I said a curt, "Sorry."

"Things must be pretty tense up there," he said after a moment. "You need to get out of the house. Come down and meet me for lunch. H'okay?"

He was trying to charm me out of my sullenness as if I were a little boy. I didn't know whether to be touched or annoyed, but I said, "H'okay."

Around noon, I wandered down to the house where John was working. It was the first time I'd taken this route since the day John had rescued me and, as tired as I still often felt, I could also feel the increase in strength and energy. Only now as I was recovering did I realize that some part of me had not believed I was going to. John was standing in the driveway behind his battered truck talking in rapid Spanish to two men wearing red DeLeon & Son baseball caps. He saw me, waved and continued his conversation. The two men—one middle-age, the other a boy in his twenties—listened to

John with almost servile deference, glancing down, nodding respectfully, but then he said something that made the younger man toss back his head and laugh. I felt a prickle of jealousy.

"Be back at one-thirty," he told them in Spanish.

The two men went off to a big wreck of a car parked beneath a jacaranda tree that had rained papery purple flowers on the windshield. As John approached me, he doffed his cap and fluffed his hair. There was a kiss in his smile.

"Hey, Henry."

"Your crew?" I asked, as the big car sputtered off, the windshield wipers scattering the jacaranda blossoms.

"Two of 'em."

"Documented?"

His smile turned wolfish. "Who are you, INS?"

"Just curious."

He threw an arm around my shoulders. "How many generations your family been up here in *el norte*?"

"Three, counting from my grandparents."

"Same here," he said, walking me toward his truck. "I bet no one asked your *abuelo* or mine if they had green cards before they put them to work in the fields or whatever. I don't either, and I pay everyone the same and give everyone the same benefits."

"I think that's great, John, really, but you know, technically you are breaking the law."

He squeezed my shoulder with powerful fingers. "I bet you wait till the light turns green before you walk across the street."

"So what's your point?"

"Nothing. I could kiss you."

"But not with the guys watching," I said.

The happiness faded from his eyes. "Hop in. I want to show you something."

"That was a lousy thing for me to say. I'm sorry."

He shrugged. "Let's get some food."

We went to a drive-in on Sunset and ordered burgers and fries and milkshakes. Then he drove up into Griffith Park toward the observatory.

"Hold on," he said, suddenly veering off the paved road into gray-green underbrush and onto a rutted dirt road that ascended an adobe-colored hill and terminated abruptly at a turnaround. Downtown unfolded beneath us in the baked brown air. Glass towers glinted through the sludge, palm trees lifted their fronds as if gasping, ribbons of freeway were clogged with noontime traffic. A coyote ran along the hill below us.

"This is some view," I said.

He slipped a tape into the cassette player and a woman, a sob in her voice, began to croon in Spanish in a style I remembered from childhood.

"Thirty years ago when I came up here with my dad, you could still see the ocean sometimes. I love this city and I hate what's happened to it." He slurped some of his milkshake and unwrapped his hamburger. "If it keeps getting worse, I'll leave."

"Where would you go?"

"Down in southeast Arizona, in the Sonora desert, where my mom's family comes from. They're Yaquis. Indians," he explained. "There's a little town down there called Bisbee built on hills. The high desert's real beautiful." He munched his burger. "It's only an eight-hour drive. We could go there for a long weekend."

"I'd like to see it. Who's this singing?"

"Daniela Romo," he said between gigantic bites. "*Tu eres mí destino.*"

"You are my destiny. Doesn't sounds as corny in Spanish."

"It's the language of love, man. How's Angel?"

"Really excited about going to the game. We watched the Yankees play last night and he told me all about Derek Jeter."

"Best short in the majors, except maybe Nomar Garciaparra."

"Angel said the same thing. Johnny, I'm really sorry about that crack I made down there. I feel like a jerk."

He wiped his mouth with the back of his hand. "Don't apologize. You were right. I wouldn't kiss you in front of my crew, they'd lose all respect for me. They're like your niece, Henry. They come from a different place and there's times you gotta go along with that."

"I don't want to start a fight, but what are the times when you don't?"

"We do work for gay guys all the time, and when we do, I tell my crew if I hear any fag jokes or any kind of remarks like that, they're gone. I tell them, these people are feeding your families, you show some courtesy." He looked at me. "That probably doesn't seem like much to you."

"I'm no militant," I said. "I understand discretion, but when I saw you, I was so happy, I didn't care who was around."

"You called me Johnny just now," he said.

"That's how you introduced yourself when we met," I said, "but you corrected yourself and said John."

"I was Johnny when I played ball," he said. "Back when I was a kid. Now I'm John."

"You can be Johnny with me sometimes."

His smile was a complex mixture of happiness and sadness. "What did they call you when you were a kid?"

"Besides *Flaco*, you mean?" I'd been a skinny-bones until I fleshed out in college. "They called me Henry."

Then he leaned over and whispered into my ear, "I'm going to call you—" and the name he chose revealed it was something he had been thinking about. Then he kissed me and we made out like a pair of horny teenagers.

When I finally came up for breath, I said, "Oh, man. That was intense."

He released a long, pent-up breath. "You thought I just brought you up here for the view?"

I began to button my shirt. "I've never made out in the front seat of a pickup truck. It's sexy, but kind of cramped."

"Next time we'll try the flatbed." He picked up what was left of his hamburger. He'd sat on it. "I guess I'll leave this for the coyotes," he said, tossing it out the window.

I rooted around the floor and found the bag with my food. "Here, mine's only a little mauled. Eat it."

"I'm not going to eat your lunch."

"You're going back to work," I said. "I'm going home to take a nap."

He took the bag. "We'll share. What's going on with your niece?"

"My sister's flying down this afternoon. We're having a family meeting." He held out the burger. I took a bite and gave it back. "I know it's not Vicky's fault that she irritates me, but honest to God, she's so passive-aggressive. Instead of saying what's on her mind, I catch these little looks she gives me. You know how she expresses disapproval of me? By doing my laundry. You should've seen her face when she tossed my boxers into the dryer. Like she should be wearing gloves."

John chuckled.

"What's funny?"

"The way she pisses you off, she could only be family." He dipped a mangled french fry into catsup. "You don't have to like her, Henry. You just have to love her."

"Where did you read that?" I said. "A greeting card?"

"*Chistoso*," he said. "You'll do it. You'll do it for Angel. You already love him, don't you?"

"It's funny how much, considering that I hardly know him."

John smiled and said, "The only time I fell in love at first sight was when I watched them deliver my son." He crumpled the burger wrapper and tossed it on the floor of the cab, which was already littered with other fast food bags and wrappers. "You want Angel to be like you."

"He *is* like me," I said.

"What does his mom want?"

"She says she wants a better life for him."

John pressed my thigh, a gesture more emphatic than erotic. "When you give him that better life, make sure she's still a part of it."

"I'm not going to kidnap him."

"Being around you, Henry, seeing what you've done with your life, he could become ashamed of her. You don't want to let that happen no matter how screwed up his mom is, because if he's ashamed of her, some little part of him will be ashamed of himself, too."

"You know what, John, not everyone needs a family for a sense of identity. Some of us create ourselves."

He looked at me and said, "You're all upset now."

"No, I'm not," I pouted.

He opened his arms. "Come here, *m'ijo*."

"*M'ijo*? I'm six years older than you," I said as I scooted across the seat.

John dropped me off to an empty house. In blissful quiet, I went into my room and took a nap. When I woke up, I heard Elena's voice. I roused myself out of bed, put on my bathrobe and emerged. At the doorway of the kitchen, I stopped. Elena and Vicky were sitting at the table drinking coffee, deep in conversation. They were at an angle from which they could not see me. My sister cupped her daughter's face as she spoke to her in a low voice. Vicky shook her head. Elena dropped her hands and slowly wept. I felt a small presence behind me, turned around, and saw Angelito. I felt momentarily nonplussed at having been caught spying, but then I remembered this kind of lurking seemed to be one of his survival skills.

"Grandma wants us to go home with her," he said in a low voice. He was carrying Homer, his finger wedged at the page where he had stopped reading.

I stepped away from the door. "When?"

"After we go to the baseball game." He looked at me.

"No one's said anything to me about you leaving," I said, trying to answer truthfully the question in his eyes. "How's the book?"

"Achilles's friend, Patro—Patro—"

"Patroclus."

"Patroclus dressed up like Achilles and Hector killed him. Now Achilles is mad."

"Patroclus was his best friend," I said. "Do you want to live with your grandmother?"

He feigned indifference. "Can I take the book?"

"Sure."

Then he said, "Will you come to see me?"

"You know I will."

"Henry?" It was Elena. "Is that you?"

I winked at Angelito. "Busted." I headed back to the kitchen, where I found Vicky stirring a fragrant stew and Elena at the sink washing salad greens. "Hi," I said, kissing her cheek. "I'm sorry I was asleep when you arrived."

She dried her hands and hugged me. "You still look tired. How do you feel?"

"Better," I said. "Hi, Vicky, that smells great."

"Did we wake you up, Uncle?"

"No," I said.

"This is the first time we've all been together," Elena observed. "Our first family meal."

Late that night, after dinner and after Vicky and Angel had gone to bed, Elena and I sat on the deck. I had dug out a dusty bottle of Scotch that had belonged to Josh from beneath the sink and poured her a drink.

"It doesn't bother you?" she asked, accepting the glass gratefully.

"I hated Scotch," I said. "Though I suppose if I'd kept drinking, I would've ended up guzzling turpentine."

"Is the sky always red like this?" she asked, looking out over the canyon.

"Usually. It's a combination of smog and city lights, I think. Angel told me you're taking them back with you to Oakland."

"That was always the plan," she said. She glanced at me. "I would think you'd be relieved. I could cut the tension between you and Vicky with a knife."

"I know," I said. "I swear I try, Elena, but we don't seem to get along. I'll miss my nephew."

"You'll come and see him," she said. "I'll persuade Vicky to let him come and visit you." She took a sip of her drink. "You know I feel about her the same way you feel about him."

"You're her mother," I observed. "I'm her faggot uncle."

She looked over her glass at me. "She pities you, you know."

"Oh, for Christ's sake. Why?"

"You seem like a lonely old man to her."

"Why doesn't she feel the same way about you? You're queer, too."

"Well, as you said, I'm also her mother. That gives me a primal claim on her. Besides, Vicky doesn't take my lesbianism very seriously. When I told her I had been a nun, you should have seen the expression on her face. It was as if I suddenly made perfect sense to her." She sipped the last of the Scotch. "If she sees you as pitiable, she sees me as sexless."

"How does she explain Joanne?"

She smiled. "Two old crones living together."

"How can you put up with that condescension?"

"I'd put up with more than that to have my daughter back. Anyway, the more time she spends around us, the more accepting she'll become."

"That's what John said."

"John? Who's John?"

"My friend," I said.

She lifted an eyebrow. "Boyfriend?"

"I'm a little old for a boyfriend, but I suppose you could call him that."

"No wonder you seem so much better," she said. "When do I get to meet him?"

"Tomorrow," I said. "He's taking Angel and me to a baseball game. It's strange to be talking to you about my boyfriend. I feel like I'm a tongue-tied twelve-year-old and you're a worldly seventeen."

She laughed. "We have a lot of years to make up, Henry, including the awkward ones." After a moment of comfortable silence, she said, "Vicky told me you looked up her criminal record, by the way, and she told me what was on it."

"I was only trying to protect you," I said. "We didn't know anything about her."

"Listen, Henry, whatever else you think about her, she's tried to be a good mother under very difficult circumstances."

"She created some of those difficulties," I pointed out.

"You mean the drugs. That was Pete's doing."

"How did she end up with such a loser?"

"She met him at a party in San Francisco when she was sixteen. She told me it was love at first sight. He'd just been released from jail so she must have looked pretty good to him, too. They came down here to live with his mother."

"Sixteen? That's statutory rape."

"If anyone had cared," Elena said. "No one did and she had already been through worse than statutory rape. Marrying Pete gave her the most stable home she'd ever had."

"From what I know about him, he doesn't seem prime bread-winner material."

"Pete didn't provide the stability, his mother did. Jesusita. Vicky stayed with her even after Pete went back to jail."

"He's spent as much of the last ten years in custody as out."

"Vicky blames his cousin, the same boy who introduced them in

San Francisco. Butch, I think she said his name was. According to her, he's always been the ringleader and Pete just goes along."

"I can't believe she's still making excuses for him."

"You have to understand, Henry, they were a family, and what that meant to her after growing up in foster homes and orphanages. He gave her the first happiness she ever had in life. The only happiness. You can't blame her for trying to hold on to it."

"Why did she come to you rather than go to his mother?"

"I think she's had enough," Elena said. "She knows she has to break the cycle and that means separating herself not only from Pete, but Jesusita, too. For better or worse, we're the alternative." She put her glass on the railing and said, "I wish we could talk all night, but I really have to get some sleep. You really don't mind me taking your bed?"

"The couch in my office will be fine for me," I said.

She kissed my cheek. "Good night, Henry. Thank you for taking care of Vicky and Angel."

The next time I saw my sister, she was shaking me awake, a frantic look on her face.

"Elena? What's wrong?"

"They're gone," she said.

9.

A SUDDEN TWISTING PAIN IN MY CHEST, AS IF I'D STRAIN-
ed a muscle, made me wince as I got up from the couch and threw
on my bathrobe. I limped across the house to the guest room. The
bed was neatly made up, the room was empty. I looked beneath the
bed where I had seen Vicky stow their suitcase. It was gone. When
I looked up, Elena was sitting on the edge of the bed.

"I don't understand it," I said. "If she was going to leave, why
didn't she just leave? Why pretend with us? It's not as if we could
have forced her to do anything she didn't want to do."

"The only way she could leave was without telling me because
she knew if we had talked it out, she would have changed her mind."

"That doesn't make sense. You offered her hope of a new life."

She smiled wearily. "At the price of her old life."

"You mean she prefers the devil she knows."

"Pete may hit her, but she doesn't feel inferior to him. Not the
way she does to us. She'd always feel like she was the poor relation."

"Are you defending her decision to go back to him?"

"No, I'm only trying to understand how she feels," she said. "So
that next time I'll know what to say to her." She stood up. "God, I
need a cup of coffee."

"I want to call Edith Rosen," I said. "She talked to Vicky yesterday. Maybe she said something to her. Come into my office. I'll put her on the speaker phone."

When I told Edith that Vicky and Angel had left, she said, "I thought there was a good chance this would happen."

"Elena thinks it was because we overwhelmed her. Do you?"

"Possibly," she replied. "On the other hand, it could have nothing to do with you. The literature on battered women's syndrome talks about three stages of abuse. Tension-building, acute explosion and loving contrition. If that's Pete and Vicky's pattern, they might be in that third stage where's he's promised to change and she's talked herself into believing him. Of course now that she's gone back to him, the tensions will start again, like clouds gathering before a storm."

"Then another explosion," Elena said.

"Another blowup may be what it takes to break the cycle, if that's what's going on," Edith said.

"You keep saying 'if,'" I said.

"I wouldn't swear that Vicky's a battered woman."

"She still had the bruises from the last beating he gave her," Elena said.

"I know, I saw them, but when I actually pressed her for details of the abuse, she was vague."

"Can you blame her?" Elena asked. "She was ashamed."

"I've been a forensic psychologist for a long time," Edith said. "I know the difference between someone who's evading a painful subject and someone who's making things up."

"You think she fabricated the abuse?" I asked.

"I don't know that," she said, a bit defensively. "But something felt a little hinky."

Usually I deferred to Edith's intuitions, but this one seemed off base. "Then she's either a pathological liar or she was playing on our sympathy," I said. "Vicky doesn't fit the profile of a pathological liar and if she wanted us to feel sorry for her, she didn't stick around for the payoff."

After a moment, Edith said grudgingly, "You're probably right. I didn't have much time with her and she wasn't particularly forthcoming."

"You have any idea where she might have gone?"

"There was one thing. She asked me to drive her to a church somewhere on Beverly. A storefront church. Pentecostal. It had a Spanish name. Iglesia de Cristo something. She went in while Angel and I waited for her. She was there for a good thirty minutes. Does that mean anything to you?"

"It's probably the church she was looking for the night she turned up here," I said, and related what she had told me. "Maybe she went to arrange marriage counseling."

"Don't be sarcastic about her faith," Elena said. "It turned her life around."

"Finding Jesus isn't what turned her life around," I said. "It was the fact that Pete was in prison. I compared their rap sheets. She does fine when he's locked up, but once he's out, she slips."

She digested this in silence.

"What about Angel?" I asked Edith. "Did you get anything helpful from him?"

"No. I've rarely met a child as self-possessed as your nephew," she said. "In the old days, they used to call kids like him 'invulnerables.'"

"What kind of kid would that be?" I asked.

"Kids who become high achievers when all the cards are stacked against them. They're not only very smart, they're able to find some inner resource that keeps hope alive for them in the most desperate situations, and without much encouragement from the adults in their lives."

"Are you saying he isn't being affected by a drug addict dad and a battered mom?"

"Of course it affects him, Henry, but it hasn't destroyed him."

"That's only a matter of time," I said. "Vicky's a write-off. We can at least save Angel."

"What are you talking about?" Elena asked.

"I know family lawyers, kids' rights advocates. We could get custody—"

"Absolutely not," she said angrily. "I'm not going to drag my daughter though a custody fight."

"Any mother who keeps dragging her child back into a dangerous situation doesn't deserve custody. Edith, what do you think?"

"Where do you think Angel comes by his invulnerability?" she replied. "Your entire family shows remarkable resilience. Look at your own life."

"Are you saying that Vicky is one of these invulnerables?"

"She survived her own traumatic childhood and has managed to keep herself and Angel intact as a family against some very tough odds."

"Going back to Pete doesn't say much about her judgment."

"Life is trial and error," Edith replied. "Vicky is still a young woman. Don't discount her ability to learn from her experiences."

"But she's had this experience over and over again."

"All that means is she hasn't hit bottom yet."

"Why should Angel have to hit it with her?"

"It's to protect him that she might finally realize she has to leave Pete for good," Edith said. "Trying to take Angel away from her would be the worst thing you could do."

"For both of them," my sister added. "Whatever her faults, she is his mother, Henry. You don't seem to understand how important that is."

Outnumbered, I conceded. "Then what do you suggest we do?"

"Edith is right, Vicky has to make her mistakes," Elena said.

"She knows we're here, and she knows she can come back. We'll just have to wait."

Edith offered any help she could give us and we said our good-byes. Elena and I continued the discussion over coffee. I was determined to make sure that Angel did not suffer further because his mother was stuck in the rut of dysfunction, but Elena was just as determined that Vicky find her way back to us on her own.

"I wanted to give Vicky the childhood I owed her, but it's too late for that," she said. "I can at least try to give the respect she deserves as an adult."

"She's not an adult," I countered. "At least she's not making adult decisions going back to this guy—"

"She loves him," Elena said, sipping her coffee, as if that settled everything.

"Oh, come on," I said. "This is pathology, not *Romeo and Juliet*."

"That's where you're wrong," she said. "You know the Russian poet, Joseph Brodsky?"

"What about him?"

She pulled her bathrobe around her shoulders and said, "He wrote that no loneliness is deeper than the memory of miracles. Isn't that what love seems like, Henry? A miracle? Something that strikes out of nowhere and transforms our life. That's how I feel about my daughter." She touched my hand. "That's how you feel about Angelito. Vicky must feel the same way about Pete. Hard to let go of an experience that powerful or the hope it will repeat itself. I see that now. There's nothing we can do to help her as long as she still has that hope."

"And Angel? He stays hostage to her romantic fantasies?"

She cocked her head and studied me. "Why do you dislike her so much?"

"She reminds me of Mom, Angel is like me, and I see history repeating itself. A kid left on his own while the woman who should be protecting him is off chasing some delusion. Religious in Mom's case, religious and romantic in Vicky's."

"What was Mom supposed to do?"

"Leave him," I said, and heard all the repressed bitterness of forty years in my voice.

"And go where?" Elena asked softly. "She had a grade-school education, no job skills and her family was far away."

"I would've starved in the street before going back to him," I said. I didn't have to say who—she knew I meant our father.

Elena closed her hand around mine. "We wouldn't have starved but something worse might have happened. Instead, she stayed with him and here we are, more or less intact."

"More or less," I said. "I would like something better for Angel."

She sighed. "What do you want to do? Take Angel away from her? That's just exchanging one kind of suffering for another."

"It would be better in the long run."

"You can't possibly know what kind of damage he would sustain if we put him through a custody fight. Besides, Henry, I know a little about family law, too, and whatever else she is, Vicky is not an unfit mother."

"She will be if she becomes readdicted to crack."

"You seem determined to think the worst of her. We're not going to interfere."

"All right, fine. What about trying to find Jesusita Trujillo? You said Vicky's close to her. Maybe we can at least maintain a line of communication with Vicky and Angel through her. That's not interference."

After a moment, she said, "No, it's not. It's actually a pretty good idea for us to get to know the other side of the family. Were you able to locate her?"

"I called off my investigator when Vicky turned up here. I'll put him back on it."

She nodded. "I'm going to fly home today. There doesn't seem much point in me staying."

"I understand. I'll let you know as soon as I find Jesusita."

She stood up. "I want you to promise me something, Henry."

I thought I knew what was coming. "I know, no interference."

"That wasn't what I was going to ask," she said. "I want you to promise me that if Vicky ever needs your help, you'll put aside your feelings and help her."

"I don't have to like her, I just have to love her. Is that it?"

"What?"

"Nothing," I said. "I promise, Elena. Whatever she needs."

Elena went off to shower and pack. I put a slice of bread into the toaster and poured another cup of coffee. The phone rang. Thinking Vicky might have come to her senses, I grabbed the receiver. It was John.

"Hey, you and Angel ready for a little *béisbol*?"

"John," I said. "Actually, there's a problem."

"What's wrong?"

I told him that Vicky and Angel had disappeared and that I wanted to spend time with Elena before she flew back north. "I'm sorry about the game. I'll pay for the tickets."

"Nah, one of my brothers will take 'em. I feel bad for Angelito. What do you think is gonna happen?"

"I think Vicky will reconcile with her husband and they'll put each other and Angel through hell."

"They're his parents, man. They won't do that."

"You're very idealistic about family," I said. "Not me. I've seen the damage it can do. Listen, John, maybe we can talk later."

After a moment, he said in a quiet, hurt voice, "I know you're feeling bad, but don't blow me off. I care about you."

"I'm sorry. I care about you, too. You know that."

"Come and have dinner with me tonight," he said. "I promise I'll make you feel better."

"What time?"

"Like around seven?"

"Good," I said. "And John? I feel better already. Should I bring anything?"

He laughed. "How about a toothbrush?"

Mount Washington was one of those neighborhoods that tourists to L.A. never see and that even most residents would have been unable to find on the map. It was a hills-and-flats neighborhood. The flats were a backwater of light industry and poor people; warehouses and small, shabby residences on treeless streets where walls were scarred by gang graffiti, and the few businesses had bars on the windows and closed when the sun went down. This was Third World L.A., populated by Central American immigrants. The men could be found standing on street corners hoping to be hired for a day's work as cut-rate gardeners or painters. Street vendors pushed their carts down the street selling *helados* and *elote*—ice cream and roasted corn. Small children with large dark eyes played in dirt yards behind high Cyclone fences. I wondered, as I ascended the street that led to John's house, whether Angelito would end up in a neighborhood like this one.

In the hills, the houses were bigger and commanded greater privacy and nicer views, but unlike comparable neighborhoods, there was not the stunning disparity between hillside wealth and flatland poverty. Rather the hills seemed inhabited by old-fashioned L.A. bohemians, the kind of people who had always given the city its reputation for benign looniness—health cultists, guru followers, past-life regressionists, mediums and spiritualists of every stripe. Their houses were hidden among the trees like hermits, or worshipfully faced the sun with broad decks and multilevel terraces where neglected gardens scented the air with roses and jasmine.

I followed John's directions to a rutted private road that plunged through a thickness of manzanita, eucalyptus and pine. His was the third driveway off the road. The driveway ascended up a small hill and dead-ended at a clearing where his truck was parked. I emerged from my car to dusty silence and still light. All that was visible of his house was a flight of redwood stairs that disappeared into a stand of pine trees, the edge of a deck and, in the shadows, the glint of glass. I climbed the first steps and discovered there was not one, but two flights of stairs. The first ended at a landing, from which I could see, in the gloaming of the trees, concrete pilings. I started up the second flight and heard music. At the top of stairs, I came out onto the deck I had seen from below. The glint of glass was revealed as a sliding door set into a wall made, like the rest of the house, of weathered redwood. Through the glass I saw a large, sparsely furnished room with a hardwood floor and a stone fireplace. I slid the door open, walked inside and called out above the music, "John?"

He emerged from the kitchen wiping his hands on a dish towel that he tossed over his shoulder. He was wearing freshly pressed khakis and a midnight-blue pocket T-shirt that showed off his biceps and broad chest. His hair was brushed and his face was shaved and he had never looked handsomer. He turned down the stereo and met me at the threshold.

"Hey," he said, giving me a hug. He had steeped himself in cologne. "You made it."

I held out the bouquet of white roses I had purchased from a flower shop where the clerk had winked and told me what a lucky gal my girlfriend was.

"These are for you."

He took them with a warm smile. "They're nice, Henry. Thank you."

I looked around the room. The ceiling went up a second level where, behind a railing constructed, he later told me, of posts salvaged from a Victorian staircase, there was a loft bedroom. I could make out the edge of a bed covered with a quilt, an iron floor lamp and an old, unpainted dresser. This room was furnished with a swaybacked brown leather sofa so old that the leather was cracked; a couple of newer armchairs, one deep green leather, the other striped canvas in a vaguely southwestern design. There was a big frayed Indian rug in front of the fireplace and a cane-backed rocking chair beside it. On the plank coffee table was a scattering of newspapers, mail, a coffee cup. Built-in bookshelves held books on architecture, landscaping and baseball, and framed snapshots that I guessed were family pictures. Off to the side a door was partly opened to reveal a smaller bedroom. The kitchen was also partly visible and I assumed there was a bathroom somewhere, but I realized that these four rooms were basically all there was to the house. The high ceiling made it seemed larger, while clerestory windows and skylights filled it with light and lightness. The air smelled faintly of lemon wood polish. Tree branches scraped gently against the outside walls.

"This is like a grown-up version of a treehouse."

John grinned. "That was the idea. I built it myself mostly out of salvaged material. I lived in a tent down where the cars are parked for months. I love it up here."

"Was this where you lived when you were married?"

"No, Suzie got that house. This is mine. I put in the second bedroom for my son when he comes down from school. Come into the kitchen with me."

The walls of the kitchen were painted a warm orange, the tile was blue and white. On the stove was a skillet with rice and peas in tomato sauce. A handpainted ceramic bowl on the counter held a green salad. There was a second, glass bowl in which two pieces of fish were marinating in a clear oil. A door opened out to the deck, where there was a grill and a small wrought-iron table set with pale green plates and blue glasses. I was aware that the things in John's house had not been chosen at random, but the effect was casual rather than calculated, and though the eye that had arranged them was masculine, it was also capable of delicacy.

John came up behind me and put his arms around my waist. "What are you looking at?"

"The guy who put this house together is an artist," I said.

"Thanks," he said, relaxing into my body. "Since I started contracting, I've become interested in all kinds of design—architecture, landscape, interiors—but I don't have the education and I'm too old to go back now. Anyway, I like what I do."

"Putting in guest bathrooms?"

He bit my ear. "They're good guest bathrooms."

"Ow, is it going to be that kind of night?"

He let go of me. "Hope so. You want something to drink? Iced tea? A Coke?"

"Tea," I said. "Can I help with anything?"

"Everything's done, except grilling the fish. It's tuna, that okay?"

"Sounds great."

He got the drinks and we went outside, where he sat me at the table, put the fish on the grill, and brought the rice and salad from the kitchen. He put the roses in a blue vase and set them on the table.

"So," he said, watching the fish. "You had a rough day."

I looked around at the sun-dappled trees, the weathered deck, the bright kitchen. "I'm happy now."

"You want to talk about it?"

"No, I'd like to forget about my family for a few hours. Is that all right?"

"Man, that's why I built this place. You can shrug everything off and just kick back." He turned the fish.

"You really don't seem like the kind of guy who needs to get away from it all."

"No? Why?"

"You're pretty outgoing. I wouldn't have figured you for someone who likes a lot of time alone."

"I never used to be," he said, smearing the fish with marinade.

"Fact, I hated being by myself. I was always looking for the party or at least someone to distract me. Hand me the plates one at a time, okay?"

He slid the fish onto the plates. I took one then the other, while he went back into the house and came out with small bowls of salsa and guacamole, a bottle of dressing and a stack of corn tortillas wrapped in an embroidered dishcloth that I knew had to have been sewn by his mother.

He refilled our glasses and we served ourselves. He lifted his glass and touched mine. "*Buen provecho*, Henry."

"*Buen provecho*, John." I cut a piece of fish with the edge of my fork.

"When I was alone, I started thinking," he said, picking up the conversation. "I didn't like to think."

"Why?"

He shrugged. "Because then I'd have to start thinking about the future, or why I had these little feelings about other guys or maybe that I was drinking too much or about my marriage. Grown-up shit. I tell you, Henry, I did not want to grow up. I figured if I grew up, I would stop having fun."

"Something change your mind?"

"No. I was right! You do stop having fun, or maybe the things that were fun when you were a kid stop being fun. For a while I just did 'em more, faster, harder, trying to get the fun back, but it didn't work. I bet you've always been the kind of guy people can count on."

"I try to be."

"Me, I was the kind of guy you could count on not to count on." He ate a forkful of rice, a piece of fish. "That shit catches up with you." He stopped eating and looked at me. "It caught up with me the night I ran into that telephone pole and almost crippled that girl. Since then I've been trying to walk the straight and narrow."

"I'm not sure about the straight," I said, "but you do okay on the narrow."

He laughed, but then in a serious voice said, "I have my slips. You gotta know that about me."

"Anyone who has standards has slips, John. Only good people worry about being good."

He smiled. "Is that why your hair is gray?"

"My hair started going gray when I was twenty-five. That was a long time ago, by the way."

"Lucky for you I like older men," he said.

When we finished eating, I helped John clear the table and together we washed up. I went to put the leftover salsa in the refrigerator. On the door, in a magnetic plastic picture frame, was a snapshot of John in a silvery-gray suit with a white carnation in his lapel, standing with his arm around a very pretty woman, a blonde about his age who was wearing a bottle green silk sheath dress. They were standing against a railing. Behind them was the ocean and sunset. I put the salsa away. When I turned, John was standing at the sink, drying a bowl and watching me.

"That's Deanna," he said. "The girl I told you I was dating."

I took the picture off the fridge. Deanna had the look of a woman who believed she'd earned the laugh lines that bracketed her mouth and wasn't ashamed of them.

"She's not a girl, John, she's a woman," I said. "You told me you thought I was real? She looks pretty real, too."

He came up behind me and took the picture. "She's good people." He stuck it back on the fridge, in a slightly less prominent spot. "You upset?"

"No. Does she know about me?"

He shook his head. "She knows I've been with guys, but she thinks it's in the past. I did too, before I met you. I was gonna tell her when things were more solid between you and me."

"That's cool," I said. "You know, John, I don't have any expectations."

"That's funny," he said, putting his arms around my waist. "Because I do."

We went into the living room and stretched out on the couch. Twilight deepened into night, the music ended. He sat up and switched on a lamp. His hair was rumpled and his shirt was lost in the cushions. I pulled him back down and he lay with his head on my chest.

"I can hear your heart," he said.

I smoothed his bristly hair. "You'll tell me if it stops."

"Don't joke like that." He lifted his head and looked at me. "The first time I saw you, I thought you were dying."

I kissed him. "I'm not dying, John."

"Are you sure it's all right for you to have sex?"

"Yeah, as long as it's not very exciting sex."

I could see he thought I was serious, but then he figured it out. *"Payaso,"* he said. "Clown."

I embraced him. "It feels good to hold you."

"You, too," he said, stroking my chest. "You have nice skin."

"You have a great chest."

"You don't mind my potbelly?"

"A little meat on a man looks good. I've always been a scarecrow."

"You got the right build for a distance runner," he said.

I squeezed a massive biceps. "And you've still got a pitcher's arm."

"That was a long time ago," he said. "I don't think you would have liked me when I was playing."

"Then I guess I should be happy that part of your life is over," I said. He stirred unhappily in my arms. "I'm sorry, John. That was a stupid thing to say."

He raised his face above mine and caught my eyes with his. The lamplight darkened their green flicker and made them even graver.

When I looked into John's eyes, I saw the depth of feeling that lay beneath the easygoing demeanor with which he faced life. Sometimes it floated closer to the surface than at other times, and I could see clearly how much it had cost him to leave behind the golden boy in the baseball uniform to assume the rigors and ambiguities of a man's life. There was sadness but also strength, gravity and grace, uncertainty but courage. As if he had meant for me to see this, he smiled slowly and pressed his cheek against mine, scorching me with his heat. I closed my arms around him. Our chests filled and emptied at the same time. When at last we untangled ourselves, my pendant had pressed a heart shape into his skin.

10.

"Good morning, Henry," Dr. Hayward said. "Nice hat. DeLeon and Son. What is that?"

"A friend's contracting company," I said. I removed the hat and put it on my lap. Hayward's office was on the fourth floor of Westside Hospital, with a window that framed the Hollywood hills when they were visible. The gray June pall that hung in the air made the row of palm trees lining Olympic Boulevard look like leftover props from a Maria Montez movie.

"Leon, that's the Spanish word for lion, isn't it?" Hayward said. I didn't know whether his chattiness was a good sign or a bad one. He had bustled in twenty minutes late with the results of my last series of tests, leaving me in his waiting room for another ten minutes before peremptorily summoning me. Now he wanted a Spanish lesson.

"Leon was one of the ancient kingdoms of Spain," I said. "DeLeon means 'from Leon.'"

He tipped back in a thronelike leather chair—no ergonomically correct furniture for the head of Westside's cardiology department. His feet, I observed, barely touched the ground. Other than the chair, the rest of his office was modest enough. White walls, framed degrees, a couple of art prints that appeared to have been selected by committee for maximum inoffensiveness. The only personal items I could see were pictures of his family—wife, teenage son, pre-teen daughter—all, like Dr. Hayward, small, cute and visibly of superior intellect.

"But it means 'lion,' too, doesn't it?"

On his bookcase was a spiffy miniature stereo system—all chrome and sleek blond wood—on which he was playing, at very low volume, a somber piece of classical music that the CD propped against the stereo identified as Mahler's Second Symphony.

"Yes," I conceded. "It also means 'lion.'"

He grinned triumphantly and flipped open my file folder. "Your results are fine. Treadmill was negative—ECG normal, no substernal chest pain reported. Your resting pulse is okay. You're taking your beta-blocker faithfully?"

"Like clockwork."

"And an aspirin every day."

"To keep the doctor away."

He smirked, flipped a page. "Lipids—well, you've got some hereditary problems there, but it seems to be under control with the Lipitor. Any chest pains, shortness of breath?"

"I did have a pain in my chest a couple of days ago that felt like a muscle spasm."

"Uh-huh," he said, then rattled off a series of rapid-fire questions as if he hoped to catch me in a lie. Fortunately, I had done at least as many cross-examinations as he, so I kept up. Then he fell silent, went back through my chart. "Well, Henry, I just don't see any cause for immediate alarm here, but if it happens again, I want you to call me then and not wait three days to report it." He cast a stern look at me. "Got it?"

"I understand," I said. As I tried to frame my next question, a chorus burst out on the CD. "I have to ask you kind of an awkward—"

"Yes, you can have sex," he said.

"How did you know I was going to ask you about sex?"

"It's a standard question," he replied. He glanced at the cap in my lap and said, "Hmpf. Did you have specific questions or should I give you my post–heart attack birds-and-bees talk?"

"All I want to know is whether I could drop dead in flagrante delicto."

"Ah, the standard lecture, then," he said. "Sexual intercourse carries a zero to negligible risk of cardiac arrest. In much older men, the beta-blocker may cause some dysfunction. Are you having trouble getting erections?"

"Uh—no," I said. "Well, yes. A bit."

"That's probably psychological, Henry. Sex is not going to kill you—well, let me amend that. Safe sex is not going to kill you. Your problems will pass. If they persist, then we'll see if there's a medical cause." When he finished, he smiled and said, "Tell Mr. DeLeon if he has concerns, he can call me directly."

"How did you know?"

"Usually it's one of the first things men in relationships are worried about after a heart attack. You didn't ask, so I drew the logical conclusion. Now you're asking, so obviously your situation has changed and"—he raised an eyebrow—"you came in wearing that very red hat."

"I'll tell John he can call you if he has questions," I said. "By the way, you scare me."

Hayward flashed his smug grin. "I want you to accelerate the pace of your exercise." He glanced at me. "Let's avoid the obvious double-entendre."

"I wasn't going there."

"Brisk walks would be good," he said. "The idea is a progressive increase. Push yourself a bit, and unless I hear from you before, I'll see you in a month."

I got up to leave. At the door, I said, "Thanks for everything, Doc."

"Enjoy yourself," he said, and as he reached for the phone, added, "safely."

. . .

On my way home, I had a thought and drove to the Beverly Center. Late that afternoon, when the sludge had finally cleared from the sky, I put on my brand-new running shoes, an old pair of running shorts and an even older T-shirt from law school, the red Stanford lettering all but faded into the gray, and drove to a nearby high school. I made my way through the red brick buildings that had served as a backdrop for more than one teen exploitation film, and found the football field. It was ringed by a quarter-mile track. I went out to field, lay my cell phone in the grass and began to stretch. Over a decade had passed since I'd stopped running, so I was surprised at how quickly I remembered the sequences of stretches but not so surprised at how much more difficult they were. I was reaching for the big toe on my left foot when my phone rang. I picked it up. It was my investigator, Freeman Vidor.

"Hey, Henry, I got the info you wanted on that lady. Jesusita Trujillo."

"A phone number?"

He chuckled. "Phone number, address, Social Security, place of employment, number of kids. Credit rating."

"Another fly caught in the worldwide web, huh? She have a son named Peter?"

"Yeah, and two daughters besides."

"I'm not at the office right now. Can you e-mail me this information?"

"Sure," he said. "Where are you?"

"At the track."

"When did you start playing the ponies?"

"A running track, Freeman," I said. "I'm going to attempt to run a mile in under a month."

"You sure you want to do that?"

"Doctor's orders."

He snorted. "Hope his med-mal insurance is paid up."

"Talk to you later, Freeman. Thanks."

I finished my stretches, stuck the phone in the waistband of my shorts and walked to the start of the track. The air smelled hazily of eucalyptus from the surrounding trees and of sun-warmed grass. As I looked down the dusty length of the track, my body seemed in some subtle way to remember all those years of starting lines at track meets. My pulse accelerated a bit, my knees bent a little, my shoulders loosened, my neck straightened, the balls of my feet seemed to touch more lightly the ground beneath them. I got into position, counted three and slowly set off.

Soaking in the tub that evening, I studied the printout of Freeman's e-mail glimpse into the life of Mrs. Jesusita Trujillo, a sixty-five-year-old widow who lived in Garden Grove and worked as a teacher's aide to supplement her Social Security. Peter, thirty-five, was the youngest of her three children. She also had two married daughters, one living in San Diego, the other in Hawthorne. She had recently taken out a loan for ten thousand dollars, using her house for collateral. Since she had no large debts, I wondered why she needed that much money. Home improvements? I would see for myself when I dropped in on her tomorrow evening. I had decided to visit rather than call, because if she was in touch with Vicky and Pete, she might refuse to see me, depending on what my niece had told her. The cell phone rang. I put the paper aside and answered it. It was John. I made him laugh with an account of my elephantine pace around the track and then I told him about my talk with Dr. Hayward.

Garden Grove was one of those suburbs that, forty years ago, symbolized to the rest of America the vacuity of life in Southern California: block after block of identical split-level, ranch-style houses on barren plots of land that had once been part of the vast citrus orchards that had given Orange County its name. The houses had not aged well, particularly in Mrs. Trujillo's neighborhood. The driveways on Avalon Road were cracked and oil stained. Paint blistered on the walls of the houses, and almost of all of them had barred windows and sat behind Cyclone fences. Those that did not were sprayed with gang *placas*. The spray-painted squiggles marked the neighborhood as the territory of the GGBoyz, and it had that unnatural stillness of a place where people feared to venture outside.

Although the houses on Avalon Road had become small, shabby jails for their inhabitants, the little yards were planted hopefully with flowers and fruit trees, hedges and flowering shrubs and bushes. Even orange trees had made a comeback. The tart-sweet unmistakable scent of orange blossoms filled the air as I got out of my car in front of Mrs. Trujillo's house, which was, like its neighbors, barricaded behind a tall fence. The gate was locked. I stood there a moment wondering what to do when the front door opened and a woman called out from behind the screen door, "Can I help you?"

"Mrs. Trujillo? My name is Henry Rios. I'm Vicky's uncle. Her mother's brother? I wonder if I could talk to you for a minute."

"I haven't seen Vicky since last time Pete went to jail."

"She was at my house until a couple of nights ago," I said. "I think she and Pete and Angel are together. I just wanted to give you a message for her, if they call you. A message from her mother."

The screen door squeaked as Mrs. Trujillo opened it and stepped out onto the sagging porch. In the twilight I could make out a small, plump woman with wiry hair and a round, once lovely face that time and hardship had dissolved into a puddle of sagging, melancholy features. She came to the gate and unlocked it.

"You better come in before someone tries to kill you," she said. "Did you lock your car?"

"Yeah. It has an alarm."

"That won't stop anyone around here."

"Bad gang problem?"

"When I was raising my kids, they used to play out in the streets. You see any kids out there now?"

I stepped into her yard. In the center of the grass was a bathtub planted with red and pink geraniums.

"I'm sorry," she said. "What was your name again?"

"Henry," I replied, smiling. "Henry Rios. My sister, Elena, is Vicky's mother, though I guess you've been the only mom she's ever really had."

Mrs. Trujillo said, "I love her like she's my own. Her and Angelito. Come in, Mr. Rios."

There was gold shag carpeting in her living room and an electric blue couch upholstered in crushed velvet, circa 1970. She wasn't being retro. On the wall above it were a series of paintings depicting a vaguely familiar landscape. After a moment I recognized them as views of San Francisco Bay from San Quentin. *Pete's prison therapy*, I thought. The television was set into a massive console and was running with the sound off. The top of the console was covered with framed photos that seemed to go back four generations, from snapshots to stiffly posed formal portraits. On the mirrored coffee table was an onyx ashtray, where a cigarette was burning. The first thing she did was to put it out and then ask me if I wanted something to drink.

"Ice water?"

"You don't want a beer?"

"I don't drink," I said.

She seemed to become a shade less wary. "You sober?"

"For a long time."

"I have iced tea," she said, definitely unbending. "You sit down. Here, turn the TV off. I keep it on for company."

She left the room. I noticed the sewing box on the floor beside the couch, and over the arm a pair of boy's jeans. A patch was half-sewn over a torn knee. I went over to the television set and examined the pictures on top of it. The oldest appeared to date from the turn of the century: a fading shot of a group of dark-skinned, Indian-featured men and women standing or sitting against a painted backdrop of a rose-covered trellis. Country people immortalized by an itinerant photographer plying his trade through the villages of Mexico a hundred years ago. I could almost see the dirt beneath their nails, feel the scratchy newness of the men's high, stiff collars against their skin, the women's callused feet wedged into unaccustomed shoes. Their eyes were unguarded but alien; the eyes of people at home in a world of which no trace now existed. I put the picture down and picked up a small snapshot that showed a pretty girl, a good-looking boy and, in the boy's arms, a baby with the grave eyes of his *mestizo* ancestors. After a moment, it dawned on me that I was looking at Vicky, Pete and Angelito. Elena had told me Vicky was nineteen when Angel was born but she scarcely looked that old. I was so accustomed to the suspicious, wary expression she wore around me that I hardly recognized this fresh-faced, hopeful girl. She was lovely. Pete Trujillo was a tall, thin boy with a face almost as guileless as Vicky's; when this picture was taken, he was already a convicted felon. He held Angel in one arm and wrapped the other around his wife's waist. A smear of tattoo was visible on his neck beneath his shirt collar, but otherwise he wasn't decked out in the usual gangbanger regalia. He looked like an ordinary Latino boy and beamed with evident pride in his little family. Only Angel, who appeared to be at most a few months old, seemed by his serious expression to have a premonition of what was to come. I heard Mrs. Trujillo enter the room behind me. She was carrying a tray with tea, sugar and a plate of Oreo cookies, which she set down on the coffee table. I handed her the picture.

"When was this taken?"

"When Angel was baptized," she said. "See, he's wearing his baptismal dress. I made it for him."

"Pete doesn't look like he belonged to a gang. He looks like a good kid."

She stared at the picture a moment longer and sighed. "He is,

Mr. Rios. He has a good heart." She returned the picture to its place and picked up another, of a stocky, handsome man with a pencil mustache and thick black hair. "This was Pete's dad, my husband, Evaristo. He worked down in the shipyard in Long Beach, with the asbestos. That's what killed him. I wish he'd been around when Pete was growing up. He would've kept my baby away from those damn drugs and his damn cousin, Butch."

"How old was Pete when his father died?"

"Nine," she said. "Come and sit, Mr. Rios."

"Please call me Henry. I mean, we are related by marriage."

"You can call me Jessie if you want, like my friends do. I brought you sugar and lemon for your tea."

I fiddled with my tea for a moment. "Has Vicky told you about Elena and me?"

"Why, no," she said, after a prevaricating pause. "Like I said, I haven't talked to her since Pete went to jail."

"I'm not the police or anything. I'm only here because Elena and I are worried about Vicky and Angel. They came to us, and I think we must have done or said something that upset Vicky because she left without even saying good-bye to her mother. We'd just like to know she's okay."

Jessie folded her hands in her lap. "That girl used to sit here and cry and ask me how her mom could have put her up for adoption the way she did."

"My sister was a young, unmarried woman trying to finish her education so she could make a better life for herself than the one we had growing up," I said. "She didn't think she could do that and raise a child. I don't think she's ever forgiven herself. Vicky's young. Maybe she hasn't learned yet that good people can make terrible mistakes and still be good people."

Jessie nodded, almost imperceptibly. Perhaps she was thinking of her son, the felon with the good heart, or maybe she was old enough to have made a terrible mistake or two herself.

"Elena did get her education. She's a professor at a college up in

Oakland. I'm a lawyer. A criminal defense lawyer. Vicky and Angel are our only family."

"I know," she said. "I know you and your sister are—" She paused. "Vicky told me about your lifestyle."

The way she hesitated and fumbled over the phrase made it clear she was loath to give offense. She was a kindly woman whom life had taught tolerance. I felt for her, barricaded in her own house, surrounded by photographs of a family that had apparently dispersed. I decided not to point out to her that only a moment earlier she had told me she had not spoken to Vicky since Pete went to jail, long before Vicky had come to Elena or me.

"I know Vicky doesn't approve," I said. "That's all right. We'd still like to help her, on whatever terms she's willing to accept help from us."

"They don't need money, Henry," she said. I could see she was struggling with whether to speak freely to me. "I made sure they're going to be all right."

"Where are they?"

She looked at me with a terrified expression. "*No puedo decir más.* I'm sorry." Now she seemed to panic. "I think you should leave, Henry."

I nodded. "All right, but take my card. Here, I'll write Elena's number on it, too. Please, ask Vicky if you can call us to let us know how they are."

Reluctantly she took my card. "It was nice to meet you, Henry."

"It was nice to meet you, too," I said, and knew that as soon as I left, she would throw the card away.

As I drove back to L.A., I tried to make sense of my encounter with Jesusita Trujillo. The problem was that it didn't make sense. Jesusita was clearly trying to protect Vicky and Angel from some danger but the only one I was aware of was from her son. I got the distinct impression, however, that she was not of this opinion. Hadn't Vicky told her about the beatings? Wouldn't they have been obvious? Well, at least I now knew why she had taken out the ten-thousand-dollar loan on her house. It was money for Pete and Vicky and Angel to start a new life. But where?

The next evening, John and I went to a movie and I stayed at his house. Dr. Hayward was right—once I was reassured I wasn't going to drop dead in the middle of an intimate act, my problem solved itself. John dropped me off the following morning on his way to work. I leaned into the cab of his truck and said, "I'll call you tonight?"

"I'm seeing Deanna," he said.

"Tomorrow, then."

He reached out and grabbed my hand. "You mad?"

I wasn't and said so. "It's just not like that. I told you I don't have any expectations. I meant it."

"I'll call you as soon as I get home," he said, in the tone of a man who had made an important decision.

I spent the rest of the day finishing my judicial application and dropped it off at the post office when I drove to the high school to run. When I got back into my car, I glanced at myself in the rearview mirror and realized I wasn't wearing the pendant Edith had given me. Then I remembered, in the midst of some maneuver in bed the night before, it had swung from my neck and hit John in the eye, so I'd removed it. I grinned, remembering. Elena said love was a miracle? This was a lot earthier, but for that reason I trusted the feelings growing between us. I didn't know where it was leading, but I had never felt so comfortable with another man. John had told me he felt the same way. That's why I thought nothing of it when he didn't call that evening. I was sound asleep when the buzz of the doorbell seeped into the dream and woke me. I glanced at the alarm clock; it was a quarter after one. I was a little shaky as I made my way to the door, looked through the peephole and saw John shivering in the yellow porchlight. His shirt and pants were stained with vomit. I opened the door and could smell the booze on his breath even before I saw his eyes.

"John?"

"Can I talk to you?"

He reeked, and behind him I saw his truck was parked half on the sidewalk.

"Come inside, man. What happened to you? I thought you didn't drink."

He stumbled into the hallway and leaned against the wall. He dug into his pocket and pulled out my pendant.

"Deanna found this by the bed. She asked me what it was. I told her about you."

The pendant slipped from his fingers. I caught it

"I guess she didn't take it very well."

"She called me a faggot," he said, beginning to blubber. "She said I was trying to give her AIDS."

"Oh, baby," I said. "I'm really sorry."

"I came this close to punching her," he said, holding up his thumb and forefinger.

"But instead you took it out on a bottle of"—I sniffed him—"tequila?"

"I puked most of it on myself."

"I can see that. Come on, let's get you cleaned up and then we can talk."

He leaned on me. "I'm sorry. I told you I had slips."

"Yes, you did," I said, steering him toward the bathroom. "I thought you meant something else." When we reached the bathroom, I asked, "Can you take a shower without drowning yourself?" I sat him on the toilet, untied his shoes and removed them and his socks. "I think you can take it from here." I ran the shower while he undressed and took his clothes while he got under the nozzle. "I'm going to put on some coffee and find you something to wear. Will you be okay in there?" There was no response. "John?"

"I'm okay," he said gruffly.

I tossed his clothes into the washing machine, found him a pair of sweatpants and a pullover, put on a pot of coffee and went back into the bathroom. The shower was off but the shower curtain was still drawn. I pulled it back. He was sitting in the empty tub, crying.

"John, why are you crying?"

"I fucked everything up," he said.

"I'm sorry about what happened with you and Deanna."

"Not with her."

I held out my hand. "Come on, baby."

He grabbed my hand and I pulled him up until we were face to face. He looked at me with bleary eyes. "I'm so sorry."

"Stop apologizing. Just get dressed and tell me what happened."

The shower had sobered him up, and in fresh clothes he was recognizable as the man who had dropped me off that morning. He slowly sipped a cup of coffee and blinked at his surroundings like someone coming out of a dream. For a moment, I thought he might be in a blackout, but when he looked at me I saw in his eyes that he was present and accounted for.

"I thought you told her you'd been with men," I said.

"I did. She was cool about it, you know. I think it even turned her on a little, but I guess she thought I was done with all that." He put the cup down on the table with a clatter. "I let her think that 'cause I thought it was over, too. Until I met you."

"You made it sound like things were winding down between you two."

"I thought they were," he said. "How was I supposed to know what she was thinking? She turned me down when I proposed and now she's screaming at me that she thought we were going to get married."

"Maybe she's been working on a different calendar than you."

"Duh," he said. He swallowed a couple of aspirin. "She didn't have to call me names and say that thing about AIDS."

"You caught her off guard," I said. "People react out of their gut when that happens."

"Don't defend her. She was a bitch." He rubbed his forehead. "I don't mean that. You're right. I took her by surprise. Man, if she took it this hard, I don't want to think what my family's gonna do."

"They also think being with guys was a phase for you?"

"Yeah, like drinking. Just me being my bad self. You shoulda seen my mom's face when she met Deanna. I bet she spent the next month on her knees doing rosaries to thank *la Virgen* that her son wasn't a *joto* anymore."

"Let's talk about the drinking," I said. "How long has it been?"

"I went on a bender when I broke up with Tom," he said. "Almost two years ago. That was it, otherwise I've been sober, but I haven't gone to meetings in a long time."

"So are you at the beginning or the end of a binge?" I asked, and then, because I heard it with his ears and it sounded harsh, added, "Look, I'm not being holier than thou, believe me. It took me four years of drinking and stopping and three rehabs to finally get sober, and then five years into it, I went out again. I can help you with this."

He held up a hand. "No, I don't want you to help me, because then what we have becomes about drinking." He gulped some water. "I know the drill. Go back to AA, get a sponsor, work the steps. I don't need you for that. This won't happen again. I promise."

"We never mean to get drunk again, but sometimes it happens."

"It won't."

"Let me finish," I said. "All I meant was that you don't have to make that promise to me. The possibility that one of us could go out is going to be there. I can accept that as long as this slip ends tonight."

"It's over."

"I'm beat. How are you doing?"

He threw his arms around me. "Can I stay here?"

"I'm not letting you drive when I can still smell old Mexico on your breath. The cops pull you over, you'd blow an oh-eight, easy."

He was sobbing and laughing. "You crack me up, Henry."

"Oh, baby." I kissed the top of his head. "Let's go to bed."

John was asleep as his head hit the pillow, snoring peaceably while his hand curled around mine beneath the sheets. There would be a lot more to talk about in the days to come, but for now I was happy he was here. Just as I was drifting off, the phone rang. It was now just before three. This could only be bad news. I reached over John for the phone and said quietly, "Hello."

There was silence on the other end and then I heard a small, soft, "Uncle Henry?"

I sat up. "Angel? Where are you? Is everything all right?"

"Uncle Henry," he whispered. "I think my mom killed my dad."

11.

John mumbled and stirred. I quietly rolled out of bed and went out into the hall. The loudness of the traffic noises at the other end of the line indicated he was calling from a phone booth.

"Where are you?"

"I'm at a g-g-gas station," he said, stuttering with fear. "The Ar-Arco at the c-c-corner of Hollywood and La Ba—La Ba—"

"La Brea. That's close by," I said. "Stay put. I'll be there in ten minutes."

"Hurry," he said.

I put the phone down and went back into the bedroom. John was still asleep, his snoring had subsided into a low rumble. I dressed quickly and stood over the bed for a second. His face was peaceful, the wide chest calmly rising and falling, one big arm was thrown behind his head, the other at his side, the fingers still half-opened where they had been wrapped with mine. He had a hero's physiognomy that would not have been out of place as an illustration in *Tales from Homer* and if I had awakened him, he would have insisted on coming with me. The temptation was great, but in the end I let him sleep. While I was no hero, I didn't run from trouble, and I had heard big trouble in Angel's cry for help. I kissed the crown of John's head and left.

Angel was standing beside the phone booth in a bright cone of light cast by the street lamp above him. I pulled into the parking space beside the gas station and got out. He was wearing the same Giants T-shirt that he had been wearing the first night he came to my house. The night was cool and damp, and he was shivering. He had on a game face, a small boy trying to project big, but when he saw me, he deflated, and I think he would have run into my arms except for that caution that rarely seemed to leave his dark eyes. Instead, he walked slowly toward me. Across La Brea Boulevard was a dumpy motel called, predictably, the Hollywood Inn that advertised X-rated cable and AARP special rates. Two shrieking black-and-white patrol cars pulled into its lot, followed by an ambulance. Angel glanced fearfully over his shoulder. I knew where I would find his mother.

I removed my sweatshirt. "Put this on," I said. He pulled it over his head and it came to his knees. I knelt down and rolled up the sleeves until his grubby fingers were visible. "Is your mother in the motel?"

"Yeah."

"What happened?"

"I went to McDonald's and when I came back, my dad was dead and my mom had a gun . . ."

He started sobbing. I pulled him close and he threw his arms around my neck and shook. The sour musk of fear emanated from deep within his body. I remembered that smell; it had clung to me for most of my childhood. I stroked his greasy hair and let him cry himself calm.

"Here, *m'ijo*, blow your nose," I said, giving him my handkerchief. He blew with a loud, damp noise. "I'm going over to the motel to take a look. I want you to wait in my car." There was a snack shop in the gas station. "Are you hungry? Do you want a soda?"

"A Coke," he hiccuped.

"Okay, let's get you a Coke."

A moment later he was sitting in my car with a Coke and a Mars Bar. I stooped so that our faces were level.

"As soon as I leave, roll up the windows and lock the doors and sit tight. I'll be back in a couple minutes. H'okay?"

He gripped the candy bar as it were a lifeline and stuttered, "H'okay."

"Remember you told me you know all the names of the presidents?"

He whispered. "Yeah."

"If you start to get nervous, just say them to yourself until I get back."

The Hollywood Inn was at the base of a rocky, eroded hill. Above were the gates of a hillside community where a star or two may have once lived. On the strength of this proximity, the motel's neon sign boasted it was "The Gateway to the Stars." The two-story building was in the throwaway style of a thousand other such places in the city. The first floor opened directly onto the parking lot, which the police had cordoned off. The second floor was set back on a breezeway where, at the moment, a few onlookers roused from their sleep stood at the railing watching the scene unfolding beneath them. I went up the stairs holding my keys in my hand, as if going to my room, and joined the clump of spectators in time to see my niece carried out of her room on a stretcher and loaded into the ambulance. Even in that glimpse I saw blood on her blouse, the pounding her face had taken, and I had to look away, turning to the floridly sunburned man beside me.

"Do you know what happened?"

"Can't say, mate," he replied, the accent Australian. "Me and the wife were sound asleep when I heard gunfire. I got up and called the police. We didn't leave the room until we heard the sirens in the parking lot."

"Gunfire? You mean there was shooting back and forth?"

"Well, there was several shots," he said. "Didn't you hear 'em?"

"I was out," I said. "I'm just getting in."

He cast a suspicious glance at me. "Well, 's over now. G'night."

He trundled back into his room. The ambulance drove off without its siren, which I took to mean that as bad as Vicky's injuries appeared, they weren't mortal. A few minutes later, the medical examiner's van arrived to remove the body of the other person who had been in the room. Angel's father, Pete. I knew that would take awhile. I didn't wait.

Angel was slouched down in the front seat, his Coke unopened, the candy bar unwrapped, muttering beneath his breath, "Johnson, Nixon, Ford, Carter—" He was practically sweating terror and I wished for one second that I could get into the car and just start driving until we reached a place where he would never be afraid of anything again. Instead, I got into the car, started it up, pulled out of the gas station and drove home.

John was sitting in the living room in his boxers drinking coffee when we came in. Angel took one look at him and ran toward him, crying. John scooped up the sobbing boy and murmured, *"M'ijo, what's wrong?"* while casting a look of confusion and concern over his head at me.

"It looks like his mother may have shot his father."

John stood up, holding the boy against him like an infant. "How did you find out?"

"Angel called me from a gas station across the street from where it happened. I went and picked him up."

"Why didn't you wake me up?"

"There was no time."

He rocked the boy. *"Pobrecito."*

"I've got to make some calls from my office. Can you watch Angel?"

"Of course," he said. "Angelito, I'm going to make you some hot milk and honey, like my mom used to make me, okay?"

The boy sobbed assent. I left them to it.

An hour and a half of calls yielded the following information: Vicky had been arrested for murder and transported to County General for medical treatment. After being treated, she would be taken to LAPD's Hollywood station for booking and arraignment at the nearby courthouse. None of the various cops I talked to could or would tell me, however, the nature or extent of her injuries, how long she would be held at County General or when she might be brought to Hollywood for booking. I worked my way up the chain of command at the station, telling each cop that I was her lawyer, and I was to be informed the moment she arrived at the station. I also warned each of them not to question her, unless I was present. This last gambit was greeted with the silent contempt it deserved. Vicky would be grilled as soon as it appeared she could answer questions. If she waived her right to counsel, it would make no difference that I had told the cops not to question her because the right had to be invoked by her, not me. Even if she asked for an attorney, they would continue to interrogate her to obtain what were called "statements outside *Miranda*." The Supreme Court had held that, while statements made in violation of a suspect's *Miranda* rights could not be introduced by the prosecution to prove he committed the crime, if the defendant testified and denied having done so, his illegally obtained statements could be used to impeach him. In light of this ruling, cops routinely ignored a defendant's request for a lawyer and continued to attempt to extract incriminating statements. I knew the cops would lay into Vicky because this looked like the kind of homicide—a spousal killing committed in a moment of passion—where the defendant was likely to confess, and she was the kind of suspect—female, minimal criminal record, confused, injured and terrified—most likely to roll. I could only hope her injuries were severe enough that she'd been given pain-killers that would either knock her out or so incapacitate her that even the cops would realize any statement she made would be worthless.

When I came out of my office, it was morning. I found John and Angel in my bedroom asleep, the boy curled up against the man. Almost as soon as I stepped into the room, John opened his eyes and said in a low voice, "Did you find her?"

"Sort of," I said, sitting at the foot of the bed. "Her husband beat her up so bad the cops took her to the hospital. She's somewhere between there and the jail."

John gently extricated himself from Angel, who looked to be in a dead slumber. "She kill him because he was beating on her?"

"That's how it looks. Did Angel tell you anything?"

"He said he went out for some food, and when he came back his dad was dead and his mom was holding the gun."

"Nothing about what led up to it?"

"I didn't ask him, Henry. He was all shook up." He looked at me. "Man, you look beat. First me dumping on you, then this. You need some sleep yourself."

"I'm going back to the motel," I said. "Can you stay here or do you have to get to work?"

He smiled. "I'm the boss. I show up when I show up." The smile faded. "Why are you going back? Won't the cops be there?"

"I doubt it," I said. "It's a simple case from their point of view. They got the victim, the suspect and the murder weapon. Whatever other evidence there was in the room would be minimal. I'm sure they're gone by now."

"Then what are you gonna find?"

"I don't know that I'm going to find anything," I said, "but I want to take a look while the scene's still fresh." I stood up. "I won't be long."

He got out of bed and drew the covers over Angel.

"He's so small," I said. "Even for his age. You can't see when he's awake because he seems older than he is, but you can really see it now." I looked at John. "I wanted to get him away from his parents, but not like this."

"You call your sister?"

"Elena. Man, I hadn't thought about her."

John put his arm around me. "You can't think of everything. I can't believe how cool you've been. I'd be running around like a chicken with its head cut off if it was me."

"This is my job," I replied. "I'll have to call Elena later. It's just as well, I'll know more then. What a mess," I said wearily. "Well, on the bright side, it's lucky you showed up last night."

He put his arm around my waist. "*Viejo*, you can look all you want, but you ain't going to find the bright side."

"*Viejo*, huh? I must look like shit."

"No, you look good to me, Henry. Go. I'll watch Angelito."

There was police tape across the door of the room that had been the last residence of the Trujillo family. A fifty-dollar bribe to the desk clerk had bought me ten minutes inside. I stooped beneath the tape and went in. The room was about the size of a small studio apartment. The tiny kitchen was piled high with fast-food wrappers and Styrofoam containers with scraps of food that released a stench into the warm, still air. A king-sized bed covered with a blue floral bedspread dominated one side of the room; next to it was a cot where I guessed Angel had slept. A sofa upholstered in avocado green vinyl, a desk, a dresser and two chairs completed the décor. Through an open door I heard water dripping: the shower or the toilet. On the white wall behind the bed was a thick, viscous splatter of blood and brain. Elsewhere on the walls were two bullet holes, far apart from each other, in no discernible pattern. The dark blue shag carpet glistened with a dark, wet stain. Droplets of blood were also splattered on the sofa and the kitchen counter. A chair had been upturned, a lamp smashed against the wall. The air still seemed to reverberate with rage. I guessed the smaller amounts of blood came from Vicky as she had been slapped around the room. She had shot him as he was coming at her from the direction of the bed, firing wildly. Two shots missed, the third hit him in the head and he fell forward at her feet.

On the dresser was a folder for Greyhound bus tickets. I opened one of them. Two used ticket stubs showed the same trip: San Francisco to a town called Turlock in the central valley taken a couple of weeks earlier. The dates seemed significant, so I stuck them in my pocket. My ten minutes were almost up. I started searching for Angel's things. Most of his clothes were in the dresser. I stuffed them into a laundry bag I had brought with me. Beneath his T-shirts and socks I found a snapshot that I at first thought was of him, but it was faded with age and I realized it was the picture of me that Elena said she had given him. I slipped it into my pocket.

On the floor was a pair of boy's jeans. I picked them up and noticed they had been recently patched at the knee. They were the same pants Jesusita had been sewing when I visited her three days earlier. In a corner of the room, I found the book I had given him, a baseball mitt and a baseball. I put them in the bag. Someone knocked at the door. I froze.

"Sir," the desk clerk said. "You have to leave now."

I hurried out of the room and brushed past him before he could object to the laundry bag.

Angel was sitting at the table, still wearing the sweatshirt I had given him and watching John cut a banana into a bowl of pancake batter. John was barefoot, wearing his jeans from the night before and an old striped button-down shirt of mine. I dropped the laundry bag on the floor.

"Hey," I said to them. "How are you doing, Angel?"

"Where's my mom?" he asked in a scared voice.

I looked at John. "The cops phone?"

"Not yet," he said.

"She's either at the hospital or at the police station. After breakfast, I'll make some calls and find out for sure and see when I can take you to see her."

He stared at me. "Is she dead?"

"No."

"Her mouth was bleeding," he said.

"I talked to the police while you were asleep," I said. "She's going to be all right. Look, Angel, later on I want you to tell me everything that happened from when you and mom left here. Is there any coffee?"

"Yes," John said. "Fresh pot. Hey, Angelito, how are you at flipping pancakes?"

"I don't know."

John pulled a stool to the stove where he had lit the griddle. "Come on, let's find out." Angel scrambled onto the stool and watched John ladle some batter onto the griddle. "See how it's making bubbles? That means it's cooking. Now, you want to flip the pancake right when it's cooked but before it burns." He slipped a spatula beneath the pancake and turned it perfectly. "Like that. Now you try."

I poured a cup of coffee. My head fell against the wall and I drifted into a half-sleep. I felt a hand on my head, fingers threading through my hair, and when I looked up John was standing beside me. He smiled, but his eyes were worried.

"You all right?"

"Tired. I smell breakfast."

He and Angel sat down with me to a pile of scorched pancakes made palatable only by mounds of butter and rivers of syrup.

"I burned them," Angel said in a teary voice.

"Hey, you gotta burn your first batch," John said. "It's like an initiation. Next time you make them, they'll be perfect."

I swallowed a bit of batter that was simultaneously charred and undercooked. "They're still better than anything I could cook."

Angel looked back and forth between us. "Does John live here now?"

"No," I said. "He just happened to be staying here last night."

I watched him working something out and waited for the next question, but he turned his attention to his food and ate as if famished.

"I brought you some clothes from the motel," I said.

He looked up sharply. "How come? When's my mom coming to get me?"

"Angel," I said, as gently as I could. "Do you understand your father is dead?"

He froze. "I saw him on the floor," he said. "His head had a big hole in it."

"Did you see what happened?" I asked him.

He looked at me, tears splattering his burned pancakes, and then tossed his fork to the ground and began to wail.

When we finally calmed him down, he collapsed in a heap on the couch and fell asleep.

John glanced at his watch. "I gotta get to work, Henry."

"I don't know what I would have done if you hadn't been here."

He grinned. "You would've managed okay. Listen, you mind if I hang on to your shirt? I'll bring it back later?"

"Yeah, sure. Keep it."

He got up, went into the bedroom for a moment, then came out carrying his shoes. He sat down again, slipped them on and tied the laces tight.

"You know what's funny, Henry," he said. "I don't even feel hungover." He glanced at Angel. "Man, this shit is for real." He looked at me. "What's gonna happen?"

"I have to talk to Vicky. In the room it looked like she shot him while he was attacking her. If that's how it went down, I can argue she acted in self-defense and maybe get her off completely. At worst, I should be able to deal her down to manslaughter. She could do anywhere from three to eleven years. It all depends on what happened in that room. I won't know until I get the police reports."

As I was explaining this to him, I realized that I had just signed on to defend my niece.

He nodded. "Will Angel live with you if she goes to jail?"

"He's got two grandmothers who have a better claim on him than me."

He stood up. "He'd be better off with you."

"John, I don't know the first thing about kids."

"He needs a man in his life. I'd help you."

"I don't know, John," I said.

His sad eyes caught mine. "You worried I'm gonna flake?"

"No, that's not it. All I'm saying is that you and I are in the first stages of something that I really want to work out but—look, it's like you said last night. You didn't want this thing between us to become about your drinking. I don't want it to become about my family. They're my responsibility."

"You don't have to take the weight alone," he said.

"Are you really ready to carry part of it? I'm not sure you know me well enough to get mixed up in this. Especially after last night."

"What does that mean?"

"It means you're not a flake, so I know you're going to want to resolve your situation with Deanna."

"Yeah," he said. "You're right. See, you wouldn't know that unless you were the kind of man who took care of business himself. But you take on too much by yourself. You got to let the people who love you help you out."

I was so tired I didn't understand at first what he was saying. "That reminds me I need to call Elena."

He stood up. "Other people love you too, man." He brushed my cheek with his lips. "I won't come over later unless you need me, but I'll give you a call. Okay?"

Then I understood. "John, thank you."

He grinned. "Later, man."

After he left, I called my sister to break the news. After a long, stunned silence, she said, "Where is Angel?"

"He's here with me. He's all right, Elena. He was the one who called me last night."

"Have you talked to Vicky?"

"No, not yet. They took her to the hospital—"

"The hospital? What did he do to her?"

"He beat her up pretty badly and the cops had to take her in for treatment before they could book her. I just called again. She's at the Hollywood police station. I'm going to go see her as soon as we finish talking."

"I'll come tonight."

"Why don't you wait a day or so and let me figure out what the options are? Come down for the arraignment."

"Do you have any idea what will happen?"

I launched into my litany. "If she shot him in self-defense, I might be able to persuade the D.A. not to file charges. Even if they do, it won't be worse than second-degree and I'm pretty sure I can deal them down. Prosecutors don't like going to trial on these kinds of cases."

"If he was beating her, of course it was self-defense," Elena said.

"Self-defense has a technical meaning in the law that's different from its common-sense definition. It has to be proportional, and blowing away someone who's hitting you is generally considered excessive."

She digested this for a moment, then said, "If she has to go jail for any period of time, I want Angel to live with Joanne and me."

"He does have another grandmother, Elena, and her claim is equal to yours."

"Henry, have you told her what happened?"

"She may already have heard from the police, but I'll phone her when we finish."

"Call me as soon as you get back from seeing Vicky. Take care of Angel."

"I will," I said.

I tried Jesusita Trujillo but reached her answering machine. Not knowing what she had been told, I simply asked her to call me about an urgent matter involving her son and Vicky and left my cell phone number.

When I emerged from my office, Angel was awake. I sat down beside him and asked, "How are you feeling?"

He shrugged. "Where's John?"

"John had to go to work. Listen, Angel, I'm going to go see your mother."

"Can I come?" he asked eagerly.

"I need to see her alone first," I said, "but depending on how she's doing, you can either see her tonight or tomorrow. I have to leave you here alone for a while, but I'll give you the number to my cell phone, and if you get nervous or upset, you can call me."

"Why can't I see my mom?"

He was a breath away from hysterics so I answered as calmly as I could. "Angel, I'm not just your mother's uncle now, I'm her lawyer, too. Do you know what a lawyer is?"

"Yeah, he defends people."

"Exactly," I said. "I'm going to defend your mother, and so I need some time alone with her to talk about what happened last night and how I can help her."

"She don't want your help."

"Did she tell you that?"

He wiped his nose with the back of his hand. "She said you think you're better than us."

I said, "Your mom and I got off to a bad start, but we're family and I'm going to do everything I can for both of you." I stood up. "I've called both your grandmothers. Elena will be here in a couple of days. I left a message for your grandmother Jesusita. I have to go. Look, I found the book I gave you at the motel. You can read it while I'm gone."

"Can I watch TV instead?"

I tossed him the remote. "I'll be back as soon as I can."

He switched on the TV and his eyes went blank.

I took one look at my niece in the holding cell, turned to the deputy sheriff and demanded, "Why isn't she still in the hospital?"

He shrugged. "They released her. You want to see her or not?"

"Of course I do."

He unlocked the cell door. Vicky was lying on a metal bed cushioned with a thin foam mattress, covered with a gray wool blanket. The right side of her face was so swollen that her eye was closed. Her head had been shaved above the ear to reveal a zigzag of stitches. Her breath was loud and raspy. I pulled a chair up to her bed and reached for her hand. Even it was bruised.

"Vicky," I said.

She turned her face painfully until she could see me. "Uncle Henry," she wheezed. "Do you know where Angel is?"

"He's at my house," I said. "He's okay. He called me last night from a gas station across the street from the motel. They were putting you in the ambulance by the time I got there."

She pulled her hand away. "I want my mom to take care of him."

"I'll tell her," I said. "She'll be flying down day after tomorrow."

With effort, she shook her head. "No. Jesusita."

She said it with no particular emphasis, which made it all the harder to hear, and I dreaded having to relay this message to my sister.

"All right, Vicky. I called Jesusita earlier, and as soon as she calls me back, I'll ask her. I'm ready to represent you as your lawyer, but only if you want me to. Do you?"

Her assent was a passive, "Yes, Uncle Henry."

"Can you tell me what happened last night?"

"I killed Pete," she said.

I waited for an explanation, but none came.

"Was he beating you?"

"He was high," she said. "He didn't know what he was doing."

"Where did the gun come from?"

"For protection. Pete bought it."

"Protection? Who was he protecting himself against?"

"Pete knew bad people," she said. "Drug dealers. Gangbangers."

"What were you doing in that motel in the first place?"

"Waiting," she said.

"Waiting for what?"

Her head lolled back and forth. "I'm tired now, Uncle Henry. When can I see Angel?"

"I'll bring him tomorrow," I said. "Listen, Vicky, try to remember what happened last night."

"I already told the police."

"You told them you shot him?"

"I had to tell the truth," she replied. "That's what Jesus would do."

"What else did you tell the police?"

"That he was smoking crack again and he was hitting me. I told them I didn't mean to kill him. I just wanted him to stop."

"When did you talk to the police?"

"When they brought me here this morning."

They would have taped her statement. "I don't want you to talk to them again unless I'm with you. Do you understand?"

"Yes, Uncle Henry."

I got up. "You rest. I'll make sure they give you proper treatment and I'll be back tomorrow morning with Angel."

A tear rolled down her swollen cheek. "Don't let anything happen to him."

Worse than this? I wondered. I said, "I promise you I won't."

12.

I LEFT THE STATION AND SAT IN MY CAR READING THE AR-
rest report. The only surprise was that the cops had not recovered
the murder weapon. I thought Angel had told me he had seen the
gun, but it had been a long, traumatic day and I may have misheard
him. There was, as yet, no autopsy report and nothing on ballistics
except that the slugs the cops had dug out of the wall came from a
.380 semiautomatic. Pete Trujillo must really have pissed off someone to require that kind of serious firepower for protection. Otherwise, the report was perfunctory. As far as the cops were concerned,
the case was open and shut. I liked cases the cops thought were
dead-bang because they didn't work them as hard, and my clients
tended to profit from the neglect.

I heard the first bars of "La Cucaracha" played on a car horn and
looked up. A roach coach had pulled up in front of the police station, where a crowd of cops and DWP workers was already waiting
for the truck. It was just now noon. I had been up most of the last
twelve hours and the world had taken on the shimmer of unreality
produced by extreme fatigue. A transvestite in a yellow wig and red
hot-pants tottered by on spike heels, deep in conversation with a
balding, middle-age man in lawyerly pinstripes. Three *cholos* passed

by dressed in baggy pants and flannel shirts, each with the same tattoo emblazoned on his neck, one of them pausing to maddog me. A young policeman stood in front of the station smoking a cigarette and lazily watching the girls emptying out of the nearby office buildings without making any attempt to hide the hard-on that tented his trousers. *This is my life*, I thought, *these are the people among whom I have spent it, prostitutes, tattooed boys with dead eyes, and horny cops.* Usually I could separate myself from the milieu in which I plied my trade, but this time, to quote the slogan of innumerable action films, it was personal. My niece had belonged to this world of the terminally damaged and now it seemed that world had engulfed her. I wanted desperately to rescue her, and not simply because I had promised Elena. Maybe I was beginning to master the paradox of family—loving without liking. Irritably, I tossed the arrest report on the passenger seat and headed off to see the D.A. to plead for Vicky's life.

"Anthony Earl," I said.

Tony Earl looked up at me from behind his battered desk in the sweltering cubicle reserved for the head of filing in the small suite of rooms comprised by the D.A.'s satellite office in Hollywood. The furniture told the story: This was a dead-end assignment for any D.A. For Tony Earl, who had, until the last election, been the big D.A.'s number-two man and anointed successor, the fall was particularly steep. Earl had been a man in a hurry, and after a series of botched high-profile prosecutions weakened the incumbent, Tony had smelled blood in the water and announced his candidacy. The D.A. was a Sicilian with a rich wife, and he fought back with one of the dirtiest and most expensive campaigns in L.A.'s history. Tony Earl had movie-star looks, a nimble mind and a preacher's eloquence. He had also had the politician's requisite rags-to-respectability story—raised in one of the worst neighborhoods in the city, he now wore two-thousand-dollar suits as though to the manor born. He was also black, and he fell victim to the silent racial civil war going on in post–Rodney King, post–O.J. Simpson L.A. One of the battlegrounds was the polling booth, where whites voted in greater and more consistent numbers than any of the city's other major ethnic groups.

The D.A. ran for reelection on the slogan, "A District Attorney for All Los Angeles." In white neighborhoods, he distributed campaign brochures featuring a picture of Tony Earl at a black bar association meeting, ostensibly to criticize Earl for being too chummy with the criminal defense bar, but the real point was that sea of black faces. City law required Earl to take a leave of absence from the D.A.'s office to run his campaign. The D.A. parceled out his duties to two deputies, a Latino and an Asian, and won in return endorsements from the Latino and Asian bar associations. Earl was squeezed in the vise of race: If he ignored the D.A.'s barely submerged race-baiting, it would doom him, but if he complained about it, he would be the one blamed by white voters for making race an issue. He complained, bitterly, and went down in the kind of decisive defeat that ends a political career.

"Mr. Rios," he replied. "Still buying your suits off the rack, I see."

He had removed his coat, revealing sweat-stained armpits and a pair of maroon suspenders. His handsome face was a bit fuller than it had been ten years ago when we had squared off in a capital case. That trial had gone on for two months before the jury finally sent my client to Pelican Bay for the rest of his life. In the courtroom, Earl was the model of prosecutorial rectitude; outside, he was profoundly cynical—his nickname for the LAPD was "the Aryan Brotherhood." He fought hard and dirty, but I had the distinct sense he was motivated less by a concern for justice than for his career. On the other hand, he was so good that when he finished his closing argument, even I was ready to send my client to the gas chamber. That I persuaded the jury to give him life instead was one of those examples of why justice is like sausage-making, a process best not examined too closely. Years later, as I stood in my polling booth, I remembered that summation and, realizing what a tough and effective D.A. Tony would make, cast my vote for his incompetent opponent.

"So this is what happened to you," I said, sitting down in a metal chair. "Why is it so hot in here?"

"Brand-new building," he said. "'Course the air-conditioning system is fucked up. Go ahead, take off that wrinkled-ass sports coat. Unless it's covering a mustard stain on your shirt."

"Who are you, Mr. Blackwell?"

"That's funny, Rios, on so many levels. I haven't seen you in a long time. Thought you were dead."

"Not yet. I don't do much trial work anymore. I'm more into appeals." I laid my niece's arrest report on his desk. "But I do have this case I came to talk to you about."

He picked up the report and flipped through it. I remembered from our trial together that he was a speed reader with near-perfect retention.

He tossed it back at me. "Why are you bringing me this low-life shit?"

"Because your name is on the door, Tony. You're the D.A. who decides what gets filed. Plus, the suspect is my niece."

He leaned back in his chair and played with his tie, a pale lavender silk number that went perfectly with the French blue shirt and the darker suspenders. "Yeah, well, all that proves is that you should choose your relatives more carefully. What do you want?"

"Reject it for filing," I said. "He was a wife-beater, she snapped. Plus, the cops did a crap job that's not going to look good if I get to cross-examine them. They didn't even find the weapon."

"Dream on, baby," he said. "All I need for what's left of my career is to start cutting deals like that. Anyway, she copped to it, Rios. Pretty stupid of her, but I'll assume she didn't have the benefit of your wise counsel."

"I'll argue self-defense."

"You do that," he said, "but last time I looked at the jury instructions on self-defense, if someone comes at you with fists you don't get to blow their brains out with a semiautomatic."

"You can if his fists can kill you," I said. "My expert on battered women's syndrome will testify that her belief that she was in mortal danger was reasonable."

He grunted dismissively. "My expert will say she wasn't. This is going to get filed as second-degree."

"That's bullshit, Tony. We both know this is voluntary manslaughter, at best."

He grinned. "I gotta to give the trial deputy something to deal."

"Then file it as voluntary and let them deal it down to involuntary."

"Yeah, right," he said. He snapped his suspenders thoughtfully. "But because I like you, I'm going to do you a big favor. I'm going to see this case gets assigned to the greenest deputy I can find. Give it to someone as their first homicide. If you can't deal some greenhorn down to involuntary, you better turn in your bar card."

"You give to it a green trial deputy and they'll be so afraid of screwing up and losing their job, they'll treat it like a capital case."

"I have great faith in your powers of persuasion," he said.

Bemused, I said, "You haven't changed, Tony. You talk like the street, but you think like a cop."

"It's payback. I still remember you beat me in that case we tried together."

I couldn't tell if it was a joke or not. "As I recall, my client was convicted."

"But you kept him off Death Row." He was serious.

I got up. "So, how's exile?"

The handsome face turned to stone. "There ain't but one rule when you strike at the king, Rios. You got to kill him. Now get out of here, I have work to do."

When I looked back he was staring into the mid-distance with a expression of bored desperation.

．．．

The day had turned muggy. By the time I pulled into my drive-way, I was ready for a shower, something to eat and a nap. Then I remembered Angel would be waiting for me. I cut the engine and sat there rubbing my temples. How was I supposed to do my work with a ten-year-old boy to worry about? *Welcome to the world of single parenthood*, I thought, and then, *Who can I call for advice?*

Angel was sitting on the deck reading *Tales from Homer*. As I stood at the doorway leading outside, I could hear him softly sounding out words. I tossed my coat aside, loosened my tie and stepped out to the deck.

"Hey, Angel," I said, sitting at the edge of his chaise.

He set the book in his lap and looked at me anxiously. "Did you see my mom?"

"Yes," I said. "She's going to be okay in a day or so. I'll take you to see her tomorrow." I tapped the book. "How far along are you?"

Reluctantly, he allowed me to change the subject. He picked up the book and struggled to pronounce Scylla and Charybdis.

"The rock and the whirlpool," I said. "Isn't there a picture of them?"

He leafed through the pages, then handed the book to me. "This one?"

I studied the wood print of the tiny ship entering a narrow strait, on one side of which were hulking rocks, and on the other a whirlpool in which the wreckage of another ship was still visible. The proverbial rock and a hard place. The place where he and Vicky had lived most of their lives.

"Why can't Ulysses go home?" Angel was asking.

I returned the book to him. "Because he angered Poseidon."

"The god of the ocean."

"That's right. Poseidon was offended by Ulysses so he put obstacles in his way to keep him from reaching Ithaca. But some of the gods were friends of Ulysses so they tried to help him overcome Poseidon's obstacles. This is a very old story," I said, "but one reason people still read it is because sometimes in life it feels like we're struggling the way Ulysses had to struggle. We have to overcome dangers and obstacles, too, sometimes alone and sometimes with the help of others. You understand?"

His dark eyes were thoughtful. "I'm not sure."

"Then think of it this way," I said. "A month ago, you and I had never met, but since then, all these things have happened to you and here you are sitting here with me."

"And you're going to help my mom and me," he mused aloud, constructing the first fragile link between the book and his life.

I wanted him to make that connection, to give him the beginning of a narrative that might help sustain him through the troubles that were coming.

He looked at me. "What's going to happen to my mom?"

"Her situation is very complicated," I replied. I loosened my tie and unbuttoned my shirt to feel the sun on my throat. "Listen, Angel, I'm going to talk to you the same way I would to another grown-up, so if there's something you don't understand, stop me and I'll explain."

"Okay," he said, half-anxious, half-proud to be addressed like an adult.

"Your mother is going to be charged with the murder of your father. I tried to stop that from happening, but I couldn't. Now we're going to the next stage, where I'll try to convince the lawyer on the other side, the district attorney, to lower the charge against your mother down from murder to something less serious. Do you understand?"

"Plea bargain," he said.

"How do you know that?"

"That's what they did to my dad."

I remembered his father had been cut an exceptionally good deal the last time he was arrested. "That's right. I'm going to try to get a plea bargain for your mother so that she'll spend as little time in jail as possible. If the district attorney won't agree, then we'll go to the next step, to a trial. I think I have a decent chance of getting your mother off completely if I can convince the jury that she shot your father to defend herself because he had been hitting her—"

"My dad never hit my mom," he said.

"What?"

"My dad loves us."

I made the split second decision that it was better to burst this illusion now than to let it harden into even deeper denial.

"Angel, I saw your mom at the jail. She'd been beaten up."

"She said he did it?"

"Yes."

He shook his head. "No way."

"What happened when you left here with your mom?"

He gazed past me at the canyon, thinking. "My dad came to get us."

"Did you know he was coming?"

He nodded, looking guilty. "My mom told me it was a secret. I wanted to go to the baseball game with you and John, but she said we had to leave."

"Where did you go?"

He fiddled nervously with the book as if he was letting me into secrets. "To Grandma Jesusita's. We stayed there that night, but the next day we had to leave again."

"You had to leave? Do you know why?"

He shook his head. "I heard my dad arguing with Grandma after I went to bed, but they were talking Spanish so I didn't understand. After breakfast, we went to a motel."

"The one where I found you?"

He shook his head. "No, a different one. Then we went to another one, then the one where—the last one."

"Do you know why you moved around so much?"

"No." He said it so quickly that I knew he was lying, but I thought if I didn't press the point, he would eventually reveal it.

"What did you do at these motels?"

He ran his a hand through his hair and it stayed up like a porcupine's quills. "Watched TV. My dad bought me a mitt and a ball and we played catch in the parking lot, but only after it was dark and I couldn't see the ball too good. We went to McDonald's. My mom said—" He stopped himself.

"What did she say?"

He flapped the pages of the book again. "My dad was shooting up."

"Using heroin?"

"He was in the bathroom for a long time. He said he was on the toilet, but when he came out, I saw his eyes." He looked at me. "I tried to find his works."

"Why?"

"I wanted to throw them away, then he would stop. I hate it when he shoots up," he said passionately. "He makes my mom cry and he promises to take me places, but he doesn't. I'm never going to take drugs."

"What did your mother do when your father started taking drugs?"

He shrugged. "She told him to stop."

"They fight? Tell me the truth."

He shook his head. "My dad would tell her to shut up but then he said he was sorry. Maybe they fought when I wasn't there."

"Where did you go?"

"For walks."

"You went for walks?"

He nodded. "Yeah. I saw the stars in the sidewalk and that place with movie-star footprints. It was cool."

"Weren't your parents worried about you?"

"I can take care of myself. Uncle Henry?"

"What, *m'ijo?*"

"Can I have some lunch?"

I glanced at my watch, it was almost three. "God, I haven't fed you yet. I'm sorry, Angel. There's a pretty good pizza place not far from here. You like pizza?"

"Yeah!"

"Come on, then," I said. "Afterward, we can stop at the video store and get some videos for tonight."

"*Phantom Menace*?"

"Absolutely," I said.

He smiled, and when he smiled he looked like an ordinary boy, not one who went on hunt and destroy missions for his junkie father's syringes. He should have been harder but only his surface innocence had been ruffled. He retained the deeper innocence that allowed him to believe he could free his father of addiction by tossing out his works and to turn flight from his desperate parents into an adventure on Hollywood Boulevard. There was no doubt, though, that he loved them—loved them enough to lie to me about his father beating his mother. I suppose that was the deepest innocence of all.

After I had put Angel to bed, I called my sister.

"You sound exhausted," she said.

"I've never taken care of a kid before," I replied. "I guess I fret more than I need to."

"Well, at least I'll be able to relieve you of the responsibility."

"That's one of the things I need to talk to you about," I said. "When I saw Vicky this morning, she told me to take Angel to his other grandmother."

"Jesusita? Did she say why?"

"I think we both know why, Elena."

She was quiet a moment. "Does she even want you to represent her?"

"Yes."

"Well, that's something, I guess," she said bitterly.

"You know, Vicky's had a rough life, I would imagine the only homosexuals she's ever met were—"

"What, Henry? Not the sterling characters we are." She was quiet again. "It took me a long time to completely come out. I told myself it was because I wanted to protect my privacy, but really it was because I was ashamed to be a lesbian. I want a relationship with my daughter. I'll meet her more than halfway, but I can't be a different person for her."

"I know. She yanks my chain, too."

"The ironic thing, of course," Elena continued, "is that I wasn't able to love and accept her until I came out."

"What do you mean?"

"I had to learn about compassion and tolerance when I came out because you can't ask from others what you're not prepared to give. I ran away from Vicky once because she wasn't the daughter I wanted. Now I understand that it isn't up to her to be who I might want her to be. It's up to me to love her for who she is."

"Even if she doesn't reciprocate?"

"Even that wouldn't matter if she would just give me a chance." She sighed. "Well, maybe I don't deserve it. It's asking a lot to be forgiven for abandoning your child."

"That's in the past. Look at everything you've already done for her."

"Family isn't a matter of credits and debits."

I didn't want to have the family values debate again, so I let it drop. "Do you still want to be here for the arraignment?"

"Of course," she said. "When is it?"

"Monday, early. Elena, I tried to intervene with the D.A., but they're going charge her with second-degree murder."

"Is that as bad as it sounds?"

I told her about my meeting with Tony Earl and explained why I still believed I might be able to deal it down to minimize any jail time she would have to serve. "We'll have to post bail," I concluded.

"That won't be a problem as long as I have a few days. Have you spoken to Jesusita Trujillo?"

"No, I left a message for her. I'll try her again when we finish."

"Maybe while I'm there, I could meet her."

"I'll try to get her to the arraignment."

"How's Angelito?"

"Remarkably adaptable," I said, and described the ordinary evening we had just had of videos and pizza. "Maybe this is what Edith meant when she called him an invulnerable."

We talked for a few minutes more and after I hung up with her, I called Jesusita Trujillo. Once again I got her machine, and I left an even more urgent message, asking her to call me at any time of the day or night. And then I staggered off to bed.

I was awakened by screaming. Even before I was entirely conscious, I was running down the hall to the guest room, where I found Angel thrashing and crying. I sat on the bed and shook his shoulders gently while intoning his name. He opened terrified eyes and began to pummel me with his fists. "Hey, hey," I said warding off the blows. "It's me, Uncle Henry. Come on, *m'ijo*, it's all right. Everything's all right." My voice finally penetrated his terror and he dropped his arms to his side, shivering and panting.

"I dreamed of my dad," he said.

"You saw him the way he was in the motel?"

He began to sob. His sobs were the existential wail of a baby that had no other language to communicate its horror and fear. He bundled himself against me. I put my arms around him and let him cry, thinking, *Better now than twenty years from now in some therapist's office.*

"That's right, *m'ijo*, you go ahead and cry," I whispered in his ear. "You've been a brave little boy but now I'm going to take care of you."

He sat back and looked at me. My T-shirt was soaked with tears and snot. "You promise, Uncle Henry?"

"I promise. Do you want to talk about your nightmare?" I asked him, handing him the box of tissues from the nightstand.

He blew his nose and wiped his eyes with the back of his hand. He said, "No," but I saw a question in his eyes.

"Is there something else you want to tell me?"

"Are you going to get my mom out of jail?"

"I don't know for sure," I said. "There's a good chance she'll have to do some time."

"A long time?"

"I don't know. Maybe just a couple of years, maybe a lot longer."

"If my mom goes to jail," he said, "can I stay with you?"

This wasn't the impulsive plea of a frightened child but something he had been thinking about. To someone else, he might have sounded cold-blooded, but I recognized it as bravery. He loved his parents, but his father was dead and his mother might be gone for a long time, so he was trying to make the best choice for himself. As I looked into his dark eyes, it also occurred to me that, just as his mother had been sizing me up, so had Angel and he had come to a different conclusion about my character. I loved him more at that moment, loved his fragility and trust, than I had ever loved another human being. If I was going to be equal to his trust, I knew I couldn't buy him off with a platitude.

"I'll do everything in my power to make that happen," I said. "But I'm only your uncle, well, your grand-uncle, and your mother has already told me she wants you to live with your grandmother Jesusita."

"I don't want to live with her," he said.

"Your mother is still your mother, even if she has to go to jail. She has the final word."

He considered this and responded, not with a child's petulance, but like a negotiator. "Can I live with you if she says I can?"

"If she says you can, then, yes," I replied. Now was not the time to explain how unlikely that was. "Angelito, wherever you live, I promise you I'll never be far away."

He nodded. "John, too?"

"That's kind of up to John," I said. "Do you want me to get you a night-light?"

"Can you stay here for a little while?"

"Yeah," I said. I noticed the book on the nightstand. "Shall I read to you?"

"Uh-huh."

I opened the book where he had folded the edge of the page and read him the story of how Ulysses outwitted the cyclops.

The next day, I took Angel to visit his mother at the Hollywood station. He seemed completely unintimidated by being in a police station. For greater privacy, I browbeat the sympathetic watch commander to let Angel see his mother in the small attorney interview room. The room was soundproofed, but equipped with a one-way mirror to allow the cops to make sure contraband was not passed. While Angel visited his mother, I stood outside reading the autopsy and ballistics reports. The cause of Peter Trujillo's death was a single shot through the back of his head. My eye stopped. The back of his head? The report asserted that the entry wound was six inches from the base of his neck and had lodged in the middle of his forehead. She had shot him while his back was turned to her. That was a problem if I was going to argue self-defense.

I looked into the interview room. Vicky was holding Angel by the shoulders, apparently berating him. He faced her down like a little soldier, but then she released him and backed away, crying. He held his martial posture for a moment longer before breaking down and approaching her. His posture communicated pity, fear and anger all at once. She wiped her tears and spoke to him again. He stared at his feet and nodded.

I was repelled by her manipulation of him and tried to concentrate on the ballistics report to keep myself from bursting into the room and lecturing her. The bullet that the medical examiner had dug out of Pete's hcad was the same caliber as the ones the cops dug out of the wall. The cops had also found a .22-caliber bullet lodged in the baseboard near the front door, but since it seemed to be unconnected to the shooting, they assumed it was from an earlier incident. I made another note. Unaccounted-for bullets was the kind of detail that made cops look stupid on the stand and confused juries into reasonable doubt.

I knew on this case there would probably not be any follow-up reports, so this was going be as good as the prosecution's evidence got. While strong, it was also entirely circumstantial, and had it only been a matter of circumstantial evidence I could have picked it apart. Unfortunately, Vicky had confessed, and now much would depend on whether I could find a plausible ground to suppress her statement. I had not yet been provided with a transcript of her interrogation and made a mental note to request it at the arraignment. I glanced into the interview room, where Angel and his mother were now engaged in an intense conversation, heads bent together more like co-conspirators than mother and child.

13.

I GAVE ANGEL AND HIS MOTHER A HALF-HOUR AND THEN I
sent him outside to wait for me while I talked to her. As soon as he
left, all the animation went out of her and she assumed a mask of
passivity, though by now I knew she was passive only as stone is passive. Her face was still swollen and gashed, the bruises even darker
and more florid than the day before, but she had arranged her hair
to cover the stitches on the side of her head and she had found lip-
stick somewhere. The shapeless jumpsuit she had been given to
wear emphasized the soft slope of her shoulders, the swell of her
breasts, and made her seem more vulnerable than ever. I was reminded of my first impression of her: a small, gentle animal with
many predators and few defenses.

"How do you feel?" I asked her.

"Fine."

"It looked like you and Angel were arguing."

She shook her head. "No, I was telling him that I wanted him to
go stay with his grandma until I get out. He doesn't want to."

"I know. He told me he wants to stay with me. I said it was up to
you."

"I don't want him to be any more trouble for you," she said.

As if that were the reason. "You know," I said, "I've called Mrs. Trujillo and she hasn't returned my calls. By now the police will have told her about Pete. Maybe she's less anxious to raise Angel than you think."

"Pardon?"

"Vicky, you killed her son," I reminded her. "She might be upset about that."

"She knows."

"Knows what?"

She stared past me at her reflection in the mirror and touched her battered face. "She knows why. She knows I'm sorry for what I did." She looked at me and said in a decisive voice. "I want to plead guilty."

"You're charged with second-degree murder. You plead to that and you'll go to prison for fifteen years to life."

That gave her pause. "What about good time?"

"Even with good time, you'll do fifteen, plus you used a gun, so that adds another five. Angel will be thirty by the time you're released." I let this sink in. "I'm not going to let you plead guilty to second-degree."

She seemed surprised by my firmness and I caught a flash of gratitude in her eyes, but then she frowned and said, "I told the police I killed him."

I shrugged. "There may be ways to get around that. Anyway, Vicky, in the law not all killings are murder. If you killed Pete in self-defense or because there was a long pattern of abuse from him, you might not get off completely, but maybe I can persuade the D.A. to let you plead to something less than murder and you won't have to spend as long in prison."

Her lip trembled and her eyes welled up. The decision to plead had been bravado; she really was terrified. "I don't want to go to prison," she whispered. "I don't want to leave Angel without his mom. It was like you said, self-defense. Pete was hitting me."

"But he had hit you before that night and you didn't shoot him then. What was different about this time?"

She composed herself. "I don't know. It happened so fast. He was coming and I saw the gun and I picked it up and started shooting. I didn't mean to kill him, Uncle Henry, I just wanted to stop him."

"There's a problem with that picture."

"What?"

"He was shot from the back, so he couldn't have been coming at you."

She glared at me. "Why are you trying to trick me?"

"I'm not," I said, "but if we go to trial, you'll have to testify, and if you lie, you will be convicted of murder. I think what happened that night was that he beat you up just like he had many other times, and you didn't fight back because you knew that was a fight you couldn't win. I think you waited until he had stopped and his back was turned and then you shot him."

"He was drinking all day and getting high. Jesusita said she would give us money to go away and start all over again, but he was going to shoot it up his arm. We started fighting and he told me it was his mother's money and he could spend it any way he wanted to." She shook her head despondently. "I wanted to be a family again. Angel needed his dad. But not like that."

"Is this what you told the cops?"

"I honestly don't remember. I was hurting and they gave me something at the hospital that made me drowsy." She looked at me. "All they wanted to know is, did I shoot him."

"What did you do with the gun?"

"It was in the room. The police don't have it?"

"No," I said. "It seems to have disappeared. Did you get rid of it?"

"No," she said. "I could hardly move."

I believed her, but it complicated matters. "All right, Vicky. Tomorrow at the arraignment, you'll plead not guilty. Your mother and I will try to get you out on bail and then we'll take it from there, one step at a time."

I looked back through the one-way glass one last time as I left. She was still sitting at the table as the deputy came in to escort her back to her cell. She still looked fragile, but also thoughtful, as if she was working something out in her head, something complex. I saw for the first time the intelligence that lay beneath the softness and realized I was wrong to have conflated her with my mother. Vicky might present herself as a victim, but that was only her protective coloration. Beneath that coloration I now detected a determination to survive that marked her as a Rios.

On the drive home, Angel turned the radio on and began to fiddle with the channels while I tried to assess how much Vicky had lied to me. After a few minutes of static and snatches of music, I snapped. "Hey, pick a station and stick with it, okay?"

He switched the radio off and said, "You can't tell me what to do."

"I just did, Angel."

He reached for the radio and I slapped his hand away. He folded his arms belligerently across his chest, stared out the side window and didn't speak to me again. I had a sudden, chilling thought of my father.

When I saw John's truck parked at the curb in front of my house, I felt seep from my shoulders the tension that I hadn't even realized was there.

"That's John's truck," Angel said, relenting.

"Yeah, but I don't see him."

I pulled into the driveway and noticed the boots hanging out of the window on the passenger's side of the truck. I parked, went over to the truck and peered in. John was stretched across the cab, the bill of his cap pulled low over his eyes. He was dressed for work in grubby jeans and yet another faded, flannel shirt, this one black-and-purple plaid.

I grabbed his boot. "Hey, no loitering."

Lazily, he flicked up his cap and smiled. John smiled so much that it seemed to be his default setting: lips parting to disclose large, slightly crooked but benevolent teeth. This smile scarcely curved the corners of his mouth and showed only a white glimmer of teeth, but revealed a happiness that excluded everyone in the world but me. I slipped my hand into the leg of his jeans until skin touched skin. He was warm. He was always warm.

"Hi, John," Angel said, coming up beside me. I dropped my hand.

John sat up. "Hey, Angel. Henry. Where have you guys been?"

"Visiting Angel's mom," I said.

The sad, squinty eyes became even narrower. "Was she okay?"

I waited for Angel to respond, but when he didn't I tried to respond for him. "It was hard to see her like that." There seemed nothing else to say on the subject, so I asked him, "Why aren't you at work?"

"I'm taking the afternoon off," he said. "You can do that when you're the boss." That comment, directed to Angel, got a half-smile out of him. John reached into his shirt pocket and flashed some cardboard. "The Dodgers are playing the Diamondbacks at twelve-thirty. I got three tickets." He grinned at Angel. "Know anyone who's interested in seeing a game?"

Angel squealed, "Uncle Henry, can we go?"

"Yeah, Uncle Henry, how about it?"

"I have to call Elena. Give me fifteen minutes. You want to come in?"

John shook his head. "Angel and me are going to sit in the truck, and if you're not back in fifteen minutes, we're taking off without you." He reached over and threw open the passenger door. "Right, Angelito?"

"You better hurry, Uncle Henry," Angel said as he climbed in.

Elena told me she'd been unable to get an evening flight and had booked a Monday morning flight, so we agreed to meet at the courthouse. There were a couple of other phone messages I had to respond to, and then I realized I was still wearing my suit, so I changed into jeans and a short-sleeved shirt. When I went back outside, John's truck was gone. I went to the curb and looked up and down the street, thinking he was pulling a prank, but I didn't see him. I stood there for a couple of minutes not knowing what to do, when I saw his truck chugging up the hill. He roared by, grinning, made a U-turn and pulled up beside me.

"We went to get some lunch," John said.

Angel held up a sack. "We got a hamburger for you, Uncle Henry."

I got in. "I thought you'd left without me."

"I wanted to," John said, "but Angelito made me come back. I don't know why 'cause I hear you wouldn't let him play the radio."

I looked at Angel who looked away anxiously.

"I was kind of a jerk," I said. "I'm sorry, Angel."

"That's okay," he mumbled.

"Thanks, John," I said.

"For what, man?"

I reached into the sack. "The burger."

Above Dodger Stadium the sky was cloudless and blue, the air was warm and the light was pure. Beside me, I heard a sharp intake of breath and then a dreamy sigh from my nephew. I looked at him. He was transfixed. Down on the field, the Diamondbacks were taking batting practice. John, who seemed almost as excited as Angel, wanted to go down to the fence and watch.

"You two go," I said. "I need to sit."

John looked at me. "You feeling okay?"

"Go on, I'll be fine."

They trotted down the steps while I looked for our seats. Down on the field, some of the Dodgers were running sprints and tossing the ball around. I watched them for a moment, but my thoughts soon drifted back to the problem of my niece's defense. Self-defense would be a hard sell because it required that both the threat and the response be immediate. Here, neither was. Pete had not been coming at Vicky when she shot him, and she had time to get off three rounds. In real time, this may all have taken only seconds; but the law operated in legal time, which, like the Twilight Zone, existed in an entirely different dimension. In legal time, all it took was a couple of seconds for someone to deliberate a killing, and that was sufficient to convert it from manslaughter to murder. She had had enough time for that. I might have to forego straight self-defense and rely on battered women's syndrome, a considerably tougher defense because it asked the jurors to see the killer and not the decedent as the victim. My presentation would have to be flawless. That reminded me of Edith Rosen's doubts about whether Vicky was a battered woman. I made a mental note to call her. Of course, even if I couldn't argue self-defense to a jury, I could use the threat of raising the defense as a bargaining chip with the D.A. Where was the gun? Hadn't Angel told me he had seen it? I realized that I had not questioned him since the night of the shooting, but now I would have to ask him some hard questions. That got me thinking about whether I had any business representing my niece at all. I worried that my personal stake in the outcome of the case would impair my judgment and cause me to miss some crucial detail. But what was my personal stake? If I got my niece off, she would probably take Angel and disappear from my life. If, as likely, she ended up having to do time, either of his grandmothers had a stronger legal claim to custody than I did. And did I really think I was equipped to raise him? All I knew about his life was that he had had the kind of childhood that turns people into psychological time bombs. How would I react when he started to go off? Did I have my own time bomb ticking away in me? Was it possible I could revert to the brutality with which I had been raised?

"Uncle Henry, John got me a baseball from the Dodgers." Angel ran up the steps holding a pristine ball. He was wearing a Dodgers cap.

I roused myself. "How did he do that?"

"He used to play with the batting coach!" Angel exclaimed.

"Yeah," John said, coming up behind me. "He was my catcher. After twenty years, he's still bitching about how I used to shake him off." He looked at me quizzically. "What's wrong, Henry?"

"Nothing," I said. "I was thinking."

John pulled another Dodgers cap out of his back pocket and clamped it on my head. "We're here to see baseball, man. No thinking. Okay?"

"Like I could squeeze a thought past this hat."

The line-ups were announced and we sat down, Angel between us. A moment later we were back on our feet for a country-western version of the national anthem. Somewhere around the rockets' red glare, Angel reached for my hand.

The D'backs won, 7 to 5, but didn't score the winning runs until the eighth inning. Angel got to shout himself hoarse rooting for the Dodgers, which, because John had played in their farm system, was now Angel's team. We were standing outside the bathroom waiting for John as the park emptied. A blond, blue-eyed boy about Angel's age wearing an Arizona cap drifted by in the passing crowd, spotted Angel and smirked.

"We kicked your butts," he said.

Suddenly it was as if I was holding an enraged dog at the end of a taut leash. Angel's body went rigid, his face became a mask, and he glared at the boy with such unblinking hatred that the kid went scrambling after his dad. Gangbangers used this stare to intimidate each other. They learned it in the prison yards, where it was called "maddogging." When the boy disappeared, the rage went out of Angel's eyes and his hand went limp in mine.

"Why did you maddog that kid?"

He seemed surprised that I knew the expression. "He started it."

"He was just teasing you, Angel."

He dropped my hand and took a half-step away.

"Where did you learn how to do that?"

After a moment of sullen silence, he said, "I got jumped."

Since I knew what maddogging was, he had used the street term for being initiated into a gang.

"Where was this?"

"At school. In San Francisco."

"Recently?"

"Last year," he said. "When my dad was still in jail."

"Why would they jump you? You're ten years old."

His expression suggested I should get out more often. "Some sixth graders did it," he said. "They wanted me to be a runner."

"Drug runner."

Again the look. "They said I could have a gun."

"These sixth graders?"

He nodded. "A semi," he said admiringly. "I told my mom and she took me out of school. Uncle Henry, are there gangs in the schools in L.A.?"

"Not in any school you're going to, *m'ijo*," I replied. "Did you want to be in a gang?"

He shrugged. "I don't know. I like school."

John emerged from the bathroom smiling. "So what did you think of your first big league game, Angelito?"

"It was cool," he burbled as if, a moment ago, he hadn't calmly been discussing semiautomatic handguns and gang initiations. John picked him up and sat him on his shoulders. Bemused, I followed them out.

When John dropped us off, I asked him to come back for dinner.

"Just for dinner?" he asked.

Angel had rushed into the house with a bladder full of lemonade.

"You want to stay over?"

"Do you want me to?"

"What about Angel?"

He smiled. "What about him? When we were down at the fence watching the D'backs he asked me if I was your boyfriend."

"He did?"

"Listen, Henry, Angelito is ten going on thirty. You know what I mean?"

I thought about the conversation I had had with him about gangs. "Yeah, but when I look at him, all I see is a little boy."

John reached across the seat and squeezed my thigh. "That's 'cause he knows he can be a little boy around you. That's your present to him."

"What did you tell him when he asked if you were my boyfriend?"

"I'll only answer that in bed," he said. "In the presence of my lawyer."

"Then I guess you're sleeping over."

He leaned his sunburned face forward. I kissed him in full view of my neighbors, none of whom were home except old Mrs. Byrne, the fundamentalist, who had long ago cast me into perdition when she discovered I was taking care of Josh as he was dying of AIDS. She had gone around the neighborhood with a petition to force me to move. She was probably watching us now from behind the lace curtains in her living room. So I groped his butt for good measure. He laughed and groped me back.

Inside, there was a surprisingly long-winded message from Dr. Hayward that amounted to asking how I was doing. Hearing him, I realized that I hadn't exercised in two days. I explained to Angel that I had go down to the high school to run and he asked if he could come with me. I agreed because I needed to ask him about the gun, and it would be easier in a setting where I was not so obviously interrogating him. I took to heart what John had told me about letting Angel be a kid. I didn't want to rob him of the opportunity if I could help it.

The light had softened and shadows began to fall across the track. A grove of eucalyptus trees released their rainy scent into the dusty air. On the football field, a group of brown-skinned men shouting to one another in Spanish were kicking around a soccer ball.

"I don't run very fast yet," I told Angel. "So don't race me."

He grinned. "You 'fraid I could beat you?"

"I'm sure of it, *m'ijo*. Let's do our warm-ups."

We plopped down on a corner of the field away from the soccer players. Angel watched me stretch and imitated what he saw. He was as limber as a cat, and showed off by grabbing the soles of his feet while I struggled to touch my toes. As I leaned over, my pendant swung free.

"What's that?" he asked.

I pulled it over my head and dropped it into his hand. "It's a heart," I said. "My friend Edith gave it to me after I came home from the hospital. For luck."

He held it in front of his face. "Is it a ruby?"

"No, I think she said it was called red jasper."

He looked at me. "How come you were in the hospital?"

"I had a heart attack," I said. "My heart wasn't getting enough

blood because there was some stuff in the veins, so it stopped working for a minute." I got up. "That's why I have to run, to keep my
heart healthy."

He looked anxious. "Are you okay now, Uncle Henry?"

"As long as I take care of myself. You like it?" I asked, referring
to the pendant.

"It's cool."

"Keep it," I said.

"Really?"

"Yeah, now let's get started."

He hung the pendant around his neck and trotted beside me. I
went slowly, but my legs were considerably longer than his and it
was a struggle for him to keep up. After three laps, I slowed to a
walk, as much for my sake as his.

"You're too much for me," I said. "Let's walk the last lap."

"How far did we run? Five miles?"

"Three-quarters of a mile."

He smirked in disbelief. The pendant hung around his neck almost to his belly button. I would have to shorten the cord. Edith
had told me always to keep it as a spare unless I met a special man.
Angel qualified. He was practically skipping beside me. I remembered that I needed to ask him about the gun. I hated to spoil the
moment, but there would never be a moment that it didn't spoil.

"Angel, I have to ask you a couple of questions about the shooting."

His pace slowed. "Like what?"

"Do you remember you told me you saw a gun in the room?"

He answered reluctantly. "Yeah."

I put my hand on his shoulder. "If I'm going to help your mom
in court, I have to understand everything that happened that night.
That's the only reason I'm asking you these questions. Not to upset
you."

"Okay," he said, shaking me off.

"The police say they didn't find a gun. Are you sure you saw one?"

"Uh-huh, it was by my dad."

"When you were in the room, where was your mother?"

"She was on thc floor." He flinched as he replied. He was seeing the room.

"Did your mother say anything to you?"

We walked a few more steps before he answered. "She told me to call you, but the phone was pulled out of the wall." He flinched, remembering. "I ran to the gas station."

"When she told you to call me, was she upset?"

"She was hurt," he whispered.

"And when you left, the gun was still there?"

He ran ahead of me. I let him go. His posture said it all: the little soldier. I knew what had happened to the gun. When I caught up with him at the finish line, he was crying and I saw the fear in his face that I had seen the night of the killing. It hurt me that I had brought it back, but there was no other way. I knelt down so we were at eye level and wiped his face with my T-shirt.

"What did you do with the gun, *m'ijo?*"

"I hid it," he blubbered.

"Did your mom ask you to do that?"

He shook his head. "No. I was trying to help her."

"I know you were."

He shook. "Are you mad at me, Uncle Henry?"

I hugged him to me and said, "No, *m'ijo*, I'm not mad at you. I love you."

"I love you, too," he whispered.

I let him go. "Come on, then, let's go get the gun."

We drove to the Arco where I had picked him up. I told him to wait for me in the car while I went into the minimart and bought a carton of sandwich baggies. Then he led me around the side of the station and pointed to the drainpipe. Gloving my hand with a baggie, I reached into the pipe, touched metal and slowly extracted the gun by its butt. I looked at it and then at him.

"This is it, Angel?"

"Yeah."

"And you found this beside your dad?"

He nodded.

I slipped the gun into another baggie, jammed it into my waistband and covered it with my T-shirt.

"Okay," I said. "Thank you for telling me, Angel. For now, this is just between you and me, okay? I don't want anyone else to know, not your mother and not John."

He nodded understanding, ready to keep our secret. I wondered how many more he was keeping. I wondered if one of them was that he knew this wasn't the gun that had killed his father.

I locked the gun in the safe in my office before John returned carrying a gym bag with his clothes for the next day, a sack of Chinese takeout and *Field of Dreams*, which he explained to Angel and me was his favorite movie. Ever. I taught Angel how to use chopsticks and we sat around the dining table passing around the little white cartons, not even bothering with plates. Angel showed John the pendant I had given him and John adjusted the length of the cord. He showed Angel the small gold crucifix he wore, which made me remember how it looked in the thicket of his chest hair when he was naked. He caught the look in my eye and grinned.

"Uncle Henry doesn't have a necklace," Angel said.

"We'll have to get him one for his birthday," John said. "When is your birthday, Henry?"

"September fourth. When is yours?"

"November seventeenth. When is yours, *m'ijo*?"

"October fifth," he said proudly. "September," he said, pointing at me, and then "October," pointing at himself and then to John, "November."

John raised his glass of Coke. *"Feliz cumpleaños a todos."*

We touched glasses. "Happy birthday!"

I had forgotten all about the gun and the questions it raised.

Much later, I watched John emerge from the bathroom wearing only his crucifix. He paused at the foot of the bed, scooped up the bedding that had been kicked to the floor and dumped it on the bed.

"Look at the mess we made," he said, perching at the edge of the bed beside me.

Yellow lamplight fanned across his wide shoulders, deepening the red in his dark flesh. The heavy mat of hair on his chest thinned to a dark line that trailed over his paunch and then thickened again around his genitals. His green eyes flicked back and forth, watching me like fish moving through deep water.

"Sometimes," he said, "I can look into your eyes and see all the way into your heart."

"You make it sound like such a long way."

"It is. You play your cards close. I understand that. You gotta be careful of who you let know your business. But sometimes I think you hold things back from me that you don't have to, Rico." Rico from Enrique, Spanish for Henry; that was the nickname he had bestowed on me that afternoon up in Griffith Park. He got into bed beside me. "You can tell me anything."

I had an image of my retrieving a gun from a drainpipe. "I love you, Johnny, but my world can be pretty scary."

He rested his head on my chest. "I don't scare easy, man."

He got into bed and we covered ourselves. I switched off the light and we lay there, bodies touching.

"Deanna called me," he said. "She wants to talk."

"Yeah? That's good. Isn't it?"

"Yeah. I'm going to have dinner with her." His hand reached for mine. "I owe it to her."

"You just told me you loved me. I'm not worried."

"Good," he said. "'Cause there's nothing to be worried about."

I was still awake when his hand fell away from mine and he began to softly snore. I thought about the gun in my safe. The .22-caliber handgun I'd recovered from the drainpipe at the gas station. There had been a .22-caliber bullet in the baseboard of the motel room where Vicky had killed her husband with a .380 semiautomatic, in what now looked less like self-defense than the shootout at the O.K. Corral.

On Monday, as Angel and I were headed out of the house to court for Vicky's arraignment, the phone rang. I let the machine take it.

14.

I REALIZED, AS I SAT BESIDE MY SISTER AND NEPHEW waiting for Vicky to be arraigned, that this was the first time I'd been back in a courtroom since my heart attack at the Court of Appeal two months earlier. This room could not have been more different than that hushed and somber chamber where the high dais of the appellate justices presumably alluded to their God's-eye view of the law. The Hollywood arraignment court was the street level of the law: a graceless square lit by fluorescent lights behind plastic panels in the low acoustic-tiled ceiling. The cheap veneers that covered the drywall were blistering, the linoleum was woebegone, and masking tape was strung across the broken seats among the plastic folding chairs in the gallery. The reek of a back alley lurked beneath the antiseptic smell of the industrial-strength cleaner with which the floor was washed. A vagrant snored audibly from one of the back rows. Voices rose contentiously or dropped to accusatory whispers and mixed with the tinny sounds of Walkmans, mothers hushing their babies and crazy street people addressing themselves at eloquent length. In the well of the court, two bailiffs lolled over coffee, every now and then barking for silence. The court clerks frantically shuffled the day's papers behind their enclosure at the right side of the bench. To the left, the court reporter chatted with one of the D.A.'s at the long table where the prosecutors sat shuffling their own files. Their paralegals staffed the phones, calling witnesses to confirm their standby status, or consoled the disillusioned victims of crimes who had come here expecting justice and stumbled into a pigpen. Across the well of the court was the defense table, where three public defenders dealt with their own recalcitrant witnesses and anxious clients. Behind their table, along the wall, was the jury box, used, in this case, not for juries but for defendants in custody, who were brought out in groups of ten through a door behind the bailiffs' station that led to the holding cells. The only decoration in the room was a gilded replica of the Great Seal on the wall behind the dais, the flags of the United States and California, and an orchid that adorned the desk of a clerk.

I had spoken to Inez over the weekend. She had received my judicial application and was going to hand-deliver it to the governor because, as she reminded me, a politician's gratitude has the shelf-life of a snowflake on a hot griddle. If she was successful and I was appointed, this would be the kind of court to which I would be initially assigned. I looked around the squalid courtroom and thought, *Yes, I would love to be the judge that presided over it.* My family, however, did not seem to find the place as inspiring.

Angel slumped on the bench between Elena and me, reading *Baseball America.* My sister sat upright with an expression of wonder and dismay. She wore a black suit, a white silk blouse, and looked, I thought, like the proverbial nun at the whorehouse.

"Is Vicky here yet?" she asked me.

"Probably in a holding cell. They'll bring her out when they call her case."

"Will we be able to talk to her?"

"No, only I can talk to her here."

"What's going to happen exactly?"

I had explained this to her before, so I knew she was asking out of nervousness. "She'll plead not guilty, the judge will set bail and a date for what's called the preliminary hearing."

"Is that the same as the trial?"

"No," I said. "The purpose of the prelim is to require the prosecution to show the judge that there's enough evidence to warrant a trial. It's pretty much a formality. Once the judge finds there's sufficient evidence, he, or she, will bind the defendant over for trial."

"What kind of time frame are we talking about?" she asked, smoothing imaginary wrinkles from her skirt.

"They'll set the prelim within ten days. Trial has to be set within sixty days thereafter because of a defendant's constitutional right to a speedy trial. The defendant can waive the right and set the trial for later, but I don't think we gain anything by doing that in Vicky's case."

"Why not?"

"It's not the kind of case any reasonable prosecutor is going to want to take to trial," I said. "If we keep it on the front burner, they'll deal it rather than go to trial."

"If it weren't Vicky, this would be just a routine case for you, wouldn't it?" she asked, not in anger but genuine curiosity. "I mean, you seem to know exactly how it will play out."

"I've been doing this for a long time," I replied. "While every case has its twists and turns, over time you get a pretty good sense of what particular cases are worth, including homicides."

"I suppose everything has its measure," she reflected. "Even the value of a life." In a low voice, she asked, "Will Vicky go to prison?"

"Very likely," I said.

She turned away, but a moment later asked, "What do you think bail will be?"

"I don't know, maybe a hundred thousand. We'll have to talk to a bail bondsman about—"

"I have it," she said.

I looked at her. "Elena, where do you come by that kind of money?"

She smiled haughtily. "Oh, really, Henry, do you imagine I spend my evenings drinking sherry and watching PBS? I manage the family investments. We've done quite well in technologies. I assume you've got a retirement plan?"

I laughed. "My plan is not to retire."

She looked alarmed and had started to reply when the bailiff rose and shouted over the throng, "Come to order. Department one is now in session, the Honorable Judge Edgar Kline presiding."

A tall, pale, rather fat young man who wore his judicial robe with the air of a high school valedictorian stepped up to the bench, lowered himself into the highback leather chair and faced the courtroom with an expression that seemed to alternate between contempt and terror. *A brand-new judge*, I thought, tossed into arraignment court by his presiding judge to sink or swim.

"Ladies and gentlemen," Judge Kline said in a surprisingly authoritative baritone. "We have one hundred and ten cases on the calendar and the sooner you settle down, the faster we'll get through them. Now, I want you all to make sure that you're where you're supposed to be. This is a criminal arraignment court. We don't do traffic tickets or settle small claims. Those of you who are lucky enough to be criminal defendants, a word. I am not interested in your life stories. All I want is to hear a plea. If you have a lawyer, I don't even want you to talk to me. If you don't have a lawyer, some conversation is inevitable, but let's keep it to a minimum." He smirked. "All right, let's begin with the guests of the county."

Ten prisoners were brought out of the holding cells; Vicky was second to the last. I heard Elena's shocked intake of breath, but it was Angel I watched. He carefully closed his magazine and lay it in his lap. As he watched her being led out in handcuffs and an ill-fitting jumpsuit, his eyes filled with horror and grief and helplessness. How much worse must it have been, I thought, when he had walked into that room at the Hollywood Inn. I understood viscerally, as I had not before, that whatever happened, he would carry the images of these days to his grave, and whatever explanation was finally adduced, it would never be enough to wipe them away.

The plump young judge showed considerably more patience than his snide little speech suggested, and a half-hour passed before he called Vicky's case.

"Victoria Trujillo," the judge intoned. "Is Ms. Trujillo represented?"

I went into the well of the court to stand beside her. "Yes, Your Honor, Henry Rios for the defendant."

Across the room, a tall blond young man in a very nicely cut suit stood up and said, "Kim Pearsall for the People."

Kline looked at him. "I beg your pardon, counsel?"

"Uh, this is my case. I mean, I'm the deputy assigned to try it."

"Counsel, this is an arraignment court, not a trial court. You do understand the difference."

"Yes, Your Honor, I worked misdemeanor arraignment court in Santa Monica."

Misdemeanor arraignments in Santa Monica? This was the greenhorn Tony Earl had promised me. He had the open, cheerful, rather self-satisfied countenance of someone upon whom life had made very few demands. Santa Monica was easy duty; he had probably gone surfing before work.

Kline was no more impressed than I was. "How very nice for you, counsel. Ms. Trujillo is charged with second-degree murder. Is there a plea?"

"Say not guilty," I whispered to her.

"Not guilty," she said.

"You'll have speak up for the court reporter," the judge said.

"Not guilty," she said in a firmer voice.

"Bail recommendation, People," Kline said, and when the young D.A. did not immediately respond, continued, "That's your cue, Mr. Pearsall."

He cleared his voice nervously. "Um, the defendant has a record and no visible means of support and no ties to the community. The People want her remanded."

"Well, not all thirty-five million of them Your Honor," I said.

"At the moment, I'm the only one of them who matters, Mr. Rios, so convince me."

"I'm not only the defendant's lawyer, I'm also her uncle. Her mother, my sister, is in court, too, as is the defendant's ten-year-old son. So, obviously, she does have family who would be responsible for her. I'd ask you to set reasonable bail."

"Your Honor," the young D.A. interjected quickly. "The defendant comes from up north, the San Francisco area, and she couldn't give the police a local address when she was arrested at a transient motel."

"I think you mean a motel for transients," Kline said irritably. "Unless the motel moves around from place to place." Pearsall, however, had scored a point and the judge's irritability reflected uncertainty. If he was a new judge, he would be very careful about setting an accused murderer loose and risk having her flee the jurisdiction. He looked at me. "How long has your client been in L.A., counsel?"

"Your Honor, about a month. In addition to me, her mother-in-law lives in Garden Grove—"

"Which is out of the jurisdiction," he said curtly. "And where does her mother live?"

"In Oakland."

He flipped a page. "Also out of the jurisdiction."

"Your Honor, she would live with me. I live in the jurisdiction."

He looked at me. "Has she ever lived with you before, Mr. Rios?"

"Yes, when she first arrived."

"And for the rest of the time in the crack motel where she shot and killed her husband," the prosecutor volunteered.

"Please," I said. "Save that for the jury."

"No," Kline said. "He has a point, Mr. Rios. Your client has no fixed place of residence, no job. You are her only tie to L.A. and it doesn't seem to be a very strong one. Her record indicates she moves back and forth between here and the Bay Area. I smell a flight risk. No bail."

"Your Honor, I'm an officer of the court," I said. "And as such I am representing that I will see that she stays in the jurisdiction."

Kline said, "It's not you I'm worried about, Mr. Rios. You can renew your bail request at the prelim. For now, she stays in jail. Let's set this for a prelim."

"Since you've denied bail, I want the prelim as soon as possible."

"Fine by me," Kline said. "How about a week?"

"A week is good," I said. "I would also like the court to order the prosecutor to comply with discovery on that date. I particularly want him to give me a tape of my client's alleged confession."

"So ordered," he said.

"Your Honor," Pearsall said. "That doesn't give me much time."

"You're not the one with the constitutional right to a speedy trial, are you, Mr. Pearsall? Discovery compliance is ordered for one week from today. That applies to you, too, Mr. Rios."

"Understood," I said.

"Next case, please," Kline said, turning to his clerk.

I waited for Vicky in the interview room, which, like the holding cells, was located behind the court. The interview room was a narrow rectangle bisected by a counter. At each side of the counter were three metal stools with a glass partition between them. On the counter were phones. When Vicky came in, we sat down on opposite sides of the counter and picked up our respective phones.

"You said the judge would let me go home," she complained.

"The problem is that the judge isn't sure where your home is," I said. "He's afraid if he released you on bail, you'd leave L.A."

"I would leave," she said. "I'd take Angel and get the hell out of here."

"Please don't say things like that. It makes my job harder."

"When can I see Angel?"

"He and your mother can visit you when they return you to the jail. Right now there's something I have to ask you about. Angel showed me the gun that he said he removed from the room the night you shot Pete. Do you remember him doing that?"

I could tell she was about to lie, but then she nodded slightly. "I didn't tell him, he took it. He was trying to help me."

"I know that. The problem I'm having is, it wasn't the gun that killed Pete. What can you tell me about this?"

"I don't understand," she said.

"Pete was killed with a three-eighty. The gun Angel showed me is a twenty-two. There was a twenty-two-caliber bullet in the wall. It looks like you both had guns and were shooting at each other."

She shook her head. "He didn't shoot at me."

"There were two guns, Vicky. The one that killed Pete is still missing. The one I have locked in my safe was fired that night, apparently at you. What else am I supposed to think?"

"I don't understand what you mean," she equivocated. "Everything happened so fast. I have to think."

"You might think about telling me the truth, niece."

The deputy came into her side of the room. "The bus is leaving."

"Tell Angel I love him," she said as he led her away. No word for her mother.

Elena and Angel were not in the courtroom when I emerged from lockup. I was on my way out to find them when the D.A., Pearsall, loped over and stopped me at the door.

"Hey, Mr. Rios," he said pleasantly. "Kim Pearsall. About that discovery? I was wondering if informally you would give me a little more time to get it together—"

I turned on him. "You send my niece back to jail in full view of her ten-year-old son and now you're asking me for a favor? Let me give you the short answer. Fuck you."

He looked as if I'd struck him. "Hey, dude, I'm just doing my job."

"Hey, dude? What do you think this is, a sitcom? If you don't produce discovery on the day of the prelim, I'll ask for sanctions. Understand? Dude?"

I left him standing there composing a retort. Out in the hallway, I saw my sister and Angel talking to a short stocky man with jet-black hair. He was wearing an old but carefully pressed dark suit, a once white shirt yellowed with many washings, and an unfashionably skinny tie. On his lapel was pinned a silver crucifix. He had stolid, Indian features and he could have been any age between forty and sixty. When I approached, he looked at me with eyes so black they appeared to be without irises.

"Henry," Elena said, straining to be polite. "This is Reverend Ortega. He said Vicky went to his church."

"You mean La Iglesia de—what was it called?" I said.

"La Iglesia de Cristo Triunfante," he said. "I came to try to help our sister but the bus was late." He spoke with a heavy accent. "I'm sorry."

"Help her how?" I asked.

"Maybe for bail—if the judge hears a minister, he says let her go and these people will take care of her."

"I was explaining that she has family," Elena said.

"We're all family, sister," he said, smiling.

"How did you know about the arraignment?" I asked him.

"Vicky called me from the jail. She asked me to come."

I could see by the expression on Elena's face that she wanted me to get rid of him so we could talk.

"Well, thank you for coming, but the judge denied bail."

"Maybe I can talk to him?"

"Vicky's already on her way back to jail," I said. "Look, I'm sorry, but I really need to talk to my sister and nephew now."

Reverend Ortega smiled at Angel. "You gonna come and see us on Sunday, Angelito?"

"I beg your pardon?" I said.

"His mother wants him to worship in our church." He studied me like a doctor making an off-the-cuff diagnosis. "All are welcome, brother."

"You know, this isn't the time or place to discuss this," I said. I handed him my card. "Call me this afternoon and we can talk then."

He took my card. His lips moved slightly as he read it. "It makes me proud to see a Latino be a lawyer. It's a good thing to know man's law, but don't forget there's God's law, too." His glance fell back on Angel. "This boy's mother, she sacrifice everything. All she wants is her boy raised Christian."

"Reverend, please, we really have to go."

He laid a hand on my shoulder. It was a strong hand, a laborer's hand. "God bless you, brother. I know you're doing your best. Good-bye, sister. Angelito, you come and see me, okay?"

Angel responded with a surprisingly warm, "Okay, Reverend."

After he left, the three of us sat on a bench worn to the wood by all the fidgeting bottoms that had occupied it before us.

"What happened with bail?" Elena said.

"You heard the judge. He was afraid she'd take off if he released her. Look, I'll ask for bail next week at the prelim. That preacher might actually be helpful." I looked at Angel. "How do you know him?"

"He came to see us," he said. "He's nice."

"Came to see you where?"

"The motel," he said. "He came and prayed with my mom and then he took me for ice cream. Is my mom coming home?"

"Not today. She sends her love," I added, not making it specific to Angel, but I saw from her face that Elena was not fooled.

"Can we see her?" Elena asked.

I nodded. "Let me just check my phone messages and we'll go down to the jail."

"I'd like some coffee," Elena said. "There was a cafeteria downstairs. Come on, Angel, let's leave your uncle to make his call."

"Bring me a cup, too," I called after them. "Black."

I dialed my machine on my cell phone and listened twice to the message, then called the return number. I was still speaking to the woman who had left the message when Angel and Elena returned. I took the cup my sister offered me without looking at her, ended my phone conversation and slipped the phone into my pocket.

"I can't go to the jail with you," I said. "I'll drop you off and you can take a cab to my house. Angel has house keys."

"What happened?" Elena asked.

"Client emergency," I said. "I'm sorry. Shall we go?"

I let Angel get a couple of steps ahead of us and, in a low voice, said to Elena. "That was Jesusita Trujillo's daughter, Socorro. Mrs. Trujillo's in the hospital."

"Why?"

"Someone broke into her house. The cops think it was a robbery."

"Was she seriously hurt?"

Angel had stopped and glanced back at us suspiciously. I smiled at him and then told Elena, "She's in a coma."

I pulled into the parking lot of Saint Francis Hospital, a rambling pink stucco building with a white cross above the entrance. Two women in dowdy clothes and the blue veils of nuns passed in front of me on the sidewalk, deep in conversation. In flower beds beneath the first-floor windows, rose bushes were in profuse bloom. On the lawn was a life-sized statue of Saint Francis preaching to stone birds perched on his sleeves and at his feet, while a live pigeon roosted on his tonsure. The day had turned into a scorcher, withering the grass. I had time to make these detailed observations because I seemed unable to get myself out of my car and across the threshold of the hospital. I could hear Hayward's voice telling me, "Everyone dies of something, Henry, and what you now know is that the probabilities are that you'll die of heart disease." The equation that kept me sweating in my closed car was: heart attack, hospital, death. I knew my anxiety was completely irrational and my sense of foreboding misplaced, that the benign glass doors of the little Catholic hospital were not the maws of death, but a good five minutes passed before I was able to peel myself from the seat and get myself through them.

I paused at the doorway of Jesusita Trujillo's room. In the corner on a table was a makeshift altar where, among flowers and candles, there were prayer cards, family pictures and handwritten petitions to the saints on her behalf. A heavy woman in a flowered blouse and stretch pants sat vigil beside the bed.

"Mrs. Cerda?" I said, stepping into the room.

The woman turned her head. She resembled her mother mostly in the lines of weary kindness etched into her face.

"I'm Henry Rios," I said.

She got up from her chair. "Call me Socorro."

I approached her and got a good look at Jesusita Trujillo. Bandages swathed her head, covering her right eye. The part of her face that was visible looked like it had gone through a meat grinder.

"My God," I said, remembering the gentle, frightened woman who, only a week earlier, had served me lemonade and told me lies. "How did this happen?"

"She had this glass coffee table. He pushed her through it, face first." I remembered the table. The glass had been very thick "They got most of the glass out, but some of it went through her skull into her brain. Even if she wakes up, she'll have brain damage."

"The police say it was a robbery?"

She looked at her mother, then said in a low voice. "The doctors say she can't hear nothing, but if she can, I don't want to upset her. Maybe we can talk outside." We went out into the hall. "A robbery, yeah, that's the what the police say. A home invasion."

"You sound skeptical."

"I believe someone was trying to rob her," she said, "but it wasn't no invasion. The police said there was no break-in. It was someone Mom knew. The neighbors know, too, but they ain't talking."

"Why?"

"They're afraid of the gangs," she said.

"That's who did it? A gangbanger?"

She rested her bulk against the wall and regarded me with exhausted eyes. "My mom knew them when they were kids, she babysat some of them. I used to warn her they were *malos*, but she said, no, *hija*, they got good hearts, it's just the drugs. She said that because of Pete, because she blamed drugs for his problems."

"Mothers have to assume the best."

She nodded. "Maybe she was right about Pete, but not those kids he ran around with. They were just plain evil. She never got your messages about Pete, Mr. Rios. They found her the night before you called. I'm sorry I didn't call before, but—"

"She was attacked the same night Pete was killed?"

"Pete was always breaking her heart. At least she didn't have to hear about the way he died."

"Were you close to Pete?"

She ran a hand across her weary eyes. "I changed his diapers when he was a baby, but I'm a lot older and I was married when he was still a *niño*. He was okay while my dad was alive, but after he died, Pete ran wild and Mom couldn't control him. His cousin Butch got Pete into drugs." She paused. "That Butch, he's a bad one. Even Mom saw it. When Pete brought Vicky home, she was happy because she thought he would settle down. Pretty soon he was running around with Butch again, and the next thing I hear from Mom, Pete was back in prison again. I can't believe Vicky killed him. She's good people."

"There's not much question about it," I said.

"I guess he finally drove her crazy with the drugs, then," she said. "I'm sorry about Pete, but putting up with him must have been real hard on her because she's a good girl. Smart, too. Where's their little boy? Angelito?"

"Staying with me," I said. "You know I'm not just Vicky's lawyer, I'm her uncle. My sister, Elena, is her mother."

"Yeah," she said. "Mom said something about how Vicky found her family. So you're her uncle. I guess that makes us some kind of in-laws. Can I give you something for her?"

"Sure," I said. "What is it?"

"The motel where I guess they were staying, they left a message for Mom, too, and said to come and get Pete and Vicky's stuff or they would throw it away. I sent my son down to Hollywood. There's just a suitcase, some boxes. They're in the trunk of my car. I figured there might be things in there that Vicky would want."

"Is your car here?"

"In the parking lot."

With Socorro Cerda's help, I loaded two suitcases and four boxes into the trunk of my car. Afterward, there seemed no reason to return to the hospital.

"If there's anything else I can do for you, Socorro, let me know."

"Well," she said. "My sister, Mary, and me, we want to bury Pete, but we don't know where his body is."

"The police didn't tell you?"

She shook her head. "I tried to find out, but I got the runaround."

"I can take care of that for you," I said. "Where do you want the coroner to release his body?"

She gave me the name of a funeral home.

"Gutierrez and Sola," I repeated, jotting it in my notebook. "I'll call you as soon as the body is released. Would it be all right if I brought Angel to his dad's funeral?"

"Of course," she said. "We're family. I've got to get back to my mom. Thank you for coming, Mr. Rios."

"I'm very sorry about your mother. I only met her once, but she seemed like a very kind person."

"That's why I don't understand why someone would do this to her." She gave me a damp hug. "Give my love to Vicky and Angel. Tell Vicky I'll try to get up and see her."

"I will. I'll bring Angel to visit you if you want."

She smiled. "You do that. I think he likes his old Aunt Soakie."

I had handled enough homicides over the years to have become friendly with a couple of the deputies in the medical examiner's office. One of them was a young lesbian who had come to me for advice when she was considering a lawsuit against the county for what she perceived to be discrimination against women in the office's promotion practices. I had helped her find an employment discrimination lawyer who had negotiated a handsome settlement. I phoned her from my car and asked for help with Pete's body. She agreed to personally supervise the release of Pete's body to the funeral home the following day. I left a message for Socorro Cerda. Traffic on the 405 came to a complete halt around the airport, a situation that usually raised my blood pressure, but I was the bearer of bad tidings, so for once I didn't mind.

15.

WHEN I ENTERED THE HOUSE, I HEARD VOICES AND THEN a familiar laugh coming from out on the deck. Elena and Angel were sitting at the table eating lunch in the shade of the canvas umbrella I had purchased the previous summer but never got around to putting up. They had a guest—John—and it was his laughter I had heard. He was talking to Elena, but when I stepped outside, he lifted his head and our eyes met. I felt as if a light had been switched on inside of me. He unfolded his slow, private smile. I looked from him to my sister, in whom, apparently, a different light had just gone on.

"Hey, Henry," he said. "Hope you don't mind me dropping in. I was going to take you and Angel to lunch, but then your sister explained you had some business so we just picked up some food from the deli."

"You know you're always welcome," I said.

"Sit down, Henry," Elena said. "Eat something."

I sat down, untied my tie and draped my coat over the chair. Famished, I served myself from a platter of sandwiches and salads. It was pleasant to sit beneath the umbrella, and a small herb-scented breeze rustled up from the canyon. I chewed my turkey sandwich and listened to Angel and John debate the relative merits of National League pitchers, a subject, I was mildly surprised to discover, on which my sister also had some emphatic opinions. For a moment I forgot about the horror I had left behind at the hospital and thought, *So this is what it's like to have a family.*

Elena had dropped out of the baseball conversation, and in a low voice asked, "Henry, how was she?"

"Not well," I replied. "Did you tell him?"

"No, I was going to, but then John showed up and, well, he seems very fond of John."

"Yes, so am I."

"I gathered," she replied dryly.

John said, "What are you two whispering about?"

I put the sandwich down. "I have some bad new about Angel's other grandmother."

Angel looked at me. "What?"

"Someone broke into her house and attacked her. She's in the hospital." I glanced at my sister. "In very bad shape."

John squeezed the boy's shoulder sympathetically. Angel looked down at the remains of his lunch, then raised his head and asked, "Does that mean I can live with you while my mom is in jail?"

Shocked, Elena exclaimed, "Angel!"

He glanced at her, but addressed me. "You said my mom wanted me to live with my grandma Jesusita, but I can't live with her if she's sick."

Elena replied, "You have two grandmothers, Angel."

Still looking at me, he said, "If I live with Grandma Elena in Oakland, I won't be able to see my mom."

"Henry works," Elena replied, matching his deliberate tone. "He can't look after you. I'm on summer break."

Angel squared his shoulders and said to me, "You don't have to take care of me all the time. I can take care of myself."

"Angel," Elena snapped, "I'm speaking to you."

He threw her a furious look. "I don't want to live with you. I hate you." He looked at me. "Don't make me go with her, Uncle Henry. I want to stay with you." Then he ran from the table, sobbing.

For a moment, no one said anything. I tossed my napkin on the table. "I guess I should talk to him." I looked at my sister. "I'll try to make him understand why it would be better if he lives with you."

She looked back at me. "Would it? Do you want him here?"

"Yes," I said. "I want him to live with me. I know it won't be easy, but we'll manage."

She folded her napkin and set it on the table. "All right," she said. "Let me go tell him."

"You know he doesn't really hate you."

She got up from the table. "Actually, Henry, he probably does just now, because he thinks I want to take him away from you. That's why I want to tell him he can stay. Excuse me, John."

A headache began to gather in the center of my forehead. I shut my eyes and rubbed the spot. I heard John get up and then his hands clamped down on my shoulders and his thick fingers began to knead me.

"Man, you're tight," he said. "Relax."

"I couldn't get my niece out on bail, Angel's other grandma's been beaten into a coma, my sister feels rejected and Angel's in hysterics. Is this what it's like to have a family? Ouch!"

"Let go, okay? Stop fighting me." He worked my neck. "Those things aren't your fault, man."

"They're my responsibility," I said. He dug deep into my muscles and my headache began to fade. "That feels great. You're really good at this."

"I've been getting massages since I played ball. I picked up the basics over the years. I like your sister. She's sharp, like you."

"Sharp as in smart or sharp as in smart-ass?"

"Both. Like you. Like all you Rioses. You're all a little too smart for your own good."

"How was dinner with Deanna?"

The massage became a ruminative rub, as if he was composing his thoughts.

"Was it bad?" I prodded.

"She apologized," he replied. "You know, for the things she said. She told me she'd been doing a lot of thinking and she figured she made a mistake with me."

"What kind of mistake?"

His hands slipped off my shoulders. "Turning me down when I asked her to marry me. She said she didn't know how much she loved me until she thought about losing me."

After a moment, I said, "I can understand that."

"She wants me to give her another chance."

I felt a pain in my chest that I knew was not angina. "Are you?"

He laid his hands on my shoulders again, but this touch was tentative, uncertain. "I want to ask you something, but you gotta think about it before you answer."

"Okay."

"Do you think we could have a future together? I mean, we've had a lot of fun, but you know we're different. You're a lawyer, I put in bathrooms in rich people's houses—"

"They're good bathrooms."

He squeezed my shoulder. "I'm serious. You're a smart man, Henry, you have a lot of class. I'm a dumb baseball player. I never went to college. I work with my hands . . ." His voice trailed off.

"You can't mean that you don't think you're good enough for me."

"Am I?" he asked in a quiet, uncertain voice I had never heard from him before.

"Are you sure it's not that you're worried about bringing a boyfriend home to your family instead of a wife?"

"I've thought about that, too," he replied in the same soft voice.

"And?"

"I could do it if I knew we were in it for the long haul."

"I figure after the heart attack that's the only haul I got left in me," I said. "As for being too good for you, John, we come from the same world."

"Yeah, Rico," he said, "but we ended up in different ones."

"You're my honey," I replied. "It is like we grew up together and then found each other again years later. I know you feel the same way. Don't tell me you don't."

"I do," he said. "I liked you the first time I saw you. More than liked you."

"I don't want to lose you."

He folded his arms around my chest. "I have to think things through. About you and me. About me and Deanna. I have a history with her."

"I know you do. And we both know two guys together is a lot harder in this world than a man and a woman. All I'm asking is if you decide you don't want to be with me, don't blame it on your not being good enough. I could accept any other reason but that one."

"We finished the job down the street," he said. "I'm going away for a few days with my dad."

"Where?"

"Every year he takes one of his boys to a father-son retreat up at a monastery in Santa Barbara," he said, releasing me. He sat down. "This year it's my turn."

"A religious retreat? What do you do? Pray? Chat about Jesus?"

"Yeah," he said, grinning. "We do all that, but then after dinner we make popcorn and play poker with the Franciscans that run the place. I'm telling you, Henry, you got to watch those *frailes* like a hawk. Bunch of cardsharks." He kissed the crown of my head. "I'll pray for us."

"You know, John, I don't really go in for religion."

"One year I didn't want to go and I told my dad, 'I don't believe in God.' You know what he said?"

"No."

"He said, 'You think God cares, *m'ijo*? Get your ass in the car.'"
He stood up and kissed me again. "I gotta go. Talk to you soon,
okay? I love you."

"I love you, too, John."

After he left, I sat there and imagined John in a smoke-filled
room dealing cards to a couple of brown-robed monks. I opened
my mouth to laugh, but a sob came out instead.

Elena found me in the kitchen stacking dishes in the dishwasher.
"You don't rinse them first?" she asked.

"Then what would be the point of having a dishwasher? You
were in there with Angel for a long time."

"We had a lot to talk about," she replied. "Did John leave?"

"Yeah. What are you looking for?"

"Plastic wrap to cover this potato salad."

"In the drawer to the right of the sink." I pushed the rack into
the dishwasher, poured some soap in and turned it on. "You were
really shocked that Angel's first reaction to hearing about Jesusita
was for himself, weren't you?"

She nodded. "It seemed incredibly selfish."

"Remember when Edith called him an invulnerable? I've figured out that what that means isn't that things don't hurt him, but
that they don't stop him. His dad's dead, his mom's in jail, and he
feels alone and scared. He's trying to cut the best deal for himself
that he can. He doesn't know how to be graceful about it because it
must seem to him his whole life is riding on making the right
choice."

She put the salad in the refrigerator, then started wrapping the
leftover sandwiches. "You have him reading Homer."

"Not exactly Homer," I said. "It's a kid's translation."

"I remember that book from when you were a child," she said.
"It's odd, Henry. You love him because he reminds you of yourself

at that age, and for the same reason my feelings about him are—I don't know. More complicated."

"How?"

"Until you were about Angel's age, you would still come to me for comfort when things got bad with Mom and Dad, but then you stopped. It was as if you had made a decision that you were on your own. I felt as if I'd failed you but I also resented the implied judgment you had made about me. I felt the same way when Angel said he didn't want to live with me."

"Funny how family members seem to know instinctively how to push the ancient buttons."

"Well, for what it's worth, I do think Angel's had enough mothering. It's better that he stays here with you. He needs a man now and he adores you."

"I never thought I'd be dad material."

"You're probably the first adult man he can imagine wanting to be like when he grows up. I mean, besides Nomar Garciaparra. That must be very powerful for a boy."

"What about Pete?"

"I don't think Pete was around enough for Angel to have felt that close to him, and when he was, he was usually on drugs. Angel really seems to have hated that."

"I know. He told me. Do you think he'll feel the same way about me when he understands homosexuality?"

She smiled. "What makes you think he doesn't understand it now? He loves John. So do you, don't you?"

"You don't miss much."

"He'd make a splendid brother-in-law."

"Well, then keep your fingers crossed," I said. "I could use a cup of coffee. Shall we make some?"

We busied ourselves with making coffee and she volunteered to find a school for Angel.

"From up there?" I asked. "How?"

"The internet, of course," she said. "I thought we might even be able to get him into summer school. He's extremely bright, but I don't think Vicky was very consistent about his education. He's going to have some catching up to do."

"I didn't get to ask you how your visit with her went."

"The usual. Stilted, difficult. My leaving her twice will always lie between us. I have to win her trust back inch by inch. By the way, if Angel's going to stay here, you have to take him to Reverend Ortega's church. Vicky was emphatically clear about that."

"Oh, come on, Elena."

"She's still his mother, Henry. You can't completely ignore what she wants for him because she's in jail."

"What about what he wants?"

"He seemed to like Ortega," she said. "Anyway, he can decide for himself when he's older what he wants to do about religion, but for now you need to do as Vicky asks. All right?"

Sounding to myself like a sullen teenager, I said, "All right. You know the guy probably preaches that gays burn in hell."

"Angel loves you, he'll work out the rest for himself," she said. "Listen, he needs some clothes, so I thought we could shop before my plane leaves."

"Yeah, and I should get him some more books to read and some toys or something to keep him occupied while I am working. What do you think he likes?"

"We'll ask him, Henry."

"Oh," I said.

Later, after Elena had left and Angel was in bed, I went through the boxes that Socorro Cerda had given me looking for a red sweatshirt that Angel wanted. At the bottom of one box I found some of Pete's papers. Parole documents. Letters that Vicky had written him in prison. An envelope with the return address of the San Francisco branch of the Drug Enforcement Agency. The DEA? I opened it. Inside was a letter rejecting Pete's application to become an informant. I looked at the date. He would have received it just before he had been released from prison. Why had Pete Trujillo wanted to become a snitch, I wondered. And why had he been rejected? I found the name of his parole officer on his parole papers and made a note to phone her.

The parole officer, a tough-sounding woman named Cahill, returned my call the morning of Vicky's prelim as I was rushing to get Angel up, dressed, fed and out the door. Between yelling at him to get ready, I tried to explain to her that I was not representing Pete Trujillo on a new criminal charge.

"Your message said you were a lawyer," she said accusingly.

"I am a lawyer but I'm not representing him—"

"Do you know who is?"

"Pete Trujillo's dead," I said. "His funeral's tomorrow, if you want to send flowers. That's not why I'm calling you. Angel, are you dressed yet?"

"What?"

"I'm talking to my nephew, Pete's son."

"I thought you said you were a lawyer. Is he really dead?"

"Yes. His wife shot him. I'm representing her."

"I'll need the death certificate to close my file," she said officiously.

"Fine. I'll make sure you get a copy if you'll just answer a couple of questions for me. Angel . . ."

"Listen, mister, I'm not your Angel."

"My nephew's name is Angel. Why did Pete want to snitch for the DEA?"

"Because he was good at it," she said.

"At being a snitch?"

"That's how he got that sweet deal when he should've gone

down as a three-striker. The DEA didn't think he was going to be able to keep his hands out of the cookie jar, so they passed. Where was he killed?"

"Here in L.A.," I said. Angel emerged from his bedroom, his hair a tangle of knots and wearing a soiled T-shirt and his pajama bottoms. "You can't go to court like that."

"You talking to your nephew again?" she asked, caustic but no longer hostile.

"Yeah, sorry. Who did he snitch on to get the Three Strikes deal?"

"His gangbanger buddies," she said. "I don't remember the details and I don't have his file with me but you could call his P.D."

"You know her name?"

"Morgan something. Lee or Yee. Chinese. I've got to go. You send me that death certificate, okay?"

Angel wandered into the kitchen and listlessly poured himself a bowl of cereal.

"Yeah," I said. "Thanks for your time."

"You know," she said. "Pete wasn't the worst bum on my list."

"I'll make sure to put that in his eulogy," I said and hung up. I went into the kitchen, where Angel was lethargically spooning cereal. I touched his forehead, he was burning up. "Hey, Angelito, are you all right, sweetie?"

He cocked his head and gushed vomit.

A few hours later, I was sitting in lockup with Vicky. Angel was home with my neighbor, Sharon Kwan. I had rushed to the emergency room, phoning the court from my car and pleading for a postponement of the prelim. At the hospital, a harried ER doctor had diagnosed a "bug" and told me to take him home and give him acetaminophen. I was explaining all this to Vicky, who seemed much less worried than I had thought she'd be.

"He gets like that when he's upset," she said.

"Like what?"

"Sick like that," she said. "He'll be okay, Uncle Henry. Probably it was because of his grandma Jesusita. He keeps his feelings all bottled up."

"These feelings ended up all over my suit."

She laughed. I had never heard her laugh before. It was a girl's giggle. "I'm sorry. I know it's not funny."

"It is funny. Now. I was running around like a chicken with its head cut off trying to figure out what to do while he's calmly puking. Then I took him to the emergency room and the doctor's looking at me like, he's just got a little temperature, why are you bothering me?"

She was laughing harder now. "I wish I'd been there."

"I'm glad to hear you say it's not serious."

She wiped her eyes. "He'll be fine."

"I'm sorry about Jesusita, Vicky."

All the mirth went out of her face. "You take care of Angel. Don't let anything happen to him."

"Of course I will."

"I wish this was over," she said.

"All rise. Department sixty-seven is now in session, the Honorable Marie LaVille presiding."

Judge LaVille, a small woman wearing round, red-rimmed glasses and with a skunk streak of white through her black hair, assumed the bench with the wry, relaxed demeanor of a popular high school English teacher.

"Good morning, ladies and gentlemen," she said. "Be seated. We're here, belatedly, for the preliminary hearing on *People* versus *Victoria Trujillo*. The complaint alleges second-degree murder. Mr. Rios, were you able to attend to your sick child?"

"Yes, Your Honor, and thank you for putting the prelim over from this morning."

The judge smiled. "You should thank Mr. Pearsall, too. He graciously agreed to keep his witnesses on call until you made it in."

The young D.A. sat at his end of counsel table scrawling notes as furiously as if he were taking an exam.

"Thank you, counsel," I said. "That was decent of you."

He looked up, nodded. "No problemo."

"Is your son all right, Mr. Rios?" the judge asked.

"He'll be fine. He's actually Mrs. Trujillo's son. My grand-nephew."

Judge LaVille looked back and forth between us. "I see. Well, I'm glad it's nothing serious. Mr. Pearsall, are you ready to call your first witness?"

Pearsall gulped. "Yes, Your Honor. The People call Officer Korngold."

The purpose of the preliminary hearing was to compel the prosecution to demonstrate to a judge that it had sufficient evidence to bring the defendant to trial on the charge alleged in the complaint. For the defense, it served to disclose the strength of the prosecution's case and provided an opportunity to develop impeachment material for trial by getting prosecution witnesses to commit to details they would not possibly remember months later when they testified at trial. Thus the prosecution's objective was to put on as narrow a case as possible, while the goal of the defense was to get away with as much as it could. My plan in this prelim was a little different. I wanted to show the newbie prosecutor how easily his case could be dismantled, so as to deal him down to a lesser charge. I gave a pass to Officer Korngold, who was the first uniformed officer on the scene, and saved my fire for the homicide investigator, a slit-eyed, gray-haired veteran named Fitzgerald. Fitzgerald knew the game, and on direct gave a dry recital of only enough facts to make out the charge. Then it was my turn.

"Detective Fitzgerald," I began, "did you recover the murder weapon?"

"No, not personally," he said.

"As far as you know, did anyone recover the murder weapon?"

"No, not as far as I know."

"Did you look for it?"

"Yes, we canvassed the area."

"Extensively?"

Pearsall was on his feet. "Objection, calls for speculation."

A good objection, had we been in a law school evidence class. But prelims tended to be pretty casual.

"Overruled," said Judge LaVille. "I think the officer knows the difference between an extensive search and a perfunctory one. Right, detective?"

He took the hint. "We conducted an extensive search of the room and the perimeter."

"The perimeter. That means you looked outside?"

"Yeah."

"And you were not able to find the weapon?"

"Your client was able to dispose of it."

"She was? Detective, isn't it true that my client had been so badly beaten by the victim that she was taken from the scene in an ambulance?"

"That's right," he said warily.

"You saw her as she was being taken away, didn't you?"

"Yes." He definitely suspected a trap.

"Was she upset? Crying? Disoriented?"

"Objection, compound question," Pearsall said.

"You're right, counsel," the judge said, "but in the interests of time, let's hear the answer."

"Yeah, she was upset and she was crying," he said. "I don't know about disoriented. I couldn't read her mind."

"Now, detective, you heard Officer Korngold testify that he was at the Hollywood Inn within five minutes of the shots-fired call."

"Yes."

"So, let me see if I understand this. In the five minutes between the shooting and Korngold's arrival, my client, beaten, upset and crying, had the presence of mind to hide the weapon so well that LAPD's finest was unable to recover it. Is that your testimony?"

"No," Judge LaVille said, "that's your testimony, Mr. Rios. You want to rephrase or have you made your point?"

"I'll move on," I said.

I had to be careful in making this argument because, of course, if Vicky had had the presence of mind to successfully hide the weapon, she would look pretty cold-blooded to a jury.

"Detective, isn't it also true that my client's hands were not tested for gunpowder residue?"

"She was injured. We had to get her to a hospital."

"And no one thought to bag her hands?"

"No," he said. "It wasn't a priority."

"So there's no physical evidence that she fired the shots that killed the victim, is there?"

"She admitted it," he said.

"I'm talking about physical evidence."

He shrugged. "She was the only person in the room. It looked like he had attacked her."

"Let me try again, detective. Isn't it true that there is absolutely no physical evidence that she fired the shot that killed him?'"

Fitzgerald stared at the young D.A., commanding him telepathically to object, but Pearsall shrugged.

"No," Fitzgerald said. "But the only explanation is he came after her and she shot him."

"Sounds like self-defense to me."

"Not when you shoot someone in the back," he replied smugly.

"Didn't you dig a twenty-two-caliber bullet out of the wall on the opposite side of the room from where the victim was standing when he was shot?"

"That was an old bullet."

"An old bullet? And what test did you perform that determined the age of that bullet?"

"The victim was killed with a three-eighty semiautomatic."

"That doesn't answer my question. How did you decide the twenty-two was an old bullet?"

"Your Honor," Pearsall said, "this is, like, way beyond my direct."

She grinned at him. "Is that, like, an objection? If so, it's overruled. Answer the question, detective. How did you determine the age of the twenty-two-caliber bullet?"

"It was an assumption," he said, with heavy sarcasm. "Based on the fact that the holes in the victim were made by a three-eighty."

"But, detective," I said reasonably, "for all you know, the victim could've fired that twenty-two-caliber bullet at my client that very night and then she fired back at him in self-defense."

"We didn't find a twenty-two-caliber weapon," he said.

"You didn't find the three-eighty, either," I reminded him. "But I'm a sport. I'll spot you the three-eighty if you'll give me my twenty-two."

He lolled his head toward the D.A. with a look of disgust. This time the kid responded. "Objection. Argumentative."

"Yes, Mr. Rios," the judge said. "That one I would save for the jury."

"Detective Fitzgerald, isn't it possible the victim's back was turned to my client because he was reaching for his gun?"

"Calls for speculation," Pearsall said.

Judge LaVille shook her head. "I think it'll pass as a hypothetical. Objection overruled. You may answer, detective."

Fitzgerald cast a contemptuous look at the young D.A. "I don't know. I couldn't say."

"Couldn't say if it was possible?"

"Anything's possible," he replied.

"Yes," I said, "but isn't it specifically possible based on the physical evidence that there were two guns in the room that night?"

He was cornered and knew it. "Sure," he said.

"Thank you," I said. "No further questions."

"Any other witnesses, Mr. Pearsall?" the judge asked.

"No, Your Honor. People submit."

"Mr. Rios."

"Defense submits."

The judge leaned her cheek against her fist. "Well, based on the People's case, I have to find there's sufficient evidence to bind the defendant over for trial but I also have to tell you, Mr. Pearsall, I wouldn't want to be in your shoes. You have the weakest of circumstantial cases of second-degree murder. I mean, the only real evidence that the defendant even shot the victim is her statement." She looked at me. "By the way, counsel, why aren't you challenging the statement?"

"Because I'm still waiting for the prosecution to provide me with either a tape or a transcript of it, as they were ordered to do last week by Judge Kline."

"I have the tape for you," Pearsall said in a subdued voice. "Your Honor, off the record for a minute."

"Actually, we're almost done," she said. "The defendant is bound over for trial to Judge Ryan in department forty-seven down at the CCB. Trial setting conference in two weeks, gentlemen? Good. Two weeks it is. We're adjourned."

Pearsall said, "Can I talk to you, Mr. Rios?"

I told Vicky, "Sit tight for a minute. I'll be right back."

I went over to Pearsall's table. He handed me a letter-sized envelope. "There's a tape and a transcript. Listen, you want to talk about a plea bargain? I can offer voluntary manslaughter."

"I'm not making any deals until I review her statement."

His tongue flicked the corner of his mouth nervously. "You wanna talk tomorrow?"

I tapped the envelope. "This must really be bad."

"Say after lunch? I'll be in my office."

"All right," I said. "And listen, thanks again for agreeing to put the prelim over."

"That's cool," he said, gathering up his papers. "I got a kid myself."

I went back to Vicky. "He wants to make a deal," I said.

"You were great," she said. "You made that police officer look like a fool."

"My specialty."

"I hope Angel becomes a lawyer or something."

"He has the brains for it. I need to get back to Angel and relieve Mrs. Kwan."

"Tell her I told her thank you for taking care of him."

"Call me when you get back to the jail. I'll put him on the phone."

Impulsively, she hugged me. "Thank you, Uncle Henry."

I held her tight. "We'll get through this. I promise."

When I got home, Mrs. Kwan, my next door neighbor, reported that Angel's fever had broken and he was asleep.

"He'll be fine by tomorrow," she said.

Just in time for his father's funeral, I thought.

Later, after I had listened to the tape of Vicky's statement and read the transcript, I realized that the reason Pearsall had been so anxious to deal wasn't my stellar performance at the prelim, but what Vicky had said to the cops who interrogated her. In her confusion and pain, she had managed to remember to say the magic words—I want my lawyer.

16.

PETE TRUJILLO'S FUNERAL WAS SCHEDULED FOR 10 A.M. at a cemetery in Garden Grove. With Angel still pale from sickness sitting silently beside me, I followed the directions that Socorro Cerda had given me through residential neighborhoods and past a warehouse district until, behind a low brick wall, a flat expanse of grass appeared. Withering bouquets of flowers and motionless pinwheels marked the rows of gravestones. A funereal border of Italian cypresses lined the drive that led to the mortuary chapel. I pulled into a parking space and cut the ignition.

"How are you feeling, Angel?"

He shrugged. "Okay."

"I didn't go to my father's funeral," I said.

"Were you sad when he died?"

"No. I didn't get along with my dad."

After a moment, he said in a tone of final assessment, "My dad was okay when he wasn't high."

I waited for more, but that was all Angel had to say about his father. It occurred to me that the real tragedy here was not Pete's death but how faint an impression he had made on his son: summarized with a single sentence. I felt a surge of tenderness for my nephew that had me smoothing his hair and straightening the knot in his tie parentally. He submitted to my fussing without complaint.

"Ready?" I asked.

He turned himself into the little soldier. "Yeah."

It was a hot, clear day, but the interior of the mortuary was chilly and gloomy in the particular horror-movie manner of such places. Heavy stained-glass windows depicting nondenominational scenes of doves and lambs filled the corridor with dense amber light, and the still air smelled cloyingly of rose incense. Outside the Chapel of Eternal Life, where Pete's service was to be held, a handful of mourners waited. Some of them appeared to recognize Angel, though no one spoke to him. I grabbed the iron handle of the door and pulled.

"It's locked," a white haired man said to me.

I glanced at my watch; it was ten. "You're here for Pete?"

He nodded. "I'm Gabe, his uncle by marriage."

"Socorro's husband?"

"The other sister. Mary. They been in there for a while now."

"Is there a problem?"

"Beats me," he said.

I knocked, not loudly, though in that hushed atmosphere it sounded as if I'd shot off a gun. After a moment, the door was cracked open and I saw Socorro Cerda's fretful face.

"We're not ready yet," she whispered, then saw me. "Henry. Can you come in here?" Then she saw Angel. "*M'ijo*, I need to talk to your uncle for a minute. Wait out here, okay?"

Gabe said, "Something going on in there?"

"No, everything's fine," she said, opening the door just wide enough for me to slip in.

The first things I noticed were the overturned baskets of flowers and then the casket. It was metal, gunpowder gray with brass fittings, and half-opened to reveal that the face and torso of the young man lying within it had been spray-painted red and the casket itself was covered with gang *placas*. A pudgy, white-haired man in a black suit, obviously the funeral director, was standing next to the casket, whispering fiercely to a dumpling of a woman who I guessed was Socorro's sister, Mary.

"What happened?" I asked Socorro.

She gestured toward the man at the front of the room. "Mr. Sola said he found Pete this way when he came in this morning. He told us we have to take Pete someplace else. Mr. Sola, this is Mr. Rios. He's our lawyer."

I tried not to look surprised.

Sola gave me a frightened look and dug a snowy handkerchief out of his breast pocket. This room was even chillier than the corridor, but he was dripping sweat.

"Listen, I don't want any trouble," he said, "but what if they come back and disrupt the service? I've seen it happen before and these people have guns."

"What people?"

"The gangs," he said. "That's who did this." He looked angrily at Socorro. "You didn't tell me he was in a gang."

Mary spoke up. "He quit the gang."

I inspected the casket. Along with the usual serpentine and illegible gang graffiti was a crudely drawn rat. As if this might be too subtle, the word that had been spray-painted across Pete Trujillo's body was *ratón*. There was a red "r" across the still, handsome face. Pete had been light-skinned and fair-haired—a *huero*, as such kids were called in my neighborhood. He looked nothing like his son.

As I was making these irrelevant observations, Mary came up to me and said worriedly, "What should we do?"

I turned. All three of them were watching me with various degrees of respect, fear and deference.

"Mr. Sola's right. Whoever did this may come back, so it's a good idea to bury Pete as quickly as possible," I said. "Close the casket, cover it with something and have a brief service at the grave site. Okay, Mr. Sola?"

"Just hurry," he said.

"Animals," Mary spat. "Why would they do this?"

I looked at the rat. "He obviously made someone very angry." I looked at Socorro Cerda, who had remained silent. "Do you know anything about this, Mrs. Cerda?"

She bit her lip and shook her head. She was no better at lying than her mother, but this was scarcely the time or place to interrogate her.

Pete Trujillo went into the ground beneath a canvas tarp as a priest mumbled platitudes to the small, nervous crowd gathered around the grave. Angel stood beside me with martial stolidity until the casket was lowered, and then he began to tremble. I reached for his head, and he threw his arm around my waist and clung to me as if he feared he would fall into the hole with his father. As the mourners turned away, a big, souped-up car painted metallic red screeched into the cemetery and pulled up at the curb a few feet from where we were standing. The car's tinted windows rolled down and ear-splitting rap music flooded the hot, still air. Suddenly, an empty tequila bottle was hurled from the car toward the grave.

"Wait here," I told Angel. I searched for Mrs. Cerda, tossed her my cell phone and said, "Call nine-one-one, now."

I approached the car. A man's face appeared at the window. He was fleshy, goateed, wearing black sunglasses and a black fedora. He had on the usual plaid shirt opened to reveal an athletic T-shirt: gang uniform. His chest and neck were covered with tattoos in the same script as the messages on Pete Trujillo's casket.

"There's a funeral going on here," I said. "You might show some respect."

"Who the fuck are you?"

"The police have been called. You should leave," I replied.

He lowered his sunglasses. His eyes were copper-colored and beautiful. "What's your name, *pendejo*."

"Rios."

"Turn off the fucking music," he said to the driver. The music stopped. He looked at me. "I just came to pay my respects to my cuz."

"Pete Trujillo was your cousin? You must be Butch."

He smiled. "Hey, the *pendejo* knows me. I'm famous all over town." He peered past me. "Is that little Angelito I see?" He shouted. "Angel! Come here, *hijo*. It's your *Tio* Butch."

"Let's leave Angel out of this," I said.

"Who *are* you, man? For real."

"I'm his real uncle and his mother's lawyer."

"Vicky? Yeah, I heard she smoked ole Pete. I didn't know the *puta* had it in her."

"You the guys who vandalized Pete's coffin?"

He looked at me disbelievingly. "What? Someone vandalized Pete's coffin?" Then, in a perfect imitation of Claude Rains in *Casablanca*, he said, "I'm shocked. Shocked, I tell you." He giggled. "Man I just come to pay my respects to my *primo*."

I spat on the ground. "That's what you can do with your respects. Get out of here."

The light seemed to go out of his eyes as his hand went to his waistband, parting his shirt to reveal the barrel of a semiautomatic.

"I'll leave when I'm ready, *puto*."

"You look like a guy with at least two strikes—you really want to go for a third?"

I took a step back from the car, ready to hit the ground, but in the distance came the sound of an approaching siren.

"Fuck," he said. "Drive." He looked at me. "You're lucky, asshole. Ask Vicky."

The car pulled a U-turn on the grass over grave markers and sped out of the cemetery. When the police arrived a few minutes later, Angel, Socorro Cerda and I were the only ones left. We walked her to her car and I asked her how Jesusita was.

"The same," she said. "Thank you for talking to Mr. Sola."

I opened the door for her, and after she got in, leaned into the window so that Angel couldn't hear and said, "Why did Butch vandalize Pete's coffin?"

"I don't know what you mean," she said. She looked terrified. "I'm sorry."

I let her go.

Kim Pearsall's office was about the size of a holding cell and almost as bleak. The windowless gray walls were bare except for the picture hooks left by the last tenant. His desk—the usual battered government issue—was covered with case files. The bookshelf behind him held paperback editions of various legal codes. Atop the bookshelf was a framed picture of a lovely young woman standing on a balcony with the Eiffel Tower in the background. The only other personal item in the room was his screen saver, which showed a little boy splashing in the surf.

"Your son?" I asked, facing him across his desk.

He glanced at his monitor. "Yeah. Derek."

"How old is he?"

"He's three. Quite the little dude."

Pearsall appeared even younger than in court. His suit coat was draped over the back of his chair, and beneath his baggy shirt were the lines of an athletic young body. His fair hair was ragged around the edges and looked soft as cornsilk. He had the clear skin and straight white teeth of a rich boy. I couldn't imagine why he was working here instead of some Westside mega-firm.

"You been out of law school, what, a year or two?"

He frowned. "Come on, dude, don't try to play head games with me."

"No, I'm curious. I could see you at a firm, not working for the D.A."

He shrugged. "I want to do environmental law. The office has got one of the best environmental enforcement units in the country."

"So they put you out here to clean up the streets of Hollywood."

"I've got to pay my dues," he said. "Put in my time."

"How are you liking it?"

He grinned. "It's a trip. So, you want to talk about a deal?"

"I want to talk about my client's statement to the police," I said. "Had you listened to the tape before the prelim?"

He gulped. "Like, minutes before."

"I'm not accusing you of anything," I said. "But you do realize that you're screwed? She asked for her lawyer and they continued to question her anyway. Clear *Miranda* violation."

"Come on, Mr. Rios—"

"Henry," I said.

"Henry, she asked for her uncle."

"That would be me. Asking for her uncle in this case was the same as invoking her right to counsel."

"How were the cops supposed to know you were a lawyer?"

"Kim, she told them," I said.

"After she copped to shooting her husband."

"They didn't give her a chance to explain before then," I said. "You listened to the tape. They scarcely gave her a chance to catch her breath. That's coercion."

"I got an argument," he said. "That's all I'm saying."

Rich boy or not, he had behaved decently when I needed to continue the prelim to take care of Angel, so I leveled with him.

"I know. You've got a pretty good argument. The cops wouldn't have known that, when she asked for her uncle, she was asking for her lawyer until she was finally able to make the connection. At that point, however, the cops were required to discontinue questioning, and they didn't. That in itself might piss off a judge enough to throw out the entire statement."

He nodded. "Depends on the judge."

"We drew Pat Ryan," I said. "She's extremely intelligent and she bends over backward to be fair, but when she has a little wiggle room, she usually gives the benefit of the doubt to the defense. I figure I've got at least a fifty-fifty chance with her of getting the statement suppressed, which leaves you with nothing. You don't have to take my word about her. Ask around in your office."

"I already did," he said. "I know her rep. Even if she suppressed the confession, I can still use it to impeach your client when she testifies."

"Why would I even put her on?"

"I listened to you at the prelim. You have to put her on to prove self-defense."

"I don't have to prove anything, Kim. You're the one who has to connect her to the shooting. Without her confession, all you've got is my client in the room with a dead body."

"One, the dead body is her husband; two, she's been beaten up; and, three, the cops get there within five minutes of the shooting," he said. "That's solid circumstantial evidence that she did him."

"Maybe in Bolivia. It's not going to impress a jury in downtown Los Angeles. Plus, Fitzgerald is an asshole of the old school. There will be black and brown jurors. All I need to do is breathe the word 'Ramparts' while he's on the stand and I'll hang the jury."

"Ramparts isn't relevant."

"Not legally relevant, but I'll get it in, Kim, I promise. Look, this is my family and I'll fight as dirty as I have to."

My intensity seemed to take him aback. "What are you looking for?"

"She pleads to involuntary manslaughter and does the minimum. Two years."

"No way, dude," he said. "She can plead to voluntary and do the midterm."

"Six years? Forget it. She pleads to voluntary and does the low term. Three years."

"She pleads to voluntary, we agree to a midterm cap and submit to the judge whether to give her the low term," he said. "That's my final offer."

The words rolled off his tongue so smoothly I knew he had rehearsed it, like a used car salesman practicing his pitch. Still, it was a very fair offer. Six years max with a possibility of no more than three. If there was any judge in the system who might be persuaded to sentence on the low end in this case, it was Judge Ryan. With a three-year sentence, Vicky would be out in eighteen months. The alternative was to press on, litigate the suppression issue and go to trial. Fifty-fifty were good odds, but this was one case I really did not want to lose, and even though I had belittled Pearsall's evidence, if he got past the suppression motion, he could get a second-degree conviction and Vicky would be looking at a minimum of twenty years. A potential twenty years versus a possible eighteen months. This was a no-brainer.

"I'll want a full-scale sentencing hearing," I said.

"Yeah, sure. We'll take the plea and send her out for a presentence report."

"I want you to stipulate that the confession was illegally obtained."

He opened his mouth in dismay. "What? Why?"

"It'll make it easier for the judge to justify sentencing Vicky to the low term if the cops were dirty."

"You want me to stipulate that the cops violated her constitutional rights?"

"This is the LAPD we're talking about, Kim. It would be shocking if they hadn't violated her rights."

He swiveled back in his chair and pretended to mull it over, but as he had already given away the store, throwing in the key to the front door would hardly make any difference. "I'll only stipulate for sentencing."

"That's all I'm asking for." I stood up. "We can advance the case to the end of the week to take the plea. I'll take care of that."

"Thanks," he said. He extended his hand.

"I want to apologize about losing it with you in arraignment court," I said, sealing the deal with a handshake.

He shrugged. "It's like you said, it's family. I don't take it personally. Hell, I'd do the same."

From the courthouse I went to the jail, where I met with Vicky to explain the deal I had worked out for her. When I asked to see her, the desk officer informed me that she had a visitor.

"This is important," I said, wondering who her visitor could be. "I'm her attorney."

"Wait here," he said. He went back to the jail. A couple of minutes later, he returned with Reverend Ortega. "She's only allowed one visitor at a time. You two work it out."

"Señor Rios," Ortega said, reaching out his hand.

"Reverend," I replied. "I'm sorry to interrupt your visit with my niece, but I have to discuss her case with her."

He nodded. "Of course. I will come back tonight."

"You visit her often?"

"Every day," he said. "She is one of my—" he seemed to be translating in his head from Spanish to English. "*¿Como se dice 'manada'?*"

"Sorry, I don't really speak Spanish."

"Baaah," he said, screwing up his face. "Baah."

"Sheep? Flock?"

"*Sí sí.* Flock." He smiled. "*¿No hablas español?*"

"Not much, I understand some."

The sheep imitation was pretty cute, and it occurred to me he might also have a homey appeal to Judge Ryan at Vicky's sentencing hearing, as long as his Christianity wasn't of the fire-and-brimstone persuasion.

"Reverend Ortega, I'd like to talk to you about maybe coming to court for Vicky as a character witness. You understand?"

"Yes, I have testified before," he said. He smiled. "You come to my church on Sunday with Angelito, and after the service, we talk. Ten o'clock. Okay?"

He had me trapped, so I agreed.

Although she tried not to show it, I sensed that Vicky was disappointed to exchange Reverend Ortega's company for mine. The moment of ease we had shared at the prelim seemed to have dissipated, so I got down to business and explained the deal.

"I don't understand. How much time in prison?" she asked when I finished.

"No more than six years, maybe as little as three," I said, "but with the time you've already spent in jail and with good behavior credits, it would be more like four years at the most, maybe as little as a year and a half. I know the judge we're going to be in front of. She'll be sympathetic to your story. I think I could persuade her to be lenient."

"Four years," she said softly.

Her face had healed and she looked very young. I remembered she was not yet thirty, and four years, if it came to that, would be a long stretch.

"You don't have to take the deal," I said. "We can go to trial. We might do a little better."

"I'll take the deal," she said.

"You're sure?"

"You won't let Angel forget me?"

"Of course not."

"Then I'll take the deal. What happens now?"

"We'll go back to court on Friday and you'll plead guilty, and then in a week or so we'll have a sentencing hearing. You'll testify about how Pete abused you. I'm going to ask Reverend Ortega to testify, and probably some other people, to show the judge that you acted to protect yourself and Angel. Then she'll sentence you and you'll start your time."

"Where?"

"That will depend on the Department of Corrections, but probably at the women's prison over in Riverside County. It's a couple of hours from here. I could bring Angel to see you a couple of times a week"

Her eyes welled up.

"Are you sure you want to plead?"

"I'm sure," she whispered.

I had planned to tell her about Pete's funeral and my encounter with Cousin Butch, but this did not seem to be the moment. I reached across the table and held her hand, hoping to console her but conscious, as I always was with her, that I was not what she wanted.

"All rise. Department forty-seven is now in session, the Honorable Patricia Ryan presiding."

Patricia Ryan was a tall, beautiful woman about whom many stories were told, some of them true. Allegedly, a successful producer of TV legal dramas had met her at a dinner party and become so smitten that he offered to build an entire series around her. She was occasionally approached for her autograph by tourists under the impression that she was Diahann Carroll or Diana Ross. She didn't really look like either entertainer, but she naturally radiated the kind of glamour that Hollywood spent millions to create. She was also one of the fairest and brightest judges on the bench, the only one whom I could have imagined on the U.S. Supreme Court. In her mid-fifties, she was still young enough for that to be a possibility, and just that morning the legal newspaper had carried the announcement of her nomination to the Ninth Circuit.

"Good morning," she said brightly. "Please be seated. Hello, Mr. Rios, it's been awhile. Good to see you."

"You, too, Your Honor. Congratulations on your nomination to the Court of Appeal."

She made a wry face. "Thanks, but at the rate the Senate is confirming the president's nominations, this may turn out to be a posthumous appointment." She glanced down at her file. "We're here for trial setting on *People* versus *Trujillo*." She looked at Vicky. "Good morning, Mrs. Trujillo."

"Good morning, Your Honor," Vicky said, awestruck. "Thank you."

The judge smiled. "For what?"

"Seeing me," my niece said.

It was exactly the right thing to say. The judge nodded. "People can get lost in the system, but not in my court. I understand from my clerk that you've worked out a plea on this case. Is that right, Mr. Pearsall?"

The young D.A. was on his feet so fast, I thought he was going to kneel. Judge Ryan had that effect on men. "Yes, ma'am."

"Gentlemen, all I know about this case is the charge, which is a serious one. May I read the police report?"

"Yes, Your Honor," I said. "After you do, may I add a couple of details that don't appear?"

"Of course," she said.

For a few minutes, the court was silent while the judge read the police reports. I glanced over my shoulder to the gallery at Elena and Angel and smiled what I hoped was a confident smile.

"Mr. Rios," Judge Ryan said, "what did you want to add?"

"Your Honor, I'm not only the defendant's lawyer, I'm also her uncle. My sister, her mother, is in the court, as is her son, my grand-nephew. I know from past experience here that you are a judge who always thinks of the human consequences of her decisions. As it happens, in this case those consequences hit pretty close to home. The People have agreed that in exchange for my niece's plea to voluntary manslaughter, we will submit to you on sentencing. I would request that the case be put over after the plea for a sentencing hearing to give you the fullest picture possible of this family tragedy."

"Mr. Pearsall, is this the agreement?"

"Yes, Your Honor," he said.

"Your Honor," I said, "I also want to mention that the People have agreed, for purposes of sentencing only, to stipulate that my client's statement to the police was taken in violation of *Miranda*."

She raised her eyebrow. "Is that true, Mr. Pearsall?"

"For sentencing only," he said.

"Well, this is an unusual case. The victim was Mrs. Trujillo's husband?"

"Yes, Your Honor."

"Are any of his family here, Mr. Rios?"

"No, Your Honor, but I hope to have one of his sisters here at the sentencing hearing to testify on my niece's behalf."

Judge Ryan nodded. "Yes, I'd like to hear her. Well, I guess all we're going to do this morning is take the plea. Mr. Pearsall, will you do the honors, please?"

"Yes. Mrs. Trujillo, would you please stand up?"

Vicky and I stood up, and Pearsall began the familiar sequence of questions with which she waived her constitutional rights.

"Mrs. Trujillo," he said, after she waived her rights, "on the charge of the voluntary manslaughter of Peter Trujillo, how do you plead?"

She seemed to hold back a sob. "Guilty," she whispered.

Pearsall turned to me. "Does counsel join the waivers and the plea?"

"Join," I said, committing my niece to prison.

"The People move to dismiss count one, second-degree murder," Pearsall said to the judge.

"Count one is dismissed," Judge Ryan said. "The defendant's plea to voluntary manslaughter is entered into the minutes of the court. How much time for the sentencing hearing, Mr. Rios?"

"I only need a week, Your Honor."

"You have it," she said.

I heard my sister quietly weeping.

"Mr. Rios," the judge said, "I'm going to give your family a few minutes together before I remand the defendant."

"Thank you, Judge."

Vicky turned to the gallery and said, "Angel? Mama?"

Her voice catching, Judge Ryan said, "We're in recess."

Late that night, after we had put Angel to bed, Elena and I sat on my deck, where she polished off the last of Josh's Scotch. The night was warm and the blaze of city lights made a red glow in the sky as if from a gigantic furnace.

"I think that's the first time she ever called me Mama," Elena said, rattling the ice in her glass. "What will you do at this sentencing hearing, Henry?"

"Try to persuade the judge to give Vicky the least time possible."

"The judge seems persuadable, " she said. "Do you want me to testify?"

"It would really help if you could track down someone from the women's shelter she was staying at in San Francisco before she came to you."

She nodded. "Yes, I have it written down somewhere. Who else will testify?"

"Vicky, of course—"

"What about her privilege against self-incrimination?"

"She waived that right when she pled. Judge Ryan will want to hear her story. She's really the only one who can tell it. What I need is to support it. I'll call Socorro Cerda, Reverend Ortega, maybe Edith Rosen. I've also got a call in to Pete's last lawyer in San Francisco, see if I can get any useful information from her to rough him up a little."

"What do you mean?"

"Sometimes you really do have to blame the victim. This is one of those times."

"Henry, remember, Angel will be there. Whatever you say about his father will remain with him for the rest of his life."

I hadn't thought about that. "You're right," I admitted. "I'll be careful."

"It's odd," she said. "I don't really have much of an impression of Pete. There must have been some good in him. She did keep going back to him."

"Aren't you the one who said it was because she dreamed of creating the family she didn't have for herself?"

She sipped her drink. "Ironically, she has created a family. The four of us. Joanne. I suppose this is what they call a nontraditional family."

"What other kind of family could you create out of material like us?"

She looked at me. "And John DeLeon? Will he be part of it?"

"That remains to be seen," I replied. "He's up at a monastery in Santa Barbarba with his dad, on a retreat. He said he'd pray for us. For him and me, I mean."

"You sound skeptical."

"I don't think God concerns Himself with the details of my love life."

After a moment, she said, "What do you think God is but the opportunity to love other people? If God's not interested in those details, then God doesn't exist."

"That doesn't sound like the God I grew up with."

She smiled. "Then maybe you need a new God."

17.

ELENA HAD FOUND A COUPLE OF SCHOOLS SHE THOUGHT might be suitable for Angel, and the next morning they went for a preliminary look while I worked. Half-a-dozen calls to friends in San Francisco yielded the name of Pete Trujillo's public defender, Morgan Yee. I reached her voice mail and left a message. Then I phoned Edith Rosen to ask her to be my expert witness on battered women's syndrome at the sentencing hearing. I wanted Edith because ordinarily she testified as the court's expert and commanded more respect than the usual hired guns who made up the expert witness circuit and would say basically what they were paid to say. BWS was a little out of her field of expertise, but I doubted that the D.A. would challenge her qualifications.

"You remember I had my doubts about whether Vicky was battered," she said.

"She killed her husband after he beat her up," I said. "Doesn't that change your opinion?"

"I'd have to know all the facts," she said. "This isn't exactly my area. There are more qualified experts."

"I want you," I said. "Judge Ryan trusts you and you already know Vicky. Will you at least read the police reports before you make up your mind? I can fax them to you now and you could let me know on Monday."

"All right" she said. "I can do that. How is everyone bearing up?"

"We've decided Angel will live with me while his mother's in prison."

"How do you feel about that?"

"Are you asking me as a friend or a therapist?"

She chuckled. "Both."

"I'm anxious and excited," I said. "I want to do right by him, but I'm not entirely sure I know how."

"You can't know that in advance," she observed. "Raising a kid is the ultimate exercise in trial and error." She paused. "The issue I see with Angel is that you're coming into his life pretty late."

"I know," I said. "I also know that he's had the kind of childhood I usually read about in probation reports, but you're the one who said he was invulnerable."

"Surviving trauma doesn't mean you're not affected by it," she said.

"You have any idea what I can expect?"

"There are effects of trauma that don't become apparent until the traumatizing experience is over. I know you'll give him a stable and loving home, but don't be surprised if he responds by acting out."

"Acting out how?"

"That's the question," she said. "One of my kids is in a really good foster home, with fine, experienced foster parents. They discovered she was hoarding food in her room. I'm not talking about candy bars, I mean a pound of lunchmeat, an entire loaf of bread, cans of soup. Her mother was a crackhead and used to leave the girl alone for two or three days at a time without any food. Now that she has access to it, she stockpiles it. Whatever Angel didn't get, he'll be greedy for."

"I don't think Vicky ever did anything like that to him."

"I agree," Edith said. "From what I saw, she was very loving, but I wouldn't say she was exactly parental. In a way, she and Angel seemed more like siblings than mother and son."

Or more like conspirators, I thought, remembering the day I had watched them through the mirror at the jail.

"You're not being very reassuring," I said.

She laughed. "Not to worry. He is a very bright and resilient boy. If you want, I'd be happy to work with him."

"I would be grateful."

"All right," she said. "You fax me the police reports on Vicky and we'll talk again on Monday. By the way, Henry, how is your health?"

"I see the doc next week, but I feel almost my old self."

"You seemed to improve dramatically after Vicky and Angel came into your life," she observed.

"Don't you start giving me the family values lecture, too," I said. "I get enough of that from my sister and John."

"All right, dear," she said. "Sometime we'll talk about denial. Good-bye."

The doorbell buzzed. I went down the hall to the front door and looked out the peephole. A white-haired, slightly stooped old man stared back. He was wearing a flannel shirt and gray work pants, but even if the clothes hadn't tipped me off, I would have known who he was from his slanting green eyes. I opened the door.

"Hello," I said.

"Mr. Rios? I'm Armando DeLeon, John's dad."

His voice was deep but surprisingly soft, with a rich timbre I associated with singers and public radio anchors. He spoke English with the rolled "r" and Spanish intonation of a first-generation immigrant.

"Is John all right?"

"Yes," he said. "He told me about you. I wanted to meet you."

"Please come in."

I took him to my office, thinking that the somber room would level the disadvantage I felt with this handsome old man. He did not appear to be angry, but I felt the tension creeping up my spine into my shoulders. Why was he here? Had John sent him? Or had he come on his own to plead the case for his son's heterosexuality? He stood for a moment, looking at my degrees, the bookshelves crammed with case reports and treatises and the piles of transcripts.

"Johnny said you were a lawyer. Criminal lawyer, yes?"

"That's right. Have a seat, Mr. DeLeon. Can I get you some coffee?"

"No, *gracias*," he said, lowering himself slowly to the sofa. "I came to talk."

John had said his father was in his seventies; now I saw they were a workingman's seventies, hard years that had left a worn-out body. He settled into the couch with a grimace.

"Did John send you?"

"John's not like that," he replied. "He says what he has to say himself."

I sat down at the opposite end of the couch and decided to get this over with. "I bet he got that from you."

I thought that, for an instant, I detected a twinkle in his eyes, but his expression remained somber.

"John says he's in love with you," he said, without any kind of emphasis.

"John's old enough to know what he feels and for whom," I said, sounding tongue-twistingly lawyerly even to myself. "I love John, too. I'm sorry if that causes problems, but really this is between him and me."

It was a challenge and I expected some heat in return, but in his mild, rich voice, he said, "Johnny's my youngest. Thank God, because if he had come first, no more kids for me. When he was a baby, he almost died. The whooping cough, they called it. When he was five, he ran out into the street to catch a baseball and a car hit him." He touched a spot on his forehead above his right eye. "You can still see the scar. Playing baseball, he was always breaking something until he finally had to quit. That broke his heart. He went wild. His mother suffered. I wasn't proud of him. Then he got married, had kids, stopped drinking. His mother thought he had straightened himself out. Next thing, he leaves his wife for a man." He shook his head. "His mother begged him to go to a priest for— what's is the word? *Para tirar el diablo.*"

"Exorcism?"

He nodded. "Me, I knew."

"You knew? What?"

"I knew what my son was. I knew when he was a boy."

"He likes women, too." I would have to tell John how I defended his bisexuality to his father.

"Con respecto, señor, usted no es mujer."

John was right, in Spanish his father was not a tired old man but a formidable patriarch.

"No," I agreed. "I'm not a woman. How did you know about John?"

Mr. DeLeon shrugged. "My brother was like John." He looked at me. "My father found him with another boy. My brother hanged himself. I cut his body down. My brother was a good boy, like Johnny. A good boy. I don't understand why he is *un homosexual*, and if I could make him different, I would. *Pero* what happened to my brother will never happen to my son. God gives us children to love, not to hurt."

"Why are you telling me this, Mr. DeLeon?"

"I don't want John to stay away from his family because he doesn't think you will be welcome. In my house, you will always be treated with respect."

We looked at each other for a moment. He was sizing me up.

"Thank you," I said. "I will always be respectful in your house and with your family."

He nodded, then stood up with a grunt. "Damn arthritis. John doesn't have to know I came to see you."

"I won't tell him."

I walked him to the door where he stopped, turned and shook my hand. *"Pues, hasta luego, Rico."*

"Mr. DeLeon," I said. He hobbled to his car and drove away.

After he left, I scribbled a note for Elena and drove to John's house. His red truck was parked in the driveway.

"Henry? I thought I heard a car." He was standing at the railing, looking down. "I just tried to call you. How did you know I was back?"

"ESP. Can I come up?"

He started down the steps as I started up, and we met halfway. He was barefoot, wearing old khakis and a black tank top. Above his right eye was a faint scar. I had never noticed it before. He had a couple of days' growth of beard and his eyes were even sleepier than usual.

"I missed you," I said.

Something in my tone alarmed him. "Are you okay?"

"I missed you," I repeated and embraced him. I held the weight of his body against mine, felt the warmth of his skin and rasp of his breath against my neck, and I was suffused with the joy that comes when everything is as it should be. "I'm glad you're back."

He stroked my hair. "I want us to be together. That's what I was calling to tell you."

John said, "You sure you have to go?"

He was lying naked on the bed, his hands cupping his head on the pillows, watching me dress. I paused and studied him. I remembered some of the boys I'd slept with in my twenties and thirties, with their hard, perfect bodies, and while perfection has its attractions, it isn't really lovable. John had golden skin and big arms, but the muscles in his chest sagged a little and there were pockets of flab at his waist and a mesh of fine wrinkles above his eyelids, reminding me whenever I looked at him that among the reasons I loved him were that he spent his days in the sun, loved to eat and was halfway through life.

"You're looking at me like you're taking inventory," he said.

"You're beautiful."

"Don't embarrass me."

I sat at the edge of the bed. "I love your body."

"I love yours," he said. He chuckled. "Man, that's a hard thing to say to another guy."

"I know, but I had to tell you at least this once."

"You tell me every time you look at me," he said. He started to unbutton my shirt.

"I can't stay," I said, stopping him. "Elena will be expecting me. We have to make a decision about where to send Angel to school, and after dinner I have to drive her to the airport. Why don't you come and eat with us?"

"I have a better idea. Bring your sister and Angel back here and I'll make dinner."

"Really?"

He nodded. "Sure. Angel can hang out and watch a game with me while you take your sister to the airport, and then you can come back and we'll all camp out here tonight."

"Angel and me stay here?"

"He can sleep in my son's room."

"I don't know, John."

He frowned. "Henry, what are you trying to protect Angel from? He knows we sleep together. He knows we're boyfriends."

"I don't want him to think there's some kind of competition going on between you and him for my attention."

"In the first place, Angel and me are buddies," he said. "In the second place, I know when to back off." He studied my face. "You have to get over this, you know. If Angel thinks you're ashamed of who you are, he won't respect you."

"Believe me, John, I know that," I said. "I'm surprised I feel this way. I thought I'd worked out being gay a long time ago."

"It's one thing when you're on your own," he said. "It's another thing when you've got kids because you don't know how something's going to affect them and you want to protect them against anything that can hurt them." He touched my hand. "Seeing two people who love each other can't hurt him."

"You're right," I said. "This can't hurt him. When am I going to meet your kids, John?"

His face darkened for an instant. "My boy comes home from Spain in a couple of weeks and he'll be staying with me till school starts. We'll all go to a game or something. He'll be cool. With my daughter, it's gonna take awhile, Henry. Maybe a long while." He smiled. "We'll work it out. So, you coming back?"

"Yeah, but we'll have to leave early in the morning, because we're going to church."

"Church? When did that happen?"

I explained about Reverend Ortega.

"That's not until ten," he said. "I'll get you out of here by then. I have to go to church myself with my mom and dad."

Thinking of his dad, I said, "I'd like to go with you sometime."

"Really? That would be great. All right, take off, man, so I can figure out what to feed the Rios family."

"Can I bring anything?"

"Something chocolate for dessert."

Angel was already excited about staying over at John's house, but when he saw it, he could scarcely contain himself.

"It's like a treehouse," he exclaimed when we pulled up in the driveway.

John called down from the railing, "Hey, Angelito. Elena. Come on up."

Angel clambered up the stairs while Elena and I followed at a more sedate pace, finishing our conversation about the schools she had visited. The most promising was a boarding school in Pasadena that had a strong commitment to "multicultural diversity."

"Particularly," Elena observed, "if the multiculturally diverse can pay the fifteen-thousand-dollar-a-year tuition."

"That's more than Stanford charged me for law school," I said. "Of course, that was a hundred years ago."

"On the plus side" she said, "the school takes in a lot of scholarship students. Black kids from the inner city and quite a few Central American kids, and they're used to working with students like Angel who have some ground to make up. They also really want him."

"Yeah, I bet a mom in jail has a lot of cachet. What did he think?"

From above us, we heard Angel giggling at something John had said.

"He's going to struggle at any school he goes to for a while," she said. "At this place, there will be kids struggling along with him and some wonderful teachers. What did he think? He loved the fact that they have a baseball team."

"What's our next step?"

"The headmaster wants Angel to come in for aptitude testing to see where he is academically. They're starting a kind of academic summer camp in two weeks, which he highly recommends for Angel. Five thousand for six weeks."

"Holy moley."

She laughed. "Didn't you know? Kids are a money pit."

"Grandma, Uncle Henry," Angel called. "Hurry up and see John's house."

"Remember how hard Dad worked to support us?" she asked. "Think of this as paying him back."

La Iglesia de Cristo Triunfante was located in a storefront on a stretch of Beverly Boulevard known as Little Tegucigalpa because of all the Central American restaurants and travel agencies that had set up shop in the crumbling, ornate one- and two-story buildings that dated back to the 1930s, when it had been the heart of a prosperous Jewish neighborhood. The buildings were now painted blue and lime and pink, but they retained their original Art Deco zigzags and chevrons. The building the church occupied was not one of the older ones, but a featureless brick square, the windows of which had been painted white with the church's name written in blue across them. On the sidewalk, a squat, dark man with a broad, impassive Indian face pushed a cart with an ear of corn painted on it and cried out, *"Elote, elote."* An old woman in a black rebozo picked out kids' T-shirts imprinted with Bart Simpson's face from a bin in front of a store that sold everything from communion dresses to velvet tapestries of John and Robert Kennedy. Mariachi music blared out from a music store. A homeless man peed into the doorway of a shuttered bank. Outside the church, women in pastel dresses wearing veils over their heads greeted each other with kisses.

"This the place?" I asked Angel.

"Uh-huh." He looked at me. "What's wrong, Uncle Henry?"

I couldn't tell him that I was afraid I would turn into a pillar of salt as soon as we crossed the threshold of the church.

"Nothing, *m'ijo*. It's just that I haven't been to church for a long time."

"Is that because you're gay?" he asked me.

"Yes," I said. "Most churches don't like gay people very much."

My nephew's expression was sympathetic. "Don't worry, Uncle Henry. Reverend Ortega is really nice." He glanced at the church. The women were going inside. "We should go before they start."

I followed him into the church. The sky did not fall.

The service was in Spanish. I struggled to follow along, then gave up and looked around the small room. The air was hot and close and reeked of perfume, hair oil, flowers and bodies from the hundred or so people crammed into folding chairs. Only the ceiling fans kept it from being really unbearable. There were more women than men, though not by much, and everyone was dressed in their Sunday best: Easter-egg colors for the women, for the men dark trousers, white shirts. There was a sprinkling of children and a surprising number of adolescents, but most of the crowd seemed to consist of people in their thirties and forties. Here and there, hefty women in late middle-age fanned themselves with fans improvised from the church bulletin and watched the proceedings with a proprietary interest; the ladies sodality, I imagined. At the front of the room was a simple altar covered with flowers, and on the wall above it a cross. On one side of the altar was the choir—ten women and four men wearing sky-blue robes—and three musicians, a keyboardist, a guitarist and a flutist. Opposite them was a podium with a microphone. The choir had just finished singing a high-pitched, piping hymn, more like a chant than a song, and now Reverend Ortega took the podium and began to read a passage from the Bible. He was wearing the same black suit that he had worn when I first encountered him at court, the same narrow, unfashionable tie.

I had formed my stereotype of evangelists from channel-surfing through the Sunday morning religious shows: white Southern men in expensive suits, with brittle, poufy hair and faces slimed theatrically with tears as they condemned people like me to the crude hells they constructed out of ignorance and fear. Sometimes the face was black, and instead of tears was frowning sternness, but the condemnation was always the same and it was animated by that purposeful energy of hatred. I expected Ortega to be the same kind of shrieker and weeper, and assumed the best I could hope for was that Leviticus was not this week's text.

I turned my attention to him. He read from Matthew about the afflicted woman who believed if she touched even the hem of Jesus' garment she would be healed. She humbly made her way through the throng that surrounded him, touched his robe and was instantly cured. Among all the people who pressed against him, it was her touch that Jesus felt and her faith he praised. I had no trouble understanding the simple Spanish of the verse or the sermon that followed. Ortega was not a weeper and shrieker. He spoke in a conversational tone, in a resonant voice and seemed scarcely able to conceal his happiness, like someone bringing you the best news you would ever receive. I thought he had to be faking it, that this bubbling mirth was an orator's trick, and perhaps there was something of that in it, but the joy was real, too. His message was not complicated: He used the story to assure his listeners that among the rich and powerful, it was the faith of the poor and the humble that pleased God best.

I thought of my niece. She'd responded to me with a passive blankness that made me wonder if she had an interior life at all. Now it occurred to me that perhaps she was like the woman in Mark's story, her blankness concealing humility and her passivity, faith. When I was with her, it often felt to me as if she had hoped for someone else. Perhaps it wasn't that she was hoping for someone else, but that she had placed her hope in someone else. I looked around the room; sweat poured down the mesmerized faces of the congregation as Ortega expounded his text. I was touched, but the mystery of faith remained mysterious to me.

When the service ended, we followed the other congregants as they filed through a door into an adjacent room equipped with an industrial stove and a double sink. Food, paper plates, cups and plastic utensils were laid out on the long counter that partitioned the room. A screen door was propped open, and through it I glimpsed a patio set up with tables and chairs and realized this must have been a restaurant. Reverend Ortega saw us and came over. He shook my hand warmly and ran an affectionate hand through Angel's hair.

"Señor Rios, I'm glad you could come. Hello, Angelito."

"Hi, Reverend," Angel said.

"Will you excuse us for a minute, Angel? Reverend Ortega and I have to talk."

Angel went off to eat. Reverend Ortega said, "Come, I have an office."

His office was a tiny room that must have been the pantry. There was just enough space for a desk and two chairs. There was a cross on the wall and a bulletin board that sagged with announcements, calendars and photographs from church socials. Reverend Ortega squeezed behind his desk and invited me to sit down.

"Did you enjoy the service, Señor Rios?"

"Actually, yes. I expected something different."

He cocked his head. "What?"

"Fire-and-brimstone. People rolling in the aisle. I'm sorry, I don't mean to be offensive."

"God hears us even when we—" He paused, and I could see him searching for the English equivalent of the word he had in mind. "Even when we whisper. No one needs to yell." He smiled apologetically. "Señor Rios, Spanish is more easy for me. If I speak Spanish, you can understand?"

"I think so, but I'll have to speak English back."

"Okay," he said. "We trade Spanish for English." In Spanish, he said, "Would you like me to be a witness for Vicky at her trial?"

"It wouldn't be her trial, Reverend. She pled guilty—admitted the crime. Now the judge will decide how many years Vicky will have to spend in prison. I know you've been talking to Vicky and I would like you to testify to help me convince the judge to show mercy."

"I understand," he said. "I have done this for other members of the church. I can tell the judge that Vicky is a good woman, a Christian, and she has a good heart."

"It would help if you could tell the judge that she is very sorry for her crime."

He gave me a puzzled look, as if working something out, and after a long moment he said, "I can testify that she did what she did to protect Angel."

"Are you saying she's not sorry that she killed Pete?"

Another long pause. Something was going on, and then I understood. "Reverend Ortega, I'm not asking you to testify to anything she told you in confidence. The law protects what she told you about the details of the killing. I only need for you to say something that will help me show the judge the killing was not an evil act."

He frowned. "Killing is an evil act, Señor Rios. I can only testify that Vicky has no evil in her heart. Everything she has done, she has done out of love for Angelito. She has sacrificed everything for her child."

We appeared to be going around in a circle, but I didn't know what it was we were circling.

"I understand that, but what I'm asking you is whether she's told you she's sorry. If she did, that's helpful. If she didn't, I won't ask you the question."

"She never told me that she is sorry," he said. He seemed uncomfortable with his answer, as if he knew it was a half-lie. "You must understand, Señor Rios, that she wanted to protect Angel."

"By killing his father?"

He was so long in responding that I thought he hadn't understood, but then he said, "Peter was not Angel's father. I tell you this in confidence."

It took a moment to absorb the information, but then I remembered the young man in the casket—fair-skinned, fair-haired, nothing like my black-haired, brown-skinned nephew. Now I understood why Ortega kept repeating that Vicky had sacrificed everything for Angel.

"Was Pete abusing Angel?"

"I cannot say more, Señor Rios. She spoke to me in confidence."

I inferred from his anguished expression that he regretted having told me as much as he had and nothing would be gained by pressuring him. Vicky had obviously told him something about the circumstances of the killing involving Angel that she had kept from me. I could assume it was that Pete had abused Angel, either physically or sexually. I made a snap decision: Whatever it was Pete had done to Angel was irrelevant at the moment. In fact, I didn't want to know. I had sold Kim Pearsall on the plea bargain by representing that Vicky had been Pete's victim and it was clear that she had been, for whatever reason. To switch my theory of the killing at this point would, at the very least, confuse the issues and might even endanger the deal. As for my personal interest in Angel, I would have to hope that as he grew to know and trust me, he would volunteer whatever had happened between Pete and him. Someday I would discover the truth of what had happened in that room, but at the moment I didn't need the truth, only a plausible and sympathetic scenario.

"I understand. I'm not going to ask you to testify, Reverend Ortega," I said.

Relief washed over his face. "That is for the best."

"Someday, though, I may return and ask you to tell me what you know, to help me raise Angel while his mother is in prison."

"I can never tell you what I know," he said. "But when Angel is safe, Vicky will tell you."

I got up. "Thank you for your time. I'll respect Vicky's wishes to bring Angel to services here."

"You are also welcome."

"I'm not a Christian, Reverend."

He started to speak, thought better of it, and let me go.

18.

THE PHONE WAS RINGING WHEN I STEPPED INTO MY OF-
fice the next morning after a long breakfast with Angel at which we
discussed the tests he would be taking later that week at his new
school. He was enthusiastic about going back to school but worried
that he would have to repeat the fourth grade. Listening to him,
one would have thought that the humiliation of being held back a
year was the most traumatizing event he had ever faced. Unless I
brought her up, he rarely spoke about his mother and never about
the shooting. He still woke up some nights screaming, but resisted
my attempts to coax him into describing the bad dreams. I clung to
the belief that his inability to talk about these things was because
they were still so fresh, but I worried that, like a splinter, the memories were working themselves deeper and deeper into his consciousness, where they would fester and become ever more difficult
to extract. Furthermore, after talking to Reverend Ortega, I had a
new fear—that the powder keg of unexpressed feeling beneath Angel was not only from the shooting but from whatever abuse he had
suffered at Pete Trujillo's hands preceding it. I didn't want my
nephew's life distorted by unexpressed rage toward his father or
drowned in alcohol, as mine had been, or for him to pick up some

other equally self-destructive club with which to beat himself. Yet I was reluctant to force him to talk. I was afraid if my timing was off, I would destroy the still-fragile bond of trust growing between us. All this was passing through my head while Angel cheerfully gobbled cereal and rattled on about the previous day's baseball scores and wondered if the school's baseball team needed a shortstop.

Still preoccupied with these thoughts in my office, I picked up the phone as it rang. It was Edith Rosen.

"Henry, I read the material in Vicky's case you faxed me and I've given it a lot of thought."

I didn't like the apologetic tone I was hearing in her voice.

"What do you think?"

"I'm still not convinced it was BWS," she said.

Ordinarily I would have lobbied her, but I thought about Reverend Ortega's intimation about the shooting, so all I said was, "Tell me why."

"Battered women don't ordinarily kill their batterers in the midst of an attack because they know they can't win that kind of confrontation," she reminded me. "These reports make it seem that Vicky shot him while he was coming at her."

"Exactly," I said. "She shot him. She didn't try to overpower him physically."

"Unless she ran out during the fight and bought the gun, she must have had it available before," Edith said. "Why did she choose that moment? Also, Henry, if he was beating her, it was very risky for her to escalate things by introducing a gun. He still had the physical advantage and he could have used it to get the gun away from her."

"She shot him in the back," I said.

Edith was silent for a moment. "Had the attack stopped or had he just turned his back for an instant?"

"I don't know," I said. "It's not clear. There's a chance he could have been reaching for his own gun."

"That's not in any of these reports," she said.

"I know. Does it make a difference to your opinion if you throw that into the mix?"

"Actually, that supports my point. If she knew he had access to his own gun, then why didn't she wait until the attack was over rather than get into a gunfight? Remember, Henry, the core of BWS is that the abused spouse has been terrorized. Someone in that kind of fear is trying to avoid confrontations, not provoke them. If she was going to kill him, she wouldn't do it while he was enraged and at his most dangerous. She would have waited until she could catch him off guard."

She was making a persuasive case and I could hear her on the witness stand, methodically discrediting my theory of the shooting.

"Is there anything else that makes you skeptical this was BWS?"

"Yes," she said. "Two things. First, she had the presence of mind to hide the gun before the police arrived. The other thing—and it's related to the first—is that she was reluctant to admit that she had killed him."

"Why are those things significant?"

"Battered women don't usually try to hide or deny what they've done. They're filled with remorse and anxious to explain it."

"She did tell the police she shot him because he beat her," I said.

"Well, no," Edith said. "I read her statement. She agrees with them that that's what she did when they put it to her in question form. That's different than making an affirmative statement."

"Not for purposes of the law."

"It is for purposes of my opinion."

"What exactly is your opinion of what happened that night, Edith? She had been beaten. There's physical evidence of that. I saw her."

There was a long, thoughtful silence on the other end of the line. "I'm not saying they didn't fight or that he didn't strike her," she said. "What I'm saying is that it wasn't something he did routinely. BWS requires a pattern of abuse, not a one-time quarrel, however violent. They were fighting about something specific and very serious."

About Angel. "You offered to work with Angel. I'd like you to start right away."

This time the silence was puzzled. Then she understood. "This is still about the shooting. You know something you haven't told me," she said in a seriously annoyed tone. "Henry, you know better than to try to withhold information from me to get favorable testimony."

"I didn't know this until yesterday."

"Know what?"

"Angel's not Pete's son. There's some suggestion that Pete may have abused him somehow."

"Sexually?"

"I don't know, Edith. That's what I'd like you to find out for me."

"Why don't you ask him?"

"I can't," I said. "I sold the D.A. this deal with Vicky by representing that she was a battered woman. It's a little late for me to change theories. I mean, if you're right and she shot him in the heat of an argument, then it really is second-degree murder. The D.A. took her plea on voluntary manslaughter."

She said, "I'm not a lawyer, Henry, but as I understand it, the D.A.'s stuck with that plea."

"That's true," I said. "Unless the plea was obtained by fraud. If I know the facts to be different from what I've represented them to be, well, you see where I'm going."

"I see why you can't ask Angel, if that's what you mean."

"Obviously I'm not going to ask you to testify. No offense."

"None taken," she said. "But Vicky will have to testify, won't she? What are you going to do about her?"

I was wondering the same thing.

. . .

And then Elena called. "I talked to the director of the women's shelter that Vicky said she went to after Pete was released," she said. "She told me something very curious."

"What?"

"Vicky said they asked her to leave because she was proselytizing. This woman said they asked her to leave because their psychologist talked to her and concluded that she wasn't a victim of domestic violence."

"How did they decide that?"

"She told me that was privileged," Elena replied. "She said if we wanted to know, we'd have to ask Vicky."

"I will," I said.

Vicky was immediately on her guard when I turned up unannounced at the jail that afternoon. "Hello, Uncle Henry," she said. "Did Angel come with you?"

"Why did you kill Pete?"

"What?" she asked, but I saw in her eyes she was scrambling for a strategy.

"The director of the women's shelter in San Francisco said you were asked to leave because they didn't believe you were a battered woman. I had a psychologist look at the police reports in this case and she said the same thing. I read Pete's rap sheet. He had never been arrested for domestic violence. I just assumed that was because you had never called the cops on him. Even Angel told me that Pete never struck you. I thought he was just covering for his father, but it's true, isn't it? Until that night, Pete had never struck you before."

It seemed at first that she would deny it, but then she gave a small sigh, as if of relief, slowly shook her head. "No."

"So why did you shoot him?"

"Why does it matter?" she replied, meeting my eyes. "I said I was guilty. Everyone's happy."

Her calm audacity rendered me mute.

"I got you this deal by convincing the D.A. that you're a battered woman. That's what you told your mother. That's what I believed. You lied to both of us. Why?"

"I wasn't lying when I said I had to get away from Pete. I needed help to do that."

"If he wasn't beating you, why were you running away from him?"

She looked away from me. "I can't tell you."

"Does it involve Angel?"

"No."

"You're still lying to me. I know that Pete wasn't Angel's father. Was he doing something to him?"

She lifted her head and stared at me. "What do you mean 'doing something do him'?"

"You know what I mean."

"No," she said sharply. "Pete never touched Angel."

"But he wasn't Angel's father."

"No," she conceded. "He wasn't."

"Listen to me, Vicky, I know you consider yourself a Christian, and maybe in your book it's all right to lie to your mother and me because we're not. But are you ready to go to court and swear before God to tell the truth and then tell more lies? Do you think I could let you do that?"

"Do I have to testify?"

"If you don't, the D.A. will know something's up. If I can't give him an explanation, there's nothing to stop him from asking the judge to give you the upper term for voluntary manslaughter. That's eleven years."

"You don't understand," she exploded. "I have to protect Angel. I'll go to jail. I don't care how long."

"Protect him from what?"

Sobbing, she buried her face in her arms. "Leave me alone. I want to go back to my cell."

I now recognized that her tears were the equivalent of a squid under attack spraying ink to escape its attacker.

I waited until the sobs subsided. "I know you don't like me and I'm sorry about that, but even you have to admit that I love Angel. You don't have to trust me about anything else, but trust me that I won't let anyone hurt him."

She raised her head and wiped her face on the sleeves of her jumpsuit. "I want to talk to Reverend Ortega."

I nodded. "You do that, Vicky, but remember, the hearing is in four days. We don't have much time to come up with a plan."

"How did you find out that Pete's not Angel's dad?"

"Ortega. He didn't mean to tell, but I kind of backed him into a corner and he blurted it out."

With a ghost of a smile, she said, "You do that good."

That evening before dinner, we went to the high school where I ran. I was up to eight laps, two miles. Angel usually ran partway with me, and then when I finished, we played catch in the summer dusk on the football field. He had a strong arm and I could already tell that he would soon outgrow my fumbling catches and wobbly returns, but for now I had just enough muscle over him not to look like a complete fool. Tonight, he dropped out after three laps and went off to amuse himself by throwing his baseball as hard and as high as he could, then dashing beneath it to make the catch. I could hear him chattering commentary to himself about an imaginary game. As I huffed around the track watching him, I wondered what it was that Vicky thought she had been protecting him from by killing Pete Trujillo. Her shock when I suggested that Pete had abused the boy seemed real enough, but by now I was beginning to realize how fluent a liar my niece could be when the need arose. Ortega, who had less invested, had not been as shocked. Of course, there were forms of abuse other than sexual or physical. Maybe, I thought, Angel didn't know he wasn't Pete's son, and for some reason Pete had threatened to reveal it. That was a weak motive for her to have killed him and it didn't explain why he had beaten her. Whatever they had quarreled about had been something that had enraged him enough to beat her. What could it have been? His drug use? That was a possibility. The three of them crowded into that cramped motel room and Pete blowing whatever money they had on drugs. Maybe she had hoped they would start a new life and instead she found herself being dragged down with him. That could've sparked a pretty nasty fight, but one that would end in a killing? And how did that protect Angel? Unless . . . good God. Was that it? I looked for Angel and saw him lying in the grass on his back watching a sliver of moon rise in the pink and violet sky.

"Hurry up, Uncle Henry," he shouted. "It's getting dark."

"Okay, this is my last lap."

He smiled. I loved him so much, but not as much as his mother who was willing to go to prison for something Angel had done.

That night, after Angel had gone to bed, I called John to get a reality check. He knew immediately something was preying on me.

"You sound sad, Rico," he said.

That cut to the heart of it. I was sad. I didn't want to believe the conclusion I had talked myself into, because if I was right, I would have to do something about it that could potentially cause serious injury to several people, all of them related to me.

"I need your advice."

"I'm here for you."

"Are you sitting down?"

There was a pause. "This is serious, huh?"

"John, I think Angel killed his—killed Pete Trujillo, and Vicky's prepared to go to prison to cover for him."

"Angelito?" He was shocked. "Did he tell you something?"

"No," I said. "I pieced it together and maybe I'm wrong. I hope I'm wrong. That's why I called you. Can I tell you?"

"Yeah, I'm listening."

"Pete Trujillo's not Angel's father."

"Angel know he's not Pete's son?"

"I don't think so," I said. "Well, he may know now, but I don't think he knew before the shooting. Pete must have known all along. I think at best he put up with Angel for Vicky's sake. He may have mistreated him, especially when he was high. Pete was a drug addict. A junkie, mostly, but I'm sure he used whatever was available. He was in and out of prison most of Angel's life. When he was on the outside, he always went back to Vicky and to drugs. Living with an addict is like watching someone commit slow-motion suicide. Every day they use, a little piece of them dies."

"Yeah," John said softly, and I remembered that, he had first hand experience with addiction.

"That's what it must have been like for Vicky and Pete. From what I've learned about him, he wasn't a bad kid. He had this evil cousin who dragged him into some serious criminal activity, but left on his own, the worst things he did were to himself. And to her."

"And Angel," John added. "Even if Pete never laid a hand on him, any kid who grows up around that kind of sadness, it hurts him."

I remembered that John had kids. "He told me once he would never use drugs," I said. "He was so quiet and serious when I first met him. You don't know how good it makes me feel when he laughs."

Tenderly John said, "I think I do."

"This last time Pete got out of prison, Vicky tried to run away from him. She took Angel to a shelter for battered women in San Francisco, but they asked her to leave when they figured out she wasn't battered. Then she appealed to my sister for help, telling her the same story—that she was running away from Pete because he beat her. In a way, she wasn't lying. Maybe she didn't know herself that she was speaking in metaphor."

"Meta-what?"

"She lied about Pete beating her to get help, but it wasn't a complete lie. What she was really saying was that he'd broken her heart, not her bones."

"Really saying it to who?"

"To herself," I said. "I think she knew if she went back to him this time, something bad was going to happen. In the end, she couldn't help herself. Pete and Angel were all she had."

"Like they say, hope springs eternal."

"Yeah, especially with junkies. They're not violent, like drunks. They're charming and tragic. Easy to fall in love in with."

"You talking from experience?"

"Yeah," I said. "But that's another story. Vicky went back to Pete and they ended up in this little motel room in Hollywood, with him using and her at the end of her rope and Angel being left pretty much on his own." I remembered how he had told me about his walks through Hollywood. "Plus Pete was turning paranoid. He had at least two guns in the room."

"He was paranoid?"

"He had reason to be. I'm not sure of the details, but I think he ratted out his homeboys to get a deal on his last felony."

"You sure one of them didn't shoot him?"

"That doesn't fit the evidence. What I think happened is that he and Vicky were fighting all the time, and for the first time in their marriage, the fights started getting violent. I figured Angel had to have been there for some of it, maybe some of it was directed at him. The night Pete was killed, he and Vicky got into a bad fight."

"How do you know that?"

"I saw her face the next day," I said. "I think Pete may even have taken a shot at her. Angel was either in the room or just returning to the room and he tried to protect his mom by picking up the other gun and firing it at Pete. Two shots were wild, the last one killed him."

For a moment, the line was quiet. Then John said, "He's just a kid, Henry."

I hadn't told him about the episode at the stadium. I did now.

"That just proves he knows how to take care of himself," John said.

"That's my point," I replied. "Angel's trapped in this motel room with these two people locked in a dance of death. He sees his mother getting more desperate and the man he thinks is his father getting crazier and crazier. Then one night, everything snaps. Pete beats the stuffing out of Vicky and then pulls a gun on her. Angel has to believe at that instant that Pete's going to kill her. She's the only parent, the only protection Angel has ever had. Simple self-preservation would have told him to kill Pete. He may even have thought if Pete killed her, he would be next. I'm not saying this is how it happened, I'm saying this is how it could have happened. Am I crazy?"

After a moment, John said, "No, you're not crazy. Is this all guesswork, or did Vicky tell you something?"

"When I found out she'd been lying about being a battered woman, I asked her about it and all she would say is that she had to protect Angel. Reverend Ortega, when I talked to him, said the same thing. He said she'd sacrificed everything to see that Angel was safe. At first I thought they meant Vicky had killed Pete to protect Angel from him, from some kind of abuse, but they were saying it as if she was still trying to protect him. I began to wonder how she could be trying to protect him from her jail cell. Then I figured it out."

"You're not sure, are you?"

"I am sure, but I don't want to be. Angel wakes up screaming in the middle of the night. The first time it happened, he told me it was because he dreamed of how Pete died. I thought he was remembering how Pete looked after he'd been shot. Now I think he dreams about the shooting. I don't know, he won't talk to me about the dreams anymore. The gun that was used to kill Pete disappeared and so did the gun that Pete used to shoot at Vicky. She was in no shape to get rid of them, but Angel was."

"You know that for a fact?"

"On the night Pete was killed, Angel called me from a gas station across the street from the motel within a few minutes of the shooting. A couple of weeks ago, he took me back to the same gas station and showed me where he had hidden the gun that I think Pete fired at Vicky. You understand, John? He didn't give me the gun he used to shoot Pete, because he can't face that. Instead, he gave me the gun Pete used, because in his mind that justified what he did."

"He trusts you. Why wouldn't he tell you the truth?"

"Because Vicky has told him to keep his mouth shut," I said. "She's ready to take the blame to protect him."

"From what? You're not going to turn him in?" When I didn't immediately answer, he said, "Hey, you're *not* going to turn him in."

"In this situation, I'm not just Angel's uncle," I said. "And Vicky's not just my niece. I'm a lawyer and she's my client. If there were no blood relation here, I would never let her plead guilty to a crime she didn't commit."

"That's her choice," he said.

"I can't allow her to make that choice."

"Man, you can't be serious."

"If I let her plead guilty, I'll be allowing her to spend maybe six, ten years in prison. That's hard time, man. She'll suffer, and when she gets out, she'll have a manslaughter conviction that follows her around for the rest of her life. She's not a woman with an unlimited future as it is. What kind of future would she have as a convicted felon? And what about Angel? What's the lesson here for him? That you never have to face up to the things you do because someone will take the fall for you? And me? I'll be an accomplice to a homicide."

"You'll destroy his life."

"I don't think so," I said. "He *is* a kid, John. He'd be tried in juvenile court. I can make the same case for him I was going to make for Vicky. He acted in defense of his mother and himself. That's justifiable homicide, and when you throw in the incredible stress he was under, no judge is going to convict him."

"Yeah?" John said skeptically. "You a hundred percent certain?"

I hesitated, then admitted, "No. There's no such thing in the law."

"So there's a chance they could commit him to, what's it called, the youth authority? Prison for kids." He paused to allow it to sink in. "Listen, Henry, you don't know that Angel killed his—Pete. You don't know that."

"What's your point?"

"Hey, man, you're the lawyer. If you can't prove it was Angel, what right do you have to sacrifice him for your theory?"

"I have no direct evidence, it's true. Only circumstantial evidence."

"That means you're guessing."

"It's an educated guess."

"It's a guess," he insisted. "You gonna go to the judge with a guess?"

Heart sinking, I thought about Friday and the sentencing hearing. "Okay, I get it," I said. "I can't prove it was Angel, I can't prove it wasn't Vicky, so I have a little moral wiggle room. But in my heart, I know."

"Maybe what's in Vicky's heart is more important than what's in your heart," he said. "She's his mother. Hey, Henry, if it was one of my kids, I might do the same thing."

"Are you serious? You'd take the rap for a crime they committed?"

"You don't stop loving your kids because they fuck up," he said. "You love them more."

I remembered that his father had said basically the same thing about him.

"How will they learn what's right and wrong if you go on picking up the pieces all their lives?"

"You don't understand," he said. "This is about settling things in the family versus letting some outsider settle them for you. Angel's gotta know what he did is wrong. He's gotta know his mother will pay for his mistake with hard time, like you said. He's a good boy, Henry, he won't blow this off. He *is* being punished. That's what those nightmares are all about. But it's in the family. Keep it there."

My years of legal training, my veneration for the law, made me want to argue the point, but something stopped me: the memory of seeing a small boy standing at my doorstep and the sensation of looking through time into a distant mirror. I saw him now as Ulysses must have seen Telemachus at the end of his long voyage, the innocent son on the verge of his own journey, who might yet be taught how to avoid the dark places. I had never wanted a family, but Angel had shown me that what I wanted was irrelevant. I carried him in my veins; I couldn't not love him.

"Henry?"

"Yeah, I'm still here. Listen, maybe you're right. Everything I told you, it's just a guess. If Vicky wants to plead to protect her son, maybe I have to let her."

"He's your boy, too." After a moment, he asked, "Should I come over?"

"No, I've got to do some work. You've been a great help, John. Really."

"All right, *viejo*. I'll talk to you tomorrow. Okay?"

"Yeah. Thanks, baby. Sleep tight."

"*Te amo.*"

"*Yo tambien.*"

He laughed. "Someone's been practicing."

I was up half the night mulling things over, going back and forth, but I could come up with no better conclusion than John's:

Put up or shut up. I couldn't put up. I still had to decide what to do about Friday. I decided on a risky tactic that involved a half-lie. I would tell Judge Ryan that Vicky's memory of the events was so unreliable that I had decided simply to submit on the police and probation reports without a hearing. She and the D.A. would naturally be suspicious after the big deal I'd made about wanting a sentencing hearing. Well, it couldn't be helped. I'd tap-danced my way through worse fixes than this, and with a lot less at stake.

I went into Angel's room. He was asleep on his back with the blankets kicked to the floor. He had never removed the heart pendant I had given him. I reached down and touched the warm stone. I covered him, kissed his forehead and then stood above his bed for a long time, silently wishing him better dreams.

19.

MY DECISION WAS STILL BOTHERING ME THE NEXT MORN-
ing, but I had little time to ponder it further because there was a crisis with Angel. He was scheduled to spend the day at the Winslow
School in Pasadena for what their fax called "placement orienta-
tion," a euphemism for aptitude tests. At breakfast, he announced
he didn't want to go. He was in a high state of agitation. I had to
coax him for an hour before he admitted he was anxious about being around kids his age. I realized as he spoke about his fears that he
had been raised almost entirely among adults in a series of welfare
hotels in neighborhoods like the Tenderloin in San Francisco. He
knew about AIDS and drugs and he may have shot the man he
thought was his father, but the prospect of being around other ten-
year-olds terrified him.

"Other kids don't like me, Uncle Henry," he said.

I resisted the impulse to sweep him into my arms and murmur,
There, there.

"Angelito, remember when we talked about Ulysses?"

"No," he pouted.

"Yes, you do," I said. "Some of the gods tried to keep him from
reaching Ithaca, but there were always other gods that helped him

and eventually he got home. There will always be people in this world who won't like you, but there will also be people who will become your friends. People who will help you through life. You won't find them if you don't get out there and look."

"I don't want to," he said.

We went back and forth for another half-hour, until finally I told him we were going and he sullenly acquiesced. As we drove to the school in silence, I reached over and grabbed his hand and gave it a squeeze. He squeezed back.

John was right: If Angel had killed Pete, it was something to be worked out in the family. The alternative was the juvenile court system, where kids didn't even have the minimal rights of adult criminal defendants, and he might end up being committed to the youth authority until he was twenty-one. Still, I could foresee for myself many troubled nights.

At first glance, the campus of Winslow School seemed as stereotypically preppy as its name. The main building was a three-story rambling brown-brick Gothic edifice, complete with ivy-covered archways set back from a quiet street that was lined with sycamore trees. It looked like a parsonage out of an Agatha Christie novel, and as we crossed the great expanse of lawn, I looked for the croquet wickets. The resemblance to an English country house ended abruptly inside, where the unmistakable smells of a school—chalk dust and wood resin—floated in the warm, bright air. The corridors were plastered with posters in English, Spanish, Chinese and Vietnamese. A portrait gallery of great men and women included Gandhi, Susan B. Anthony, Dolores Huerta and Harvey Milk. We found the room where I was to deliver Angel. A sturdy young woman in dreadlocks and a tie-dyed T-shirt that she must have found in a raid on her grandmother's closet took custody of him. I stayed for a few minutes until the scared look went out of his eyes, gave him a kiss and told him I would pick up him at four.

On my way out, my cell phone rang.

"Hello," I said.

A woman replied, "Mr. Rios? I'm Morgan Yee. You wanted to talk to me about Pete Trujillo. Sorry I didn't call back sooner, but I've been down here in L.A. and I just picked up my messages. How is Pete?"

"I'm afraid he's dead."

"Wow," she said. "So his homeys finally got him."

"I beg your pardon?"

"His homeboys. The Garden something gang. How did it happen?"

"If you're down here, I wonder if we could talk face to face."

"Sure," she said. "I have an argument in the Court of Appeal at one-thirty. If you want, I could meet you for lunch around noon."

"That would work. Where?"

"The Court of Appeal's in the state building. I think there's a cafeteria in there."

"All right. I'll meet you in the lobby in front of Ronald Reagan."

"Huh?"

"Just ask the security guards."

At noon, I stepped into the Ronald Reagan State Office Building on Third and Spring, a place familiarly called Ronald Reagan S.O.B. A bronze bust of the former president graced the atrium, flanked by two ficus trees that appeared to be dying. A tall, sinewy Asian woman in a gray suit was standing beside the bust, talking on a cell phone. I paused and looked up at the skylights that flooded the plant-filled atrium with light. From the courtyard came the murmur of the fountain that emptied into a reflecting pool, where a massive bronze bear hunted bronze fish against the background of a brilliantly painted mural depicting scenes from the state's history. The last time I had seen that mural was from a gurney as I was being carried out of the Court of Appeal into an ambulance. I had forgotten that, but now, looking at the depiction of the Golden Gate Bridge, the terror of those moments swept through me. I breathed deeply, letting it go. The heart attack seemed like an event from another life, as if I had emerged from those seconds of death at the hospital a man reborn. Certainly, my life was very different now, for I had been, perhaps, at my most solitary point; but now I had this family, this child to care for. This was the last thing I would ever have expected, but I was grateful for it. I was glad to be alive, as perhaps I had not been before the heart attack, because, in retrospect, I saw that I had run out of reasons for living.

Morgan Yee cocked her head, gave me a narrow look and mouthed the words, Mr. Rios? I nodded. "Gotta go," she said into the phone. "No, I'll get a cab from the airport. Kiss, kiss."

She snapped the phone shut and extended a big hand with what I recognized as a weightlifter's calluses. Beneath her suit I discerned the lines of a powerfully developed body.

"I'm Morgan," she said.

"Henry." Her handshake was bone-crunching.

"You okay? You look like you saw a ghost."

"I'm fine. You found Reagan."

She laughed and pinched the Gipper's bronze cheek. "Oh, yeah. He actually looks more lifelike here than in life. Is he still alive or what?"

"I think the answer is 'or what,'" I replied. "You're too young to remember the Reagan years."

She rolled her eyes. "Don't go all golden oldie on me, Henry. I'm thirty-five, old enough to remember the Gipper. Can we eat? I'm starved."

In the second-floor cafeteria, Morgan hit the salad bar hard, erecting a precarious pile of vegetables, greens, tuna and cottage cheese that dripped off her plate. I put my burrito on her tray and paid for our food. We went out to the tiny sunbaked patio from which we had a view of L.A.'s skid row, a collection of liquor stores, cockroach cafés, a couple of homeless shelters and the spire of the abandoned Catholic cathedral, Saint Vibiana. The sun blazed through the fetid air.

Through a mouthful of salad, she said, "Why did they build this place in the slums?"

"The state workers were supposed to be the advance guard of gentrification," I said. "The attack faltered on the winos and crack-heads."

"Tell me about Pete."

"I was going to ask you the same question."

She tackled the mound of salad. "No, I mean how was he killed?"

"Shot dead in a motel room. The cops charged his wife. She's my client."

She swallowed. "Vicky. She couldn't kill Pete," she said. "They were like Romeo and Juliet, except Romeo was a junkie. Studmuffin, though—not that I think that's what she saw in him. She was a serious chick. I guess she thought she could change him. The love of a good woman, all that crap. I could have told her she was wasting her time."

"Because he was a junkie?"

She nodded. "People think heroin's like some Billie Holiday song. Kind of sad and romantic. That's such crap. Billie died chained to a hospital bed. You're better off blowing your brains out than sticking a needle in your arm. See where it got Pete."

"On the phone you said he was afraid of his homeboys. Why?"

She plopped a cherry tomato into her mouth. "He ratted them out to save himself from a three-strikes sentence."

So I'd been right in my reading of his rap sheet. "What happened exactly?"

"He got picked up for possession of just enough heroin for the cops to bother charging him and then they discovered he had two strikes."

"Juvie stuff."

She nodded. "Yeah. He and this cousin of his robbed a grocery store and on the way out shot a customer. The cuz did, not Pete. Pete was not a macho guy. A follower from the word go. The cuz gets this brilliant idea that in juvie court each one will claim the other did the shooting, and that way he figures the judge will let them both off." She smirked. "So the D.A. moves for separate trials and they both get nailed, and Pete ends up with two strikes. When he picks up this possession charge, suddenly he's looking at twenty-five to life. That's when I got the case."

"Was it your idea for him to snitch?"

"I tried to get the strikes struck. When that didn't work, I sat him down and explained the facts of life. They had him on the possession charge, they had him on the strikes. It was bye-bye, baby, and I was all out of ideas. Then he says Butch is part of these *narco-trafficantes* who bring heroin in from Mexico and distribute it up and down the state through Latino gangs. I told him if he was willing to roll on them, I might be able to save his ass. He didn't go for it at first."

"What convinced him?"

She pushed her plate aside. "Vicky. She told him it was better for him to snitch and take his chances on the outside than die of old age in prison. She's a smart chick. What she was doing with a loser like him is beyond me. Anyway, with Pete's information, there were drug busts from San Diego to Sacramento that actually put some dealers out of business. For a while, anyway."

"Was Cousin Butch among them?"

"He got away. Pete says he has hideouts in Mexico. There are a couple of arrest warrants out on him."

I thought about his antics at the cemetery. He was back, and not exactly lying low. Which made him either arrogant or stupid or both.

"Do you know what Butch's real name is?"

She thought about it for a moment. "It was a kind of unusual name. Oh, yeah, Narciso. Narciso Trujillo."

"Narcissus. The guy who fell in love with his reflection. They named the flower after him."

"Butch is no flower," she said. "With all his strikes, next time he gets picked up, he'll be serving time into his next four incarnations. Pete was more scared of him than anyone because Butch wasn't just a homey, he was family. Pete figured snitching on Butch made him a double traitor." She reached into her briefcase, extracted a pair of sunglasses and a bottle of Evian water. She put the shades on. "When you told me Pete was dead, I was sure it was Butch who killed him. He tried once before."

"When?"

She chugged some Evian. "Pete was shanked in the yard at San Quentin. Another couple of inches, they would have hit his heart. He told me the guy that did it was Mexican mafia carrying out a contract for Butch's gang. The Garden something."

"Garden Grove boyz," I said.

"Yeah, that's it. I got Pete out of Quentin and he served the last few months of his sentence in the high-power unit of San Francisco jail. Total isolation, that's what it took to keep him alive. When he was released, witness protection was supposed to set him up with a new identity and reunite him with Vicky and their kid. What's his name?"

"Angel. Did they?"

"In a half-assed way. They put him on a bus to some town in the central valley, where they gave him an apartment and a job and a couple of phone numbers to call if he got into a jam."

"Turlock?"

"Turlock. Yeah, that was it. He called me once to ask me to help him get a gig with the DEA after they turned him down. That was the last I heard." She glanced at her watch and stood up. "Look, Henry, I gotta get ready for argument. I'll be back in the city tonight if you have any more questions. I can tell you one thing, though—if Pete is dead, Cousin Butch is behind it."

"Would you be willing to testify in Vicky's trial if I needed you to?"

"Hey, if you can get my testimony past a hearsay objection, I'd be happy to. You got a business card?"

We exchanged cards.

"Thanks, Morgan," I said. "Good luck with the C.A."

"I figure if they don't fall asleep on me, that's a win," she said and headed briskly into the building.

I sat on the patio as flies buzzed around the ruins of Morgan's salad. Less than twenty-four hours ago, I'd become convinced that Angel had shot Pete Trujillo. When John had floated the idea that the shooter was one of Pete's gang buddies, I'd dismissed it because it didn't fit the evidence. Now I had to rethink it all. Could Cousin Butch have come to the motel, beaten up Vicky and killed Pete? How would he have found them? If Pete had been released through witness protection, there would have been no record that some prison trustee could've looked up and passed along to a gangbanger on the outside. But Butch had another access to information about Pete. Their family. Jesusita Trujillo. She had been beaten the same night that Pete was killed by someone whom she had willingly admitted into her house. Mrs. Cerda thought her mother's attacker was a gang member, someone her mother knew from the neighborhood. Could it have been Butch? But if it had been Butch, why would Vicky take the rap for him? I didn't think I'd get the answers I needed from her. There was one other possibility. I dug through my wallet for his number. I got his pager and punched in my number. A few minutes later, he called back, and after I explained to him what I wanted to talk to him about, he reluctantly agreed to meet me.

He was wearing the gray uniform of a janitor with his name stitched across his breast pocket. In the sleek Westside shopping mall where he pushed a broom, he was just one more black-haired, brown-skinned menial worker, all but invisible to the trendy lunchtime crowd that packed the boutiques and restaurants. He clasped my hand warmly, but his eyes were worried.

In Spanish, he said, "Señor Rios. I can only talk a few minutes before I have to go back to work."

"I only need a few minutes, Reverend Ortega. I thought you were a full-time preacher."

He smiled. "My people are poor. I work here to support my family." He gestured toward the food court. "May I buy you lunch?"

"Thanks, but I've eaten. You go ahead."

He lifted a grease-stained brown bag. "This is my lunch. Shall we sit down?"

I bought a cup of coffee and joined him at a table that looked down on six levels of stores that sold such essentials as German nose-hair clippers and two-thousand-dollar Italian suits made of wool so fine you could a read a paper through it. There were no children or old people among the hundreds of well-dressed shoppers; just sleek, well-groomed youngish white people whose eyes seemed to register nothing but the next purchase. The only conversations going on were into cell phones. I looked at Ortega's face, the dark skin pitted with acne scars, the thick eyebrows wild as an Old Testament prophet, and thought that in his homeliness, humility and forbearance he must represent everything the mall mannequins were desperate to escape. He was not simply of a different ethnicity than most of them, he was of a different species. There were vast divides of education and experience between Ortega and me, but we were at least of the same genus.

"Vicky didn't kill Pete," I told him as he munched a homemade taco of chorizo fried with eggs and potatoes. "Pete's cousin Butch is the murderer. Why is she protecting him?"

He chewed and swallowed deliberatively. "How do you know this?"

"Please, Reverend, there's no time. Unless I get the whole story by Friday, she'll go to prison and her husband's murderer will go free."

"Her sacrifice is not for him, it is for her son."

"I don't understand. What does Angel have to do with this?"

"This man, Butch. After he killed her husband, he told her if she went to the police he would come back and kill Angel, too. His own son."

I don't know which bit of information stunned me more. "Angel is Butch's son?"

"Vicky told me that when Pete went to jail for some little crime, he asked Butch to take care of her for him. Butch tried to turn her into a prostitute and he made her sleep with him. She became pregnant with Angel."

"So Pete must have known."

He shook his head. "He only knew Angel was not his son. She told him that she had been raped, but would not tell him who did it."

"Was she afraid he would go after Butch?"

"She was more afraid of Butch. He is an evil person, Señor Rios. A man who would threaten to kill his own son."

"So she pled guilty to protect Angel from Butch."

"To save his life."

"Does Angel know who his father is?"

"She never told him," he said. "But you know Angelito is a very intelligent boy who does not tell everything he knows."

"I can't let her go to prison to protect this thug. She's innocent."

He regarded me gravely. "I agree with you. I tried to convince her to tell you the truth, but she is afraid that you would make her tell the police Butch killed Peter, and Butch would hurt Angel."

"You said yourself he is an evil man. He has to be stopped. I can protect Angel and Vicky."

"She will not tell the police about Butch."

"Then I'll have a find a way so that she doesn't have to."

"You can do that?"

"I can try," I said.

As I drove to the jail to confront Vicky, I began to formulate a plan. The young cop at reception was surprised to see me without Angel, and so was Vicky when they brought her into the interview room. We sat down. I launched into it, to catch her off guard.

"I know Butch killed Pete. I'm not going let you take the rap for him."

"Butch? No, I did it."

"Stop it, Vicky. Ortega told me and he told me why. You think you're going to prison to protect Angel? No, you're protecting Butch. Is that what you want? For the man who killed your husband to go free to kill again?"

"You don't know what he's like," she said fearfully.

"I do know what he's like," I said. "He came to Pete's funeral."

I described how Butch had desecrated Pete's body and then showed up at the burial. She lowered her head as if to ward off blows.

"Animal," she said with quiet fury.

"That's what your Aunt Mary said," I replied. "I think she and Socorro knew that Butch was behind it. I also think they knew he's the person who attacked Jesusita. You know that, too, don't you?"

"Yes," she whispered. "When you told me about Jesusita, I knew it was Butch."

"That's how he found out where you and Pete and Angel were staying."

"She only told him because he beat her up."

"He put her in a coma. Don't you see, Vicky? He's psycho. You can't protect Angel from him by going to prison, because sooner or later Butch will figure out what I figured out—you told Angel that Butch killed Pete."

"How did you know?"

"Because you love him too much to let him grow up thinking that his mother killed the man he believes is his father."

"I know it was wrong to tell him," she said, her eyes filling. "He's already been through so much."

"Butch will come looking for him. You won't be able to help me protect him if you're in prison, but you and I and Elena can make sure nothing happens to Angelito."

She wiped away the tears and nodded. "Tell me what to do."

"What really happened that night?"

"It's a long story, Uncle."

"I've been waiting a long time to hear it."

"I was in San Francisco waiting for Pete to get out of jail. Jesusita called me and told me that Butch had come back from Mexico and found out that Pete was still alive. They tried to kill him in prison."

"I know. His P.D. told me they shanked him in the yard."

"Jesusita called to warn me that Butch knew where I was living, but it was too late. He found me and beat me."

"Why?"

"It was a warning, to Pete," she said. "I went to the shelter, but when they told me to leave, I knew I had to go somewhere where Butch couldn't find me. I never told anyone that I had my mom's address, so I went there."

"Until Pete was released," I guessed. "Then you rejoined him."

She nodded. "Miss Yee, she got him in witness protection and they sent him to this town. Turlock. He called his mom and told her where he was and she told me."

I remembered the bus tickets I had found at the motel. "Why did you come back to L.A.?"

"We didn't know no one in Turlock. Pete got depressed and started using again. He lost the job they got him and we ran out of money. I was afraid he would start stealing again to support his habit, and go back to jail. I didn't want to come back to L.A. because of Butch, but we didn't have nowhere else to go. To be safe, we split up. Pete went to his mom's. I took Angel and we found you."

"Then what happened?"

"Jesusita told Pete she would borrow some money on her house and give it to us to go away. That's what we were waiting for when Butch came." She bit her lip. "Jesusita was the only one who knew where we were. It's my fault Butch hurt her."

"What happened when he came to the motel?"

"Pete was spending all our money on drugs. They were going to evict us. We were fighting all day. He hit me. He never hit me before. But Pete was different than before. He was so scared all the time that he bought a gun. I was afraid of what was happening to him. That night, after he hit me, I told Angel to go wait in the car and I started to pack. This time I was going to leave him for real and go back to my mom. Pete started crying and begging me to give him another chance." She shook her head. "I told him I had had it, that when we got the money from his mom, he'd just shoot it up. Someone knocked at the door. I thought it was the manager because we were so loud, but it was Butch. The next I knew, Pete grabbed his gun and started shooting. Butch started shooting back. I got down on the floor and covered my ears. Butch jumped Pete and knocked the gun out of his hand. Then he made him get on his knees. Pete was begging for his life. Butch shot him. It happened so fast I didn't even have time to scream."

"Where was Angel?"

"I don't know. Butch dragged me around the floor by my hair." She winced at the memory. "He was calling me names and slapping me around. He dragged me over to Pete and said, 'Bitch, this is what happens to snitches.' He told me if I went to the cops, he would come back and make me watch him kill Angel before he killed me. I swore I wouldn't tell anyone if he would leave us alone. He said he would be watching me. Then he raped me."

"God."

"He came on my face, to humiliate me. Then he left. I wiped

him off, and then the next thing I remember is the police and the ambulance."

"What did you wipe your face with?"

She looked at me as if I were crazy. "What?"

"This could be important."

"A T-shirt or something. I don't remember exactly."

"Ortega told me something else. He told me that Angel is Butch's son. Is that true?"

"Yes," she said. "I met him and Pete at a party when I was seventeen. They were close, like brothers. Pete got picked up on some warrant and had to go to jail. Butch said he would take care of me."

"Ortega said he pimped you."

"That's when I learned what he was really like."

"Did he rape you back then, too?"

She shook her head. "I thought he loved me. I was only nineteen. I was stupid. I was stupid about Butch and Pete. The only good thing I ever got out of either of them was my Angel." She looked at me, alarmed. "You have to swear you won't tell Angel who his dad is."

"That's between you and him."

"You think I'm a bad mother."

"I think you've done everything you can to protect him," I said. "Now I'm asking you to let me help."

She was silent a moment. "Remember when you said I didn't like you?"

"That doesn't matter as long as you can trust me."

"Pete was a *joto*."

I stared at her. "Pete was a homosexual?"

She nodded. "His mom knew. She tried to tell me when Pete and me moved in with her, but I was young, I didn't understand. One night, he came home late. I heard his car in the driveway, but he didn't come inside for a long time. I went to see if he was okay. There was another man in the car and Pete's head was in his lap doing—you know. Pete swore that was the first time and begged me not to tell anyone. I never did, but I know there was other times, other guys. I thought you must be like Pete because you're gay, too."

"Like Pete how?"

"Weak. But you're not. You're a man."

I accepted the oblique apology. What she had told me explained much of her antagonism toward me, but I knew there were other things that divided us, basic differences in temperament. Maybe we could work them out over time. Maybe not.

"I'm going to try to do something in court on Friday to get the charge against you dismissed without you having to roll on Butch, but someday you may have to testify against him. Are you willing to do that?"

"I'll do whatever you tell me to," she said simply.

"All right, Mr. Rios," Judge Ryan said. "You convened this little meeting. What do you want to talk about?"

She spoke lightly, but with an undertone of judicial annoyance. She had expected to be on the bench conducting Vicky's sentencing hearing. Instead, I had corralled Kim Pearsall as soon as he had entered the courtroom and asked Ryan's clerk if we could speak to the judge in chambers. As she gazed at me over her half-glasses, I could hear the ticking of her patience.

"Your Honor, I want to make a motion to withdraw the plea."

Pearsall exclaimed, "What!"

She lifted a restraining hand toward him and said to me, "Henry, this had better be good."

"If I can just explain."

"You do that."

For the next half-hour, I laid it all out for them, from Pete's decision to roll on Butch and his gang to the shooting in the motel and Butch's threat. I told them that Morgan Yee was in her office in San Francisco ready to corroborate my account of Pete's plea and its consequences. I showed them an incident report from San Quentin about the prison stabbing, provided them with the name of the agent in witness protection who had arranged to move Pete to the central valley. I told them that I had gone through the suitcase from the motel and found a sweater with blood and semen stains that I had sent out for preliminary DNA analysis and that I expected the semen sample would yield Narciso Trujillo's DNA. I showed an affidavit from Socorro Cerda recounting the events at the cemetery and the attack on her mother.

"So let me understand," Judge Ryan said when I finished. "You want to withdraw the plea and go to trial with this new evidence." She glanced at Pearsall. "Based on his offer of proof, counsel, you're going to have a hard time convicting."

"I can't present this evidence at trial," I said.

Ryan raised an eyebrow. "You have evidence exonerating your client, but you won't put it on?"

"Judge, this evidence is not sufficient by itself to prove that Butch killed Pete. My niece would have to testify, and I can't let her do that while Butch remains at large."

"She fears retaliation?"

"Exactly."

The judge tapped a manicured finger on her desk. "Then what do you propose to do, Mr. Rios?"

"Your Honor, I'd like you to grant the defendant's motion to withdraw her plea and then suppress her confession." I turned to Pearsall. "You don't have a case without the confession. You announce that you're unable to proceed for lack of evidence, and then Judge Ryan dismisses the charges."

"Dude, that's crazy," he said, forgetting in his excitement where he was.

"Whatever that means," Ryan said. "I think I agree. A dismissal under those circumstances is not an acquittal. Why would you want that?"

"It's the only way to get her out of jail and to get the cops to re-open the investigation and catch Butch." I pushed the pile of documents at Pearsall. "I'm practically making your case for you."

"What if it turns out you're just feeding me a line? Your client gets a walk."

"No," I said. "A dismissal for lack of evidence before trial doesn't create double jeopardy, and there's no statute of limitations on murder. You can refile on Vicky at any time, with the original second-degree murder count or any other charge you think you can prove. Am I right, Your Honor?"

She mulled it over. "Yes, he's right, Mr. Pearsall. If I let her withdraw her plea, you're not bound by the plea bargain if you decide to recharge her later." She looked at me. "And you'd risk that?"

"She didn't kill him, Judge."

Pearsall said, "His client confessed. All this stuff"—he brushed the documents—"this is circumstantial. If you suppress her confession and dismiss the case, and then it turns out she did kill the dude, even if I can refile against her, I won't have her confession, and that's my best evidence."

"If you refile the charge, the next judge won't be bound by Judge Ryan's ruling and you can try to get the confession in," I said. "Plus, even if you can't use it in your case-in-chief, you'd still be able to impeach her with it if she testified."

"Very clever," Ryan said. "You've covered all the angles, Mr. Rios, except one. What if the police can't build a case against this other suspect except with your client's testimony? If she refuses to testify, he'll get away with murder."

"Butch has got two outstanding arrest warrants as it is, and a rap sheet for serious and violent felonies a mile long. It's just a matter of time before he's picked up for something, and next time he's convicted of any felony, he'll go to prison for life under Three Strikes. If you want to tack on this murder charge at that point, I'll persuade Vicky to testify. He's not going to get away with anything."

"If you expect me to stick my neck out on this case," Judge Ryan said, "I want to hear from your client what happened that night. No offense, Mr. Rios, but you are her uncle. You may be too close. I want to judge her credibility myself."

"Off the record?" I asked.

"I won't request the reporter, if that's what you mean," she said, "but I will make her take the oath, and if I think she's lying, she's not the only one who's going to be in trouble, Henry. You'll be facing a contempt charge. Understand?"

"I understand, Your Honor."

"Fine," the judge said. She buzzed the clerk and told her to have the bailiff bring Vicky in.

"In the matter of *People* versus *Trujillo*," Judge Ryan said from the bench, "the defendant's motion to withdraw her plea is granted. I also grant defendant's motion to suppress her confession based on a violation of her *Miranda* rights during the initial police interrogation. I base that decision on the transcript of the interrogation. Mr. Pearsall, are the People ready to proceed to trial?"

"Not at this time, Your Honor. Without the statement, the People are unable to proceed due to lack of evidence."

"In that case," the judge said, "I will dismiss the charges in the interests of justice pursuant to Penal Code section thirteen-eighty-two. I add for the record the following: This dismissal does not constitute double jeopardy, and if the People develop further evidence against the defendant, they are free to refile the original charge of second-degree murder or any other charge they believe the evidence will support. Do you understand that, Mrs. Trujillo? This is not a factual finding of innocence. The People could refile charges if they find other evidence against you."

"Yes, Your Honor," she said.

"With that understanding, then, the charges are dismissed. The defendant is ordered to be released forthwith. We're adjourned."

20.

THE SECRETARY IN CHARGE OF THE APPOINTMENT OF judges occupied a small corner office in the state capitol building in Sacramento. From his windows, a wedge of the verdant park that surrounded the building was visible. It was October and the grass was littered with red and yellow leaves. The secretary was a beetle-browed man named Ben Cohan, who had exchanged his partnership in a big L.A. firm for this unimposing cubicle because, along with his view of the park, the office had one other advantage. His next-door neighbor was the governor. Cohan was also undoubtedly aware that his immediate predecessor in this office now sat on the state supreme court.

"So, Henry," he said. "Your application was very impressive. You also have quite a friend in Inez Montoya. There are a couple of questions I have to ask. You know the governor doesn't have a litmus test on any issue, but he does want to know whether his judicial appointments can carry out the law, particularly the death penalty."

Inez had warned me this question would be asked, but to her credit didn't try to prompt me with the politically correct answer.

"The death penalty is immoral."

Cohen gave a look of annoyance, as if we were actors on stage together and I'd flubbed my line. "But constitutional."

"Yes, it's constitutional."

"You realize as a trial court judge you have to accept the U.S. Supreme Court's conclusion about the constitutionality of the death penalty."

"I learned about stare decisis in my first year at law school," I said.

"Would your personal feelings prevent you from imposing the death penalty if a jury came back with it?"

"I took an oath to uphold the law when I became a lawyer. I knew when I swore that oath there would be times I couldn't square what the law requires with my personal beliefs. That's the deal I made twenty-five years ago. I've tried very hard to keep up my end."

He tapped a pencil on a stack of folders. "Everyone knows how strongly the governor feels about the death penalty. Most of the people who've sat in your chair tripped all over themselves to assure me they're pro-death, because they think that's what I want to hear."

"I'm not someone who tells people what they necessarily want to hear," I replied. "I would think that would be a virtue in a judge."

He opened the top folder and skimmed a couple of pages. "This is your application," he said. "Very eloquent, but a little ambivalent, too. Why do you want to be a judge, Henry?"

"I'd be good at it," I said.

He smiled. "That's it? You want the job because you're qualified?"

"Isn't that enough?"

He closed the folder. "In a perfect world. In this world, you're going to get the job because you have a Spanish surname, a powerful politician friend and you're gay." He laughed. "Your candor is contagious, Henry. I better keep you away from Joe." Joe Rafferty, a.k.a. the governor. "Would you still take the job on those terms?"

"The important thing is not how you get the job, but how well you do it," I replied. "If people want to think I got the job as a token, let them. I'll prove them wrong."

Cohan said, "I'm sure you will. This interview's a formality. Next week, the governor will be announcing a dozen judicial appointments. You'll be one of them." He stood up and extended a slender pale hand. "Congratulations, Judge Rios."

"Thank you," I said, shaking his hand. "Tell the governor I won't ever give him reason to regret this."

Cohan raised an eyebrow. "Actually, Henry, I'm thinking you'll be a pain in the ass. Go for it."

Inez's office was as lavish as Cohan's had been austere, and as far from the governor's chambers as she could get and still remain in the building. Her office was circular, with high ceilings and marble columns flanking tall, narrow windows with blue velvet drapes. The walls were painted a soft yellow, the parquet floors were covered with massive Oriental carpets and fighter jets could have landed on her desk. She was wearing a red linen suit over a white silk blouse, and I reflected that with each electoral success she became better-looking. I had just finished telling her about the interview with Cohan.

"Congratulations," she said. "You deserve the job."

"That doesn't seem to be why I got it, but thanks. This is all your doing."

She lit a cigarette. "On those mornings when I need help looking myself in the mirror, I'll remember that I made you a judge."

"I hope you don't have those mornings very often, Inez."

She waved away her smoke. "That's what I love about you, Henry. Your innocence. In the little Mexican village where you and I would have lived a hundred years ago, you would have been the priest."

"And what would you have been?"

"Someone's wife," she said. "The mother of his thirteen children. Instead, I'm raising millions of dollars to get myself elected to the Senate. I'm going to make it, too."

"I know you are."

She waved her cigarette. "Unless these kill me first. You do a good job in superior court, and when I get to the Senate, I'll put you up for the federal bench."

"There are no known gay federal judges."

"There ain't no lady Mexican senators, either," she said. "You got to get over letting other people tell you what you can be."

"Check," I said. "You've stuck by me for twenty years, Inez. I've never been exactly sure why."

"You're my conscience," she said. "Plus, I fell in love with you the first time we met. At that public defenders' conference in Monterey, remember? You were everything I wanted in a man. Smart, brave, good-looking, Latin."

"And gay."

She shrugged. "I won't tell you how many hours I cried over that. Well, I was only twenty-four. I got over my broken heart, but you never forget the first boy you love. Right?"

I smiled. "Right."

"Speaking of boys, are you still dating that guy you told me about? John?"

"Yeah."

"When do I get to meet him?"

"Next time you come down to L.A., if you have time."

"Hey, if he's half what you tell me he is, I'll make the time." She stubbed out her cigarette. "Seriously, Henry. I'm happy you've found someone." She looked at her watch. "I have a meeting. I'll call you."

I got up. "Thanks again, Inez. I won't let you down."

"I'm holding you to that," she said.

My plane out of Sacramento was delayed, so I used the time to make some calls. The first was to Kim Pearsall. Two days earlier,

Butch Trujillo had been arrested for armed robbery and attempted murder at a convenience store. He had been captured on tape shooting the clerk, who had just emptied the cash register and the safe. Pearsall wanted to tack Pete's murder onto the charges. I had had a long talk with Vicky the night before and was calling him to give him her answer. He wasn't going to like it. She was still afraid of Butch, and she worried that if she testified against him, his gang-banger friends would go after her or Angel.

"Back in July, you told Judge Ryan that Vicky would testify if Butch was in custody," he said.

"I know what I said, but I didn't expect he would be stupid enough to get himself arrested so soon. I mean, Vicky's just now getting her life together again. No one in his family knows where she's living or where she's working, and she doesn't want them to find out. If she testifies, they'll know she's still in L.A."

"You want him to get away with murder?"

"The robbery's dead-bang, right?"

"Yeah, we have him on video. The clerk survived and he's already made an ID, and this time we got the gun. A three-eighty, in case you're interested. Probably the same one he used to kill your dude."

"He's a three-striker. You convict him of the robbery and he's going away for life. It wouldn't matter if you charged him with the Lindbergh kidnapping"

"The Lindbergh kidnapping? What's that?"

"Never mind. The bottom line is that Vicky won't testify."

"I could make her."

"You could get her on the stand, you can't make her talk."

"Damn it, Henry, we had a deal."

"The safety of my family is more important," I replied, then relented. "Look, Kim, convict him, put him away for life, and then we'll talk again. Maybe I could persuade her to testify at that point."

"I'm holding you to that," he said.

"You're the second person today who's said that to me."

"I got priority," he replied, and hung up.

   . . .

I thought about my niece on the plane back to L.A. She and Angel were living in an apartment about ten minutes' walk from my house, and she had gone back to work as a maid at the downtown Sheraton. Both Elena and I had tried to persuade her to go back to school, get her GED and train for a real career, but she claimed to be happy cleaning rooms in a hotel. Often she worked double shifts, and when she did, I picked Angel up from school and brought him to my house. Vicky had also thrown herself into Reverend Ortega's church, and while Angel would go to services, he resisted her attempts to get him involved in the youth group or prayer meetings or Bible class because it cut into his school studies. This was a source of friction between them—for which, I knew, she blamed me. Fortunately, Reverend Ortega assured her that Angel could be a good student and a good Christian. I suspected the second part of the formulation was wishful thinking on the Reverend's part, but I was in no hurry for that fight and was relieved that Angel still uncomplainingly went to church. Between my niece and me, there remained some unbridgeable gap of temperament. She put up with me for Angel's sake and I put up with her for Elena's because the two of them had become closer. I know they spoke by phone every day, and Elena and her partner, Joanne Stole, usually came down once a month. We had tense little dinners, just like a real family. Still, it had been Vicky's decision, after Jesusita Trujillo died, to cut off her ties with Pete's family and throw in her lot with the Rioses. For Angel's sake, of course; it seemed that our entire little family revolved around the boy.

At least Vicky liked John, but then, everyone liked John. Accustomed as I had been to the endless dramatics of my life with Josh, filled with hidden meanings and misunderstanding, it was a great relief to be with someone who was pretty much what he appeared to be. When I had mentioned this to him, he had laughed and told me that I was complicated enough for both of us. Actually, though, the older I get, the simpler things seem to me. Where once I would have spent hours wondering about the meaning of life and my place in it, now I am more apt to wonder what to give Angel for dinner. A much smaller question, to be sure, but one to which there is at least a concrete answer.

I came into my house and heard the TV going.

I called out, "Have you done your homework?"

"I'm doing it," Angel said.

I came into the living room and found him with his math book opened in his lap while he watched a playoff game between the Giants and the Braves.

"I can see that. Who's winning?"

"Giants, eight to six. I'll do my math when the game is over. Mom's working night shift so I'm staying over, okay?"

"What do you want for dinner?"

"Pizza. Is John coming over?"

"Not tonight."

He glanced at me. "How come you and John don't live together? Then he'd be here all the time."

"We probably will someday, but for now we each have reasons to have separate houses. How was school?"

"Ssh. The game's starting. I'll tell you after. Sit down and watch, okay?"

I took off my coat and tie, kicked off my shoes and sat down beside him. I draped my arm around his shoulder and he scooted up against me. Barry Bonds came to the plate, and on a full count sent a ball sailing over the wall at Pac Bell Park and into San Francisco Bay. Angel, cheering for the California team even if it wasn't the Dodgers, hooted happily.

"That's going to be me someday, Uncle Henry," he said excitedly.

"I know," I replied. "And I'll be in the stands cheering."

ACKNOWLEDGMENTS

THIS BOOK BRINGS TO AN END THIS SERIES OF MYSTERIES and my career as a mystery writer. In past books, I have thanked the many people who have helped me. Again I thank my agent, Charlotte Sheedy; my editor, Neil Nyren; my trusted colleagues, Katherine V. Forrest, Paul Reidinger, Robert Dawidoff; and all the other people who have helped bring these books to print over the years. In the writing of this particular book, I am also indebted to my dear friend Dr. Rod Hayward, for explaining to me the clinical aspects of myocardial infractions, and to Greg Wolff, who was kind enough to share his personal experience of recovery from an M.I. It also seems appropriate to give thanks to my readers, who, by your support, have created a place for these books in the tumultuous literary marketplace.

Michael Nava